BOHEMIA BLUES

by

Lucy Lakestone

VELVET PETAL PRESS

Florida

Published by Velvet Petal Press, Florida

Learn more about the author at LucyLakestone.com

Jacket design, shell and beach photography
by Sky Diary Productions;
additional photo by Lorand Gelner

ISBN: 978-1-943134-04-5

First edition

PART 1

*N*ever date a drummer.

Seriously. I once dated our guitar player. He had kind of an ego, but at least he showed up for gigs after I dumped him. The bass player was laid-back while we hung out, but that might be because he, of all the guys in my band, partook most heavily during weed breaks while I drank cocktails. And the other member of Ez and the Emeralds, the banjo-guitar-flute-triangle-cowbell-playing Emerald, was even less interested in a commitment than I was.

Usually I was only too happy to play the noncommittal role, which was why I tended to date losers to begin with. And to be honest, "date" was a strong word for what you might call my flirtations with my bandmates.

But drummers? This was the second drummer I'd, er, played with (fool me twice), and he gave paradiddling a bad name.

Ez and the Emeralds had been doing really well in Bohemia — Ez, that's me, or Esme to a few friends, or Esmerelda to my parents when they were pissed off. The band had finally graduated from Bohemia Beach bum bars to pretty decent venues. We'd had a guy sniffing around from an Orlando-based record label who wanted to have a meeting next week. And tonight we were playing Calista Goode's photo gallery opening in the Bohemia arts district.

We were set up against the backdrops and under her photo lights; there was a badass portrait of me in the exhibit in the lobby. We couldn't ask for a more enthusiastic audience. Some people were actually listening to us, not just talking. Groupie Gary (I always called him that, though not to his face) wore what I had to admit was an especially cute grin as he nodded along near my keyboard. People were even dancing, at least when I wasn't wailing like I was now. I'm sure the champagne was helping the mood. At least, it was helping me.

This was an *awesome* gig. I wouldn't say that any of us were giving up our day jobs, not that I'd ever admit I had one. But everything had been going great. Until now.

Stuart, the drummer and my latest flirtation of interest, was having a meltdown. Perhaps I should say my former flirtation of interest. I'd told him before the gig that his temporary home on my couch was no longer available to him, and he took it kind of hard. I didn't know how hard until he started breaking sticks, missing beats and generally pissing off the Emeralds. The crowd hadn't noticed yet. I was trying not to. One more tune after this, and we'd be outta here.

This wasn't an easy song for me, and playing this electronic keyboard instead of a piano — I always preferred a piano — made it even harder. It switched between four-four and six-eight time, which is already a bitch, and I had to hit a challenging range of notes in quick succession while keeping the emotion in check. Because sometimes, this stupid rock ballad, with all its wrenching confessions of isolation, penned in a moment of weakness, made me cry.

I closed my eyes and concentrated, shutting out the party noise, the lights, the skittering, uneven beats from Stuart. I could hear the other guys powering through, trying to keep with me, keep us all together. But if I was the heart of this band, and I'm not going to deny it, the drummer was supposed to be the heartbeat, and it sounded as if Ez and the Emeralds were having a heart attack.

A mighty crash halted me in mid-chord. Guitars screeched to a halt. I opened my eyes and turned around.

I wasn't the only one. Pretty much everyone stopped what they were doing and turned to look at Stuart, who was in the process of knocking over his ride cymbal and high-hat. He stood to face the murmur in the room, the trailing notes of interrupted laughter, and pointed at me.

"You have *no right* to sing about being alone," he screamed, his shaggy, dirty-blond hair flopping about his ruddy face, his mustache and goatee. "You have *no right* to whine. Because that's exactly what you fucking want!"

Dude, I was as stunned as anybody in the room.

So stunned I barely ducked in time when he threw his sticks at me.

The room erupted in shouts. Gary was the first to leap in and grab Stuart, and the rest of the Emeralds followed suit, practically dragging him out the back door.

"Damn," I whispered to myself, and I heard my voice go out on the mike. Not so professional. I scanned the crowd. At least half of them were looking at me, and Calista rushed up to me, cute in her lacy blue and white dress, her put-up blond hair looking electrified as usual. We'd known each other in high school but only got to be real friends over the past few years.

"Are you OK?" she asked.

"Fine," I said, sounding cooler than I felt. "Sorry to fuck up your party."

Cali shook her head with a small smile and nodded toward the crowd, whose interest was returning to drinks and chatter. "Honestly, I think they're just happy they're the ones who will get to tell the story. Sorry," she said to my frown. "It's really all right. This is the art crowd. They've seen worse."

A rock tune started over the speakers, and the music instantly reestablished the party mood, knocking the record back into its groove.

"Wyatt put the music on," Cali explained. "I hope you don't mind."

"It's either that or I wrap with a solo 'Star-Spangled Banner.'"

She laughed. "Maybe another time. It's all good. You were amazing tonight. Are you sure you're OK? What was his deal?"

"He's a drummer," I said with a shrug, not wanting to get into it. I preferred a sense of mystery, even with people I considered my friends.

Cali's ice-blue stare suggested I wasn't as mysterious as I wanted to be.

"Let me know if you want to talk about it," she said.

I shrugged again as her tasty boyfriend, Wyatt, a surfer and photographer, came up and grabbed her around the waist.

"Everybody OK?" he asked.

"A-OK," I insisted.

"Good," Wyatt said. "Your guys just called your drummer

a cab. I think they are, uh, taking a little smoke break outside before they break it down."

"Why am I not surprised?" I asked. "I guess that means I'll have a glass of champagne."

"Definitely," Cali said. "We're turning up the lights in a few minutes anyway, so you might as well relax. In fact, you can come back tomorrow to pack up your stuff if you want."

"That sounds like a great idea." I clasped my hands together, hoping to stop the slight tremor before anyone saw it. I needed that champagne more than I cared to admit. "Just give me a few minutes to think about where we're getting our next drummer."

Wyatt chuckled, and Cali kissed his cheek. Freaking sweet couple. If they weren't so nice, they'd make me want to throw up.

I strolled over to the refreshment table and helped myself. There wasn't a lot left in terms of snacks or drinks, but a couple of bottles of champagne were still chilling. I filled a glass, knocked it back and filled it again.

"You must be done for the night," came a friendly voice from behind me.

I turned. It was Gary, his long, brown, bouncy curls unruly around his slender face, a touch of elfin mischief about his features.

I shot him a cool stare. "The more I drink, the better I sing."

"I thought it was, the more everyone else drinks, the better you sing," he joked, crossing his arms. He seemed nervous. He always seemed a little nervous around me. I wasn't sure why. I mean, he was cute, handsome even. Tall and wiry, but that was OK. And everybody knew he was one of the best potters at the Bohemia School of Art and Design.

But Gary Gorski was probably my only groupie, so I guess that explained his nerves.

"So are you OK?" he asked.

"I wish everyone would stop asking. But thanks for taking down Animal."

"The Muppet drummer? Yeah, Animal's a lot nicer than that guy."

"Speaks better English, too," I said, and Gary laughed. He had dimples when he laughed, dimples you could swim in, and a sparkle in his eye. He was really too nice for me, but he *had* come to my rescue. That was worth something.

"He's an ass," he said. "I mean, I hope you and he aren't — but —"

"We were," I said without emotion, pushing the mink-brown, diagonal bangs of my short, mod haircut out of my eyes. "We were — whatever. But he's definitely an ass."

"Good. I mean, you're right." Gary looked uncomfortable.

"The only trouble is, that ass was sleeping on my couch, and that makes it kind of awkward to go home right now. I told him to get out earlier, but he still has a key."

"Want me to take you home? I can make sure he's not hanging around. He didn't seem all that sane earlier."

"He never does."

Gary's eyes were full of concern. Maybe I needed to throw him a bone. He was always mooning after me like a lonely puppy. I could give him a thrill. Might as well live up to my rep.

I drained the second glass of champagne.

"I have an idea," I said. "Why don't you take me home?"

"That's what I said." He looked confused.

I slipped my arm in his, enjoying the bewitching as the champagne started to take the edge off. And to be honest, he felt kind of comforting, warm, his arm more muscular than I would have guessed. Must be all that kneading clay.

"I mean, take me to *your* home," I murmured, looking up at him under my eyelashes.

Gary's eyes grew wide. "I'd love to!"

I'm pretty sure he squeaked.

GARY LEFT to get his van while I shotgunned another glass of champagne. Then I went to the tiny parking lot out back to talk to the guys. There was a flash in the western darkness and the distant sound of thunder. The storms in the forecast were finally about to arrive.

"I've got to get out of here," I told them. "I'll pick up my keyboard tomorrow."

"Forget it, Ez," said Robby, the guitar player, a thin, long-haired guy with a closely shaven beard and mustache who totally looked the part. "I've got it. You OK?"

"I'll be OK if everyone stops fucking asking." Even in my tipsy state, I realized they were all giving me a look that wasn't pure concern. There was something accusatory in it. "Sorry, I'm drunk and pissed off."

There was a beat, an exchange of glances. While none of the Emeralds were currently smoking, the doobie cloud hung around them like a leather jacket that had survived a Phish concert tour. But this was more than fuzzy pot brain. They all seemed out of sorts.

"We don't need this kind of drama," said stocky, perpetually high bass player Ace (aka Ace the Bass), long white-blond bangs hanging in his face.

I crossed my arms. "No, we don't." I looked around, met

each of them eye to eye. "You think *I'm* responsible for this drama? Stuart's the one who lost his fucking mind."

"You don't think you helped him along?" Robby asked. "Just a little?"

"Don't listen to them," said Banjo Brian, the short, sprightly utility Emerald with the dark buzz cut. "It's not her fault," he told the others. "Ez is cool. You guys know that." *Brian, the only one less committed than I was when it came to my little distractions.*

Robby looked at his feet and kicked an imaginary pebble. "Whoever's fault it is, now we need another drummer."

"Again," Ace said, referring to Drummer No. 1, he who shall not be named, with whom I also dallied but who really left because his job moved him to South Carolina.

I glared at Ace.

"Chill, guys," Brian said. "We'll find one. Craig's List, and we'll have somebody by next weekend."

"We'd better find someone, and quick," Robby said. "We have a gig at The Junction Box on Friday."

"I can fill in if I have to," Brian said. "I can play more than triangle and bongos, you know."

"But we need you on banjo and stuff for 'The Sound,' " Robby said. Robby was always talking about our Sound, especially since the record label guy said he wanted to meet with us.

"We'll find someone," I said, and then the alcohol and general irritation in my bloodstream prompted me to say more. "In the meantime, I don't want to hear any more bullshit about this being my fault. Stuart is a freak, and he's out, and that's it. Of course, if you guys don't want me —"

"I didn't say that," said Robby, as Ace shook his head and echoed, "No way."

"OK." Inside, I breathed a sigh of relief. I'd tested my status as queen of the band and avoided a coup.

The sky released another ominous rumble as Gary popped out the back door. "Ready?"

There was something refreshing about his inherent optimism. A nice change from these losers. And he always had a smile for me. I'd like to give him the satisfying evening I seemed incapable of having myself.

"Be right there," I said with a little wave.

He smiled and vanished inside again.

When I turned to say goodbye to my bandmates, all of them — even Banjo Brian — had expressions that ranged from disbelief to knowing cynicism. Robby shook his head.

I gave them all the cold-bitch stare that usually knocked everybody down, but this time, they didn't look away.

"Shut up," I finally said. Then I whirled and headed back into the gallery.

~

"WHERE'S THE PUPPY?"

Gary glanced over at me from the driver's seat of his nearly windowless white van, which was rattling through downtown Bohemia to wherever his place was supposed to be.

"What do you mean?" he asked over the stereo. It was rocking some band so obscure, even I'd never heard of it. Gary had unforeseen musical depth.

"You know, white van. Puppy. Sorry. Bad joke."

"Oh, I get it," Gary said, laughing nervously. "I always thought that was kind of a sick gag, and you're the first person to even mention it to me. I use this van for my real job."

"Which is what?"

"I work at the school, but I also do some high-end construction stuff, like carving architectural foam and specialty plasterwork. It still pays more than pottery. And I'm not in the habit of picking up anyone, especially with the help of a puppy, trust me."

"Except me. And you didn't even need the puppy."

He flashed a grin at me, the lights of downtown sliding over his face in charming patterns as the first drops of rain hit the windshield. There was a flash off to the west and, a moment later, a roll of thunder, louder than before.

"It's coming," he said. "But we're almost there."

I sat back and tried to relax. Gary was kind of a relief from the boys in the band. I didn't owe him anything, at least, nothing except my rescue tonight. And he seemed all too happy to be my knight. I'd make him happy, give him just enough of what he needed, what all the guys needed, and then I'd put him off and be on my way home.

We were looping around the harbor road to the side where most of the docks were located. Gary pulled up in the small parking area and practically jumped out of the van. I had my door halfway open when I found him at my side, offering a hand to help me out.

"Well, aren't you gallant." I noted how smooth his hands were, maybe from the clay.

He just grinned at me again. "This way."

The rain was getting heavier, spattering my silky black pants and jacket, and I had no idea where we were going. There were no houses or condos or apartments over here. Most of that was just across the water, on the other side of the small Bohemia Harbor, along with a few bars and restaurants. I clutched my tiny purse and followed Gary down a few steps and to the plank walkway that led from dock to dock. All of them were packed with impressive-looking boats that creaked in the wind.

"You live on a boat?" I asked.

"Almost," he said. "It's just ahead."

All I saw was a tall shack. Just beyond it, Gary took a left, and we were walking next to it, out on a broad dock. The shack, I realized, was built over the water, and it was a lot nicer than it looked from the back. Lit by the few lights along the docks, its weathered paint gave it a shabby chic look. There was a door on the side next to a window. A grill stood outside the door, along with a pair of muddy work boots, rickety shelves covered in plants, and a pet's water bowl.

I would have kept exploring, because the dock extended around to the water side, but the rain suddenly got a lot harder.

I wordlessly followed Gary as he unlocked the door and went inside.

He flipped a switch, and a floor lamp came on, a funky thing with five bendy arms sporting different colored cones shielding the light bulbs. It illuminated a space at least as funky as the lamp.

"This is your place?" I couldn't keep the surprise out of my voice.

"Yeah, isn't it great?" He tossed his keys on the square wooden table, which looked almost as antique as the plank ceiling above, weathered to gray and peaked in the middle. As I looked up, I heard the pattern of the rain increase to a steady drumroll of sound, and thunder rattled the roof.

A handful of candle lanterns hung from the beams, and Gary set to lighting them. He was so tall, he didn't need a ladder. I would've. But there *was* a wooden ladder, leading to a small loft space at one end of the shack. The loft was suspended over a tiny bathroom, a closet and a minuscule kitchen. I thought I caught a movement in the dark opening that led to the loft and looked more closely. A ginger cat appeared at the top of the ladder.

"Punky!" Gary called out. "There you are, girl. Come on down." He turned to me after lighting the last of the candles. "That's Pumpkin Spice. It's a good thing I got her inside earlier. She'd be soaked by now. She does love hunting the rats, though."

"Rats?" Now I looked around with trepidation.

He laughed. "Not in here. Outside, around the docks. Don't worry."

I examined the space more closely, rats or not. The curtains on the wall opposite the loft almost covered sliding glass doors that led out to the dock and the water. There was an air-conditioning unit set in another wall (that explained the comfortable temperature); a small stereo system on an old sideboard, complete with turntable; a fishbowl on the kitchen counter with one beta fish inside and a screen over the top; more cat bowls on the floor; a fast-looking bicycle in the corner; and a black futon. There were a few paintings and an eclectic collection of ceramic vases that, I suspected, he'd made himself. My gaze was drawn again to the top of the ladder, where Pumpkin Spice was nimbly descending. Halfway down, she leaped into Gary's arms.

"Good girl," he said idly, stroking her as he wandered over to the sliding glass doors. I could hear the purr from across the room. Then again, it wasn't a very big room.

Gary pulled the curtains all the way open so I could see the dock, a few chairs and planters, and the rain-blurred lights of the harbor beyond.

"Bitchin' view," I commented, drawn to his side. A brilliant flash of lightning across the water almost blinded me for a moment, and thunder crashed again.

"Yeah, I love it here. If the rain weren't so noisy, you'd hear the water, too. It's peaceful, usually." There was an awkward pause. "Want to sit down?"

"OK." I moved back to the futon, kicked off my sandals and sat, shrugging off my damp jacket and tossing it aside. He tried not to be obvious as he looked me over, but I know he noticed my clingy bronze silk tank and the fact that I didn't wear a bra under it. I didn't have enough boobage to make one worthwhile when I had that rocker image to live up to.

He was in a black T-shirt and jeans, jeans that fit his lanky form very well, I might add.

He put down the cat and turned on the stereo. He set the needle onto a vinyl disc, unleashing a gong, strings and then a throaty, exotic voice that started at an ethereally high pitch before lowering into a mellow lament.

"Yma Sumac?" I asked.

"I knew you'd know her."

"Which album?"

He looked at the album sleeve. "*Voice of the Xtabay*. This one is 'Taita Inty' — Virgin of the Sun God."

How apt, I thought.

"I kind of dig the old tiki tunes from the Polynesia craze," Gary continued.

"Who doesn't?" I joked.

"Well, yeah, but I'm weird, and you're a musician. Actually, I'm kind of a musician, too."

"I'm sorry to hear that."

He laughed. "I fool around with drums and ukulele. Nothing serious."

"Oh, God, no, not a drummer, too."

"I swear." He put his hands up as if in surrender. "I do not have the drummer gene."

"You know about that, huh?"

"Don't you remember? I was in the high school percussion section."

"Oh, yeah." Sometimes I forgot about those few years at Bohemia High after our family left Miami. We'd moved for reasons I didn't enjoy thinking about, and I was always on the fringes then. I hadn't bothered joining high school band. I was mostly trying to find garage bands to sing with. "I didn't go to a lot of concerts."

"Or football?"

"Hardly ever. But I remember you guys were pretty good."

"You should've been out there with us," Gary said, sitting next to me. "Though I guess it would've been hard to carry a piano around the field."

I laughed. "And you already had a glockenspiel player."

"Oh, man, she was evil."

"So am I," I said idly.

"No, you're not!"

I smiled at his befuddlement. "Got anything to drink?"

"Only beer. That OK?"

"A thirsty girl can't be picky." With that, another round of lightning and thunder shook the building, and the rain hammered harder as Yma trilled her high solo. Gary sprang up and headed for the fridge. He was back in a moment with a couple of Bohemia Brewing Red Ales in glistening bottles.

"Nice." I took a swig as he sat again, this time almost imperceptibly closer to me. It was kind of cute. He was kind of cute. Well, really, no *kind of* about it. He just wasn't the type

I usually went for: loser or asshole. He was, like the beer, nice. Unlike me. Might as well get on with it.

"So what's a nice guy like you doing bringing home a girl like me?" I teased, leaning into him.

"Oh, not you, too. I am not nice," he said, pushing his shoulder into mine.

"Oh, you're not nice?"

"Fuck, no," he said.

"You doth protest too much." I took another swig of beer with my right hand and ran a finger along his thigh with my left. "You were pretty nice to take me home."

"I — I — oh, I was only too glad — "

An almost simultaneous flash of lightning and crash of thunder interrupted him, and I jumped. The lights flickered and went out, and Yma Sumac droned to a halt. Only the candles lit the space now. I heard the cat meow and saw her sprint back up the ladder to the loft.

Gary slipped an arm around me, protectively, I thought. And — yes, it was nice. I tilted my face up toward his and kissed him on the cheek. He closed his eyes and opened his mouth slightly, his breathing agitated as I moved closer. His expression was surprisingly sensual. The flickering candle-light brought out the fine bone structure of his cheeks, his strong chin, his long lashes, the sweet symmetry of his mouth.

Whoa. I'd never been attracted to Gary.

I put down my beer and kissed his cheek again, and then the corner of his mouth. That did it. He turned to me abruptly and caught my lips with his, and his molten need was a shock to my senses. My lips felt as if they were burning. He slipped his arms around me, awkwardly there on the futon, and I felt how strong they were, all muscle. *Holy shit.*

This must be what happened when you threw clay and did real physical work all day.

A flame flickered in my core as lightning and thunder exploded outside, rattling the shack. I pressed against Gary, his long, lean body. His tongue delved into my open mouth, sweeping against my tongue in a lover's caress. *What the hell? This was hot.* And it was never supposed to be hot with Gary.

I moaned a little and pressed harder against him, and I suddenly felt his hands on my shoulders, his arms stiff as he pushed me away.

"What?" I asked, breathless.

"Do you smell something?"

"There's a slight possibility I smell like champagne."

"No." He stood, leaving me to half fall into the space he'd just occupied. "You don't smell that?"

The yowl of the cat prompted me to look up. She leapt from the loft straight to the floor and then to the door, scratching wildly. And that's when I noticed a brighter light coming from the loft.

"Smoke!" Gary said.

"Fire!" I shouted, standing, pointing up at the loft.

"The lightning!" Gary said. "Get out! Make sure Punky goes with you!"

"Come on!" I shouted as I grabbed my purse and the beer. I left the jacket. There was a whoosh as a whole corner of the building above the loft burst into flames. The cat leapt away from the side door and hurled herself across the room and against the sliding glass doors.

"Hurry, Gary!" I yanked the glass doors open amid a rush of angry heat and devilish orange light. The cat hurtled out and down the dock like a shot. I ran after her for a few steps in the downpour, then turned around. The whole roof was on fire, and the structure was engulfed in smoke. Lightning lit the roiling cloud briefly, and thunder echoed around me, ghostly cannon fire I could feel in my bones.

"Gary!" I screamed into the rain and smoke. I took a step toward the shack, trying desperately to see him.

A black shadow materialized in front of me as the entire structure went up in flames — Gary, stumbling toward me, the fishbowl in one hand, a leather-bound notebook in the other and a vase under his arm.

"Ez?" His eyes were wild.

I hugged him as relief flooded me. He didn't hug me back. In shock, I guessed. Well, that, and his arms were full. *Damn.* The fire was roaring now, lighting up the raindrops like an Impressionist painting from hell. This was not what I signed up for. And Gary — Gary had just lost everything.

"Can you call 9-1-1?" he asked hoarsely. "Otherwise, the whole dock might go up."

"Shit. Yes," I said, pulling my phone from my purse and dialing. I asked for the fire department, then held it out to Gary so he could give them the address.

In a minute, a siren began its eerie wail in the distance. Gary led me farther down the dock, calling: "Punky! Punky!" He turned to me. "Are you sure she got out?"

"Like a cat out of hell."

"That about sums it up." Gary turned down a walkway that led back to solid ground. He set down the fishbowl and vase and stuffed the notebook in his back pocket. We sat on a low stone wall and watched his shack burn. The flames reflected strangely in the fishbowl. Even the beta seemed agitated, swimming back and forth.

I handed him the beer.

Gary looked at it in a daze, and then he laughed. He tilted

the bottle against his mouth, his eyes closed, his features shifting and intriguing in the fiery light, and drank until it was empty. "This is why I love you."

"What?" *What did he just say?*

"There's the fire truck," he said, seemingly oblivious.

The truck rolled up, lights strobing, followed by an ambulance and a rescue truck that threw bright white spotlights on the scene as the firefighters worked. One of them checked with us to make sure we were OK while the rest doused the flames. Within thirty minutes, Gary's tiny house was a smoking heap of beams and charred, twisted strips of metal roofing, half-falling into the water. The rain had probably helped keep the fire from spreading to the dock, but it didn't help Gary.

"Man, I'm sorry," I said, my vision blurred by the rain and flashing lights. I felt a sudden chill despite the warm evening, soaked through, barefooted and bare-armed as I was.

"Well, it wasn't much to lose," he said philosophically, damn near as optimistic as he usually was. "And we're alive. But I need to find that cat."

"It was your home."

"I *am* kind of pissed to lose the vases. But any that didn't break would've survived the fire. I'll come back and look tomorrow."

"Really?"

"I fire some of them at over two thousand degrees. But chances are they're shattered or in the water by now. Funny," he said, staring into the smoldering mess. "I always liked fire. Getting a kiln stoked for raku is one of my favorite things."

"Why save this one?" I gestured to the vase that sat next to us, tall and slender, its color vaguely green in the spotty light.

"It's the glaze. Something I'm working on. This is the

closest I've gotten to — oh, hell, I suppose it's not the time for chemical analysis."

"What about the notebook?"

"Uh, drawings, designs. Notes on glazes. That kind of thing."

Interesting priorities. "But you lost all your clothes — and all your stuff — "

"Fucking inconvenient," he said with a shrug, his tone a little more ragged, the tension seeping through. "At least I got my keys. That's what took the extra minute. Though the house key isn't much good anymore." He stood. "Punky!"

I stood with him, and we split up, calling out for the cat. After a few minutes of walking on the docks, between the creaking boats amid now-intermittent raindrops, I heard Gary yelp.

"OK, gotcha, girl," he said, and I looked several berths down to see him extricating a terrified, sodden orange cat from his mop of wet curls. I laughed softly, wondering that I could find humor in the situation.

"Got her?" I called out.

"Yeah." He walked toward me, cradling the thoroughly miserable Pumpkin Spice. "Can you pick up my vase and the fish? And then — "

He seemed at a loss.

"And then you're coming home with me," I said simply.

GARY INSISTED ON DRIVING, which was probably just as well, since it was his cantankerous old van and I was still technically tipsy. But now I knew that nothing sobers you up as fast as being forced to flee a goddamned fire. Gary was subdued and quiet as he drove.

I held the fishbowl on my lap, and the cat cowered in the back. I directed Gary into downtown Bohemia but away from the main drag of clubs and restaurants as we made our way to my place.

I lived in an art-deco building with pink stucco walls not far from the Bohemia School of Art and Design, where Gary spent a lot of his time. My building used to be a small hotel, and over the years, it had been renovated to accommodate two apartments per floor — six in all, a mix of one- and two-bedrooms. Mine was a one-bedroom. It was cheap, with checkerboard tile floors and drafty windows, but it was mine, and I loved it.

Gary parked on the street, and the awkwardness of the situation, combined with the shock of what had happened, made this abruptly quiet moment feel more strange than either of us would acknowledge.

"At least you don't have any luggage," I quipped.

He allowed a small smile. "Unless you count a cat and a fish."

"They don't have luggage, either."

"They just have me."

"Come on up," I said, getting out of the van with my tiny purse over my shoulder and the fishbowl in my hands. He grabbed the cat.

I set down the fishbowl so I could unlock the front door, then grabbed it and led him inside. I glanced at the apartment to the right — that's where Julio lived with his mom, and the little rascal was always bugging me for piano lessons. At least now he should be asleep and not keeping his usual hawk eye peeled for my irregular appearances.

Gary and I headed up to the second floor.

My apartment door was ajar.

"Shit," I whispered.

"Uh-oh — do you think your drummer — uh — "

"Stuart? Maybe." *Fuck this fucking day.*

He took the fishbowl from me, set it on the floor and thrust the cat into my arms. "Hold her tight. She's kind of freaked out." And then he went right into the apartment.

"Gary!" I called, shocked and alarmed.

Thirty more seconds ticked by. "Gary!" I called again.

I heard his voice from within. "Fellini fan, huh?"

"What?" I pushed open the door and walked in with the cat.

"The poster," he said, staring at the movie poster over the couch. In vivid brushstrokes, it showed the dancing blond movie star in the foreground, while the blue-shadowed reporter, smoking, looked on, larger than life in the background. It was the only decor in my living room, which adjoined a kitchenette.

"So I'm nuts about *La Dolce Vita.* What's the verdict?"

"You probably don't want to go into your bedroom just now," Gary said, more seriously.

"Oh, fuck."

"Pretty much," he said. "Sorry. Give me Punky." He took the cat, and I walked into the bedroom.

Every dresser drawer was pulled out, and half the clothes had been yanked from them and strewn around the place. The bed had been tossed, too, at least a lot more so than I usually left it in the mornings. The chaos was reflected harshly in the mirror on my closet door. And what was that red stuff?

Gary appeared in the doorway with the cat in one hand and the fishbowl in the other. "I think it's ketchup."

"Oh, hell." I looked more closely. He was right. Ketchup had been squirted all over my clothes and the bed. Good thing I was out of mustard. "That bastard." I felt my hands trembling and squeezed them together. "I need a drink."

I turned and pushed past Gary.

"Put down that fish, will you? He's probably getting seasick," I said irritably as I opened the kitchen cabinet that held the liquor.

That *used* to hold the liquor.

"Son of a bitch!" I said, just standing there, gaping in disbelief at the empty cabinet.

"We should call the police," Gary said. He set the fishbowl on the beat-up coffee table, shut the apartment door and put down Pumpkin Spice, who immediately shot under the couch. I didn't blame her.

"What for? They'll laugh at this. Vandalism and a few liquor bottles."

"So you can get this on record in case you file a restraining order," he said, his voice even and strangely comforting.

At his kindness, and the generally fucked-up day, hot tears pricked my eyes. I refused to give in to them. For Christ's sake, Gary had just lost his whole house. I noticed his state of dishevelment, his damp hair and sooty clothes. Still, a strength emanated from him, a core of calm.

"All right," I said wearily. I moved to the couch and pulled the phone out of my purse. "Second 9-1-1 call of the night. Awesome."

Gary sat next to me as I made the call, and fifteen minutes later, a police officer, petite as I was but with spiky blond hair and a sympathetic attitude, arrived to take the report. Her partner, a stocky man who looked as if he'd seen everything, took a few photos to document the mess. Gary shadowed him, taking shots with my phone while I talked with the female officer.

"We'll have to interview him," she said. "If he denies this, there's not a lot we can do except list him as a suspect on the report. But since you were living together, the crime becomes more serious, especially if we can prove it's part of a pattern of domestic violence."

I frowned. "I don't intend for it to become any kind of pattern at all. He's out of my life."

"But if he does anything else, you need to report it so you can get a restraining order. For now, you might want to get this lock changed if he still has a key. Though I'm not sure you're going to get someone this late on a Saturday night."

She was wrong. The twenty-four-hour locksmith I called after the police left would be glad to come out and change the lock — for five hundred dollars. I laughed and rang off.

"That's just not going to happen, especially when it looks like I need to buy a whole new wardrobe, too," I told Gary, who'd retrieved the cat and was petting her in a way that suggested he was getting more comfort than she was. We sat hip to hip on the couch. Feeling his warmth through my silky pants gave me comfort, too. I stared around at my mini stereo, my narrow bookcase, my coffee table, the soft chair, the poster. At least those were OK. "I'll call somebody else in the morning."

"There's a guy I've used who's pretty good and open on Sunday. I'll give you the number. But I don't think you — we — should stay here tonight," he added. "I mean, I could probably handle your ex, but you're kind of dealing with a psycho. And your bed's full of ketchup."

"Kinky," I joked, and the corner of Gary's mouth quirked up. I reached out a hand and touched his dimple, and we held each other's eyes for a moment until the cat squirmed and jumped out of his arms again.

I recovered myself. "Maybe it's time I start calling some friends."

"Don't," Gary said. "There's another place we can go."

"Where?"

"My mom's house in Bohemia Beach."

WHEN GARY SAID *HOUSE,* I was picturing a nice little bungalow or '60s rancher, the type you see all over the barrier island.

I wasn't picturing the freakin' Barbie beach house, vintage edition. It wasn't hot pink, but it had levels and sprawl and all kinds of space-age charm, at least as far as I could tell in the dark as we pulled past the gate — Gary had to type in a code — and into the driveway.

"You like going from one extreme to the other, huh?" I asked.

"What do you mean?"

"Mansion to shack."

"I like — liked living small," he said. "Though, I admit, I still keep a few things here."

"Clothes?"

"Maybe a pair of jeans and some T-shirts. No, it's more like fun stuff. Like my drum set."

"That sounds practical," I said drily as we got out of the

van, my toes cool in the flip-flops I'd scrounged from my closet. I had the fishbowl again, along with a bag that held a few clothes that hadn't been contaminated by ketchup, and he had the cat and his vase.

"You just don't like drummers," he teased back, and I chuckled. It felt strange and necessary to laugh, given the shitty night we'd had.

"I have my reasons. So your mom's going to be OK with this?"

"Of course she will. And she'll even give you your own room, more's the pity."

Gary, back to flirting. Maybe the universe was returning to normal.

He used a key to get us in the front door, which was flanked by panels of light-green glass etched with sea creatures. The spacious, two-story foyer was dominated by a winding staircase, the kind with open steps. The rest of it melted into the shadows, suggesting many rooms beyond.

"Do you want a drink now?" he whispered, setting down Pumpkin Spice, who took off up the stairs. "Before we — you go to bed, I mean?"

I smiled at his correction. "The answer to that question is pretty much always yes." I set the fishbowl on the hall table next to a bonsai in a beautiful blue-glazed ceramic dish — made by Gary, no doubt — put down my bag and followed him.

We walked through a large, dimly lit kitchen with bright yellow cabinets, groovy hanging globe lights and yellow leather barstools at the center island ("It got stuck in the 1970s and never came out," he explained) to a hallway and then another room at what felt like the back of the house. He flipped on the light to reveal a den with wood paneling, heavy curtains, a pool table, couch, comfy chairs, bookshelves and a big globe on elaborate wooden legs. He went right to the globe and flipped it open, revealing a handful of bottles and glasses inside.

"Awesome! I always wanted one of those," I said.

"Looks like we have vodka, gin, bourbon, tequila and — Bailey's. Not much of a selection."

"Most of the major food groups. I'll have tequila." Tequila always eased my worries, even when nothing else would. "You got ice?"

"Sure." He took one of the glasses and went to a spot under the bookshelves where a mini-fridge had escaped my attention. He added ice to the glass and got himself a beer.

In a minute, I was taking a long sip of the tequila, followed by a long, slow breath.

I opened my eyes to see Gary staring at me, amusement on his face. "Feel better?"

"Marginally."

He grinned and sipped his beer. "Why don't we sit out on the deck? The rain's stopped." He parted the curtains and opened the glass sliding doors that had been hidden behind them.

The roar of the ocean, which I'd noticed dimly in the driveway, hit me like a sweet, familiar song. I didn't get out to Bohemia Beach, Bohemia's sister city across the lagoon, nearly enough these days, what with my day job and rehearsals and gigs.

I followed Gary out to the deck, which appeared to run the length of the house. We sat on a couple of damp Adirondack chairs, watched the scudding clouds and listened. There was no moon, nothing to alleviate the darkness out here, but a few stars shone in the clearing sky. The humid warmth of Florida spring hung in the air, promising hot days ahead.

"It's really pretty out here," I said. "It's like you don't have many houses around. It's nice."

"That's because we own — or my mom owns — the equivalent of about ten lots, with this house right in the middle. A thousand feet of beachfront. Someone in our family has owned this land since 1915. There used to be a lot more, but it's been sold off over the years."

"This is where you grew up?" I asked.

"Yep, this is it."

"I never took you for a rich kid in high school."

"By then, I wasn't." He stared out at the tumultuous, dark water.

"How so?"

"By then, my father had left my mom for one of his patients, and the money got pretty thin. But Mom grew up in this house, and she wanted to keep it, and the alimony was just enough to let her."

"Your dad sounds pretty shitty."

Gary laughed. "The King of Shitty."

"What kind of patient?"

"Plastic surgery."

"Lovely," I said, feeling a slow dissolution of my tension as the tequila entered my bloodstream.

"I suppose she was, if you like boobs that look like concrete basketballs."

I almost choked on the liquor. "Oh, fuck, that's an image."

"Tell me about it."

I heard a sound behind me and turned. The sliding door opened, and a woman walked through it, dressed in a thick pink terry robe and slippers. Her curly reddish-brown hair flew around her face in the breeze. "Gary?"

She looked just like him. Or, I should say, he looked just like her, only her features were a shade more delicate, her hair more red.

"Mom? I didn't mean to wake you," Gary said.

"You didn't. The cat did. And who's this? Oh, wait, I know you, don't I?"

"Ez Falcon," I said, standing and shaking her hand while hanging on to my drink. I'd waited a long time for it, and I wasn't letting go now.

"Esme, wasn't it? At Bohemia High? Gary used to talk about you. I'm Ginny Gorski."

"Nice to meet you," I said.

Gary stood and gave her a hug. She wrinkled her nose. "Have you started smoking?"

He looked confused, then sniffed his shirt. "Oh. That's from the fire."

"Fire?" she asked in alarm.

"It was a pretty small fire," he said, trying to ease the blow.

"It was a pretty small shack," I couldn't help but add.

"Your house?" Ginny looked stricken. "Are you OK?"

"I'm here," he said. "The house is gone."

"Oh, honey," Ginny said, giving him another hug. This time she hung on a little longer, and Gary gave me a helpless smile over her shoulder.

"And Ez had some trouble tonight, too. It's a long story. Do you have a room where she can stay? And my usual, if it's available?"

"We're a bit full right now. Why don't we give Ez the lunar bedroom? You can sleep on the couch in the den for tonight.

Be quiet, if you can. I don't want you to wake up Grandma or Aunt Johanna. Your cousin Kayla has the guest room. It's spring break."

"Do grad students get spring break?" he asked.

"She does, apparently," Ginny replied. "I'm so glad you're OK, honey. You can tell me all about it in the morning."

"Thanks, Mom," Gary said, and she left us there on the deck.

I knocked back the rest of my drink, feeling the fatigue of the crazy evening weighing me down. "Ready if you are."

"I suppose," he said regretfully. "This isn't how I wanted the evening to end."

"Maybe it's not over," I teased, thinking about what I might be able to do to make him feel better. I mean, that's how I'd started the evening. I'd wanted to give him a thrill. And then there had been his kiss — *ay caramba,* that kiss — and then all hell had broken loose. I had no plans to be Gary's girlfriend, but he was a guy, and guys had needs, and I didn't mind helping out the ones I liked. To a point.

He looked skeptical and a little sad as he followed me into the house. I grabbed my bag in the foyer, and he led me up the stairs and down a hallway to a modest bedroom. An entire wall inside was covered with a mural showing the moon — or, at least, the lunar horizon — with a half-lit Earth floating in space beyond.

"The lunar bedroom," I said.

"Shhh," he whispered, closing the door behind us, then added quietly: "Don't want to wake up Grandma. She's in the next room, but then again, she's almost deaf without her hearing aids, and selectively deaf with them."

"Then we can make all the noise we want," I said slyly, sitting on the bed and giving it a bounce or two.

"Don't tease me, Ez," Gary said mournfully. "You have no idea how much sexual frustration I experienced here on the moon, staring at these walls as a teenager. I don't want to compound it."

"Come here." I patted the mattress. "You've had a hard day."

"So have you."

"I think yours was much harder," I said, lightly inflecting *harder* to see if I could, as they say, get a rise out of him.

His eyebrows lifted ever so slightly, and he took a step toward me, uncertain again.

I stood and stepped into his personal space. He froze. "Let's get these smoky clothes off you," I murmured, grasping the hem of his T-shirt and pulling it over his head as best I could, given how tall he was.

I almost didn't realize I'd dropped the shirt to the floor, I was so distracted by his chest. Where did all those muscles come from? He'd always been the skinny guy, and the baggy T-shirts gave me no clue. And now, he was so — so —

Ever so slowly, I lifted my hands and laid them gently on his belly, then slid them up and over his nipples to his firm pecs. He sucked in a breath and gazed down at me with a look that was somewhere between alarm and pure lust.

Oh, those eyes. I'd always thought Gary had brown eyes, maybe lighter than mine, not that I'd ever looked closely. But they were something else altogether. They were hazel, dark amber flecked with emerald and streaked with bronze, altogether beautiful, like light on the lagoon early in the morning.

And right now, they were on fire.

He bent down over me, lifted my chin with one finger and touched his lips to mine.

Hot! was all my mind could articulate as I tasted his mouth on mine, his tongue against mine, beer and smoke and, God, *longing* as the kiss intensified. This could all go somewhere fast, suddenly too fast for me, supposedly the fastest girl in Bohemia.

I pushed against his chest and sat hard on the bed, breathing fast, staring up at him.

"Ez?" he asked, concern in his voice.

"I just need a minute."

"OK." He sounded amused and still aroused. And then he sat next to me.

"You're a good kisser," I said as matter-of-factly as I could.

"Am I?" He ran a hand through my long bangs, the layers of my haircut, and kissed my neck.

Oh, shit. I was supposed to be the one in control here. And my control was gone.

No. It wasn't. I'd lay hands on the man and he'd go home — er, go back to his couch happy.

I took a deep breath, turned toward him and reached for the button on his jeans.

He jumped up. "Whoa. I mean, yeah, but whoa."

"I just want to make you feel better."

"I feel — Ez, this is not how I want this to go down."

"Speaking of going down — " I shot him a coquettish smile.

He blanched. "You're killing me."

"That's not the idea."

"But it's the reality. You have no idea how much I want — look, I'm going to leave now, and you have to promise me something."

I was breathing more normally again. He was the one off-kilter now. The way it should be. "OK, I'll bite."

"You'll go out with me. Dinner. And we'll talk. Tomorrow night, OK?" He let out a sigh. "I've been wanting to ask you that for so long."

Which was exactly why I'd never given him the time of day. And now I was going out on a date with Groupie Gary.

I AWOKE to the sound of the ocean in my ears, stimulating and lulling, rhythmic and chaotic at the same time. It took me a moment to remember where I was, how I got here.

Damn it.

It all came back, the fire, the mess in my apartment, which I'd have to deal with right away, especially the lock. And then the strangely intense moments with Gary, about the last guy I ever thought I'd wake up thinking about.

I slipped out of bed, sans clothes — my usual habit — and pushed open the curtains just an inch or two on what I now realized was a sliding door that led to a deck that overlooked the beach. *Nice.* The waves glinted in the morning sun, all kinds of beautiful.

I sifted through my bag and figured out what to wear out of the few things I'd salvaged from the ketchup attack. Today it would have to be an old Ramones T-shirt and shorts. Cotton undies and bra. Comfort for the battle. I threw the clothes onto a chair, contemplated the lunar mural and paused. I thought I heard a noise outside my door.

"Is someone there?" I asked.

"It's Gary. Sorry. I need to get in there for a minute. I was hoping you'd gone downstairs already."

"OK, just a sec." I pulled the comforter off the bed, wrapped it around myself and opened the door.

Gary was there. In a towel. His hair was wet, and his face was bright red.

"I swear, I didn't want you to see me like this," he said, and then his eyes just about popped out of his head at my minimal attire.

"What can I do for you?" I asked in a sultry tone that was only slightly mocking.

"I just need something from the closet." He averted his eyes as he brushed past me. *How cute.*

The white towel was knotted at his waist — his nicely tapered waist — but he clutched it anyway, as if it might fall. And it *was* hanging pretty low on those tantalizing hips. I admired the view, the elegance of his long, trim body, as he opened the door to a closet, stepped in and closed it behind him.

I laughed. "I didn't know you were in the closet, Gary," I said. "Not that there's anything wrong with that."

"Put on some clothes," he said, his voice muffled through the door.

"If you insist." It took me just a minute. "It's safe, Nature Boy."

"Oh," he said, cautiously popping his head out the door. "I like that song. Nat King Cole's, especially."

"That's gorgeous, but Ella's is pretty sweet, too."

He emerged in jeans — an irrepressible part of me wondered if there was anything under them, since I doubted he stored underwear in the closet — with a heather-gray T-shirt in his hand. I got another look at his spectacular chest, at the corded muscles of his arms, and again, I was shocked at just how sexy this new Gary was. Or, at least, new to me. I hadn't noticed him this way — well, ever.

I think he noticed me looking. Bashful again, he slipped the shirt over his head. *Too bad.*

"I think my mom's making breakfast," he said. "I smell French toast. Might as well get a bite before facing the day."

"You mean, before facing what's left of your house and what's left of my clothes? Not that you need to help me with that — you can just drop me off so you can deal with your stuff."

"I can provide moral support. And I'd like it if you came along to the docks. You know, in case I get trapped under the debris," he joked.

"OK," I agreed, strangely pleased that he wanted me along, and touched, too. It wouldn't be easy for him to revisit the charred remains of his house. "Let me call the locksmith first."

I made the appointment for an hour from now, then called my landlady to give her a heads-up. She was sympathetic and asked that I drop off a key at her office Monday, and that was that.

We had just enough time to grab a quick breakfast and found a crowd at the oval, wooden table in the yellow '70s kitchen. Gary introduced his Grandma Helen, a sharp-eyed lady with severely short white hair and Ginny's nose; cousin Kayla, whose long hair was golden brown and who, I was told, was about to get her master's degree in film production; and Kayla's mom, Aunt Johanna, who looked a lot like her sister Ginny. And helping Ginny cook was a man Gary didn't know, either, judging by how high Gary's eyebrows stretched in surprise at meeting him.

"This is Jay," Ginny Gorski said by way of scant introduction.

Jay, who almost certainly had spent the night, was somewhere in the neighborhood of fifty with a nice head of silver-streaked brown hair. Maybe it was the shirt and the tan, but he looked like a golfer. Of course, being a musician unused to the civilized classes, I saw most middle-aged, well-groomed white guys as golfers.

"Nice to meet you, Gary, Ez," Jay said pleasantly. "French toast?"

"And bacon," I said, sniffing the divine aroma as it sizzled on the stove. I didn't care if bacon killed you. I figured it was an even exchange for not smoking. And I was willing to share with Pumpkin Spice, who was sneaking bites from Ginny's not-so-subtle handouts.

Over breakfast and fresh-squeezed orange juice from Harvey's Groves, Gary told the story of the fire. And then, as if eager to explain that we were not an item, he said that I'd had a break-in at my apartment and didn't want to stay there till the lock was fixed. I appreciated that he didn't mention that I really had a psycho ex-boy-toy who still had a key to the perfectly fine lock. That would have been a little too much information to dump on the family who'd just put me up for the night.

And what an interesting family. Discounting interloper Jay, as friendly as he was, there was a warm, feminine aura to this household. I didn't know how long this many women had lived in this place — and Kayla, who seemed pretty cool, was just visiting — but I had a feeling the estrogen levels explained something about the sweet streak in Gary's personality.

"So what do you do, Ez?" Ginny asked me.

"I'm a musician."

"Do you make a living doing that?"

"Not really. Not yet. I have to resort to more unpleasant methods of making money."

"Contract killings?" Kayla joked.

"Almost as bad," I said, not elaborating.

"We should go meet the locksmith," Gary interrupted.

"Good idea. Thanks for letting me stay," I said to Ginny.

"Any time," she replied with an impish smile and a glance at her son. "Gary, you're coming back later, right?"

"I think I'll have to stay here for a bit till I find a place, if that's OK."

"Sure, sweetheart. Let me show you out."

I figured this was code for "Let me talk with you in private," so I ran upstairs to get my bag. Halfway down the stairs, I heard Gary and his mom — somewhere in the hall-way, I thought — and stopped, not sure if I should barge into the conversation.

"So who is Jay exactly?" Gary was asking.

"He's the insurance rep for the museum. That's how I met him. And he's a good man, Gary. We're getting pretty serious."

"How serious?"

"Really serious. That's what I wanted to talk to you about. That and the house."

"What do you mean?"

"If I marry Jay — "

"*Marry* him?"

"If I marry Jay, the alimony goes away," his mother contin-ued, undaunted. "And I don't think I'll be able to keep the house, with the taxes and the insurance and just maintaining this old thing."

"You've maintained it this long," he said. "Don't you think there's a way?"

"Not without the alimony money. You know I hated using

that money to keep it, but I wanted to stay here while you were in school — and the property has been in our family for so long."

Gary sighed. "I'd hate to see it developed."

"I know," Ginny said ruefully. "Every month another condo developer makes an offer out of the blue, but I've always turned them down. If the dunes, this beautiful piece of beach, are destroyed, it will break your grandma's heart."

"But you have to live on something," he acknowledged.

"We'll need the money to find a place for all of us. Jay doesn't make that much, but he's open to having a place, maybe a duplex, where we can all live near each other."

"He's not into polygamy, is he?" Gary joked.

"*Gary,*" she admonished. "Honestly, I'm not sure what to do, but I wanted you to know what was going on."

"You should do what makes you happy, Mom," he said after a moment. I decided it was a good time to stop skulking and headed the rest of the way down the stairs.

I saw them down the hall, just off the foyer. They glanced up at me, unperturbed.

"What makes me happy doesn't matter," Ginny told Gary. "Not when so many people are depending on me."

"It'll work out. Aunt Johanna has a job."

"A part-time nonprofit job helping mentally challenged adults make crafts? She'd make more at McDonald's."

"You have a job."

"Another nonprofit job. Being secretary to the museum board has never paid all that much."

Gary looked down for a moment. "Let me think about it. But sometimes, you have to do what you have to do. Don't rush into anything, OK?"

Her laugh was dry. "I've waited this long to get serious

about someone. I'm not rushing. But the older you get, the more you realize that life is short." She glanced at me again. "You'd better go."

"OK, Mom. Love you." He hugged Ginny, then met me in the foyer.

With one hand, I rubbed Gary's back through his T-shirt, trying not to be distracted by the spark of heat I felt when I touched him. "Sorry — I heard some of that."

"It's OK. Mom is so open about everything. She doesn't mind. I don't mind. But that *was* kind of a surprise."

"Life's full of surprises right now, that's for sure."

"A lot to think about," he agreed.

"Shall we see what's next?"

"By all means," he said with an ironic smile. "Your place first."

THE LOCKSMITH WAS WAITING outside my building, sitting in his truck, playing with his phone. As he went to work swapping out my lock, I started sorting my clothes into piles — trashed, possibly washable, and ketchup-free. But first, I stripped the bed and threw out the sheets and the comforter; even bleach couldn't erase the bad memories there. Gary helped me put fresh sheets on, and then he sat on the edge of the bed and bagged the trash, listening to me mourn some of my favorite outfits. Still, probably a quarter of my clothes had escaped a dousing by being at the bottom of the pile or left in the closet. At least I'd have something to wear to work for a couple of days while I did some shopping.

"So is your Aunt Johanna married?" I asked as I worked.

"No, she never was. Kayla was one of those family

surprises, is how I heard it. Aunt Jo struggled for years as a single mom, even lived with my grandmother for a while, and then when my dad left, my mom invited both my aunt and grandma to stay. It helped with the bills, and my aunt took the nonprofit job she has now instead of working multiple waitressing jobs."

"That must have sucked. Sorry to be gossipy, but does that mean Kayla doesn't know who her father is?"

"I don't know. We're fairly close, but she never talked about it."

"Fair enough." I tossed another of my performance blouses on the keeper pile — a sparkling sheer black number I was relieved to find free of condiments. It was one of my favorites. But this poor purple one — I tossed it to Gary, and he stuffed it in the garbage bag.

"How's your sister?" he asked.

"Which one? Isabel or Reya?"

"I only knew Isabel, the younger one. You all seemed close. Reya graduated before you even came to Bohemia, didn't she?"

"Yeah, that's right." I was amazed he remembered that. "Isabel has her troubles."

"I'm sorry."

"Me too." *Izzy and Esme, singing together.* Those days were long gone. But I owed her a visit, especially after Mama's latest email. Another month, another rehab.

"She always struck me as a little wild," Gary said.

"Unlike me," I quipped. She had her reasons. We both did. I tried to change the subject. "How do you like Jay?"

"You met him the same time I did," he said, a touch of irritation in his voice. "How did *you* like him?"

"He seemed pleasant enough. He cooked me breakfast. I can't say that of any man I've known up till now."

Gary smiled. "I make a pretty mean omelet."

"I thought we were having dinner."

"At least," he teased, catching a red-splattered white cotton blouse that had gone to meet its maker.

I raised an eyebrow at him and put the last empty drawer back in my dresser. I was nearing the end of the piles. I found a couple of pairs of jeans that I thought might clean up with the help of stain remover, along with several shirts I was willing to try to save, and those went into a laundry basket. I rinsed them out, used half a bottle of Shout on the stains and hung them over the shower curtain rod to marinate. The leather jacket would be fine, I was pretty sure. My nicest pants, two miniskirts and my one decent dress had never left the closet.

Still, Gary now held a bursting-at-the-seams trash bag full of my clothes, and I felt a new wave of anger at Stuart. What an asshole. He'd seemed so — pliant before. And pretty competent with his hands, as one might expect from a drummer. Still, that had been a lousy reason to keep him around for as long as I did.

"You OK?" Gary asked, catching my angry expression.

"I will be," I said. "Let me check on our locksmith."

The locksmith was setting the last screws, and he handed me two shiny keys and a bill — a much more reasonable amount than the other guy had quoted at midnight. I paid it and gathered up my purse.

"Ready to face the ruins?" I asked Gary.

He tried unsuccessfully to smile.

Several minutes later, we were back on the edge of Bohemia's harbor. Rows of boats with shiny chrome trim or sky-piercing sails and rigging stretched along the docks; beyond, more boats and buildings gleamed across the sunlit blue water. As we parked in the same place as the night before, I wished I could have seen Gary's place in daylight. It must have been charming, and the view would have been spectacular.

Instead, now there was a heap of blackened beams and twisted metal and debris, and someone had ringed it all with caution tape.

"That looks pretty dangerous," I said as Gary gingerly approached.

"Danger's my middle name," he said, lifting the tape and stepping into the ring of fire.

Or the ring of charcoal.

I reluctantly followed and helped him sift through what I could, staying away from where part of the structure was falling into the water. Little was left of the furnishings. Gary seemed focused on finding his vases, and he did — three broken ones and two perfectly intact, if a little dirty. He also grabbed a few plates that he'd made and the cat's metal food bowls.

But most of his stuff was not that impervious to fire. The clothes were gone — even a ketchup attack would have been an improvement — as were a few pieces of important paperwork, memorabilia and his prized stereo.

"Aw, shit," he said, picking up a twisted metal rod.

"What's that?"

"It was my bike's handlebars, I think," he said. "I loved that thing. Yeah, here's the rest of it. A skeleton."

"R.I.P."

It was strange to find bits of barely identifiable objects — canned goods, a lampshade, a microwave oven.

"Hey, look at this!" I called out, lifting a warped black circle from the wreckage.

"The last of the vinyl," Gary said mournfully from the other side of the pile, where he'd been kicking aside blackened planks in vain hope of finding more salvageable items.

I looked more closely at the disc, focusing on the charred label. I could just make out the letters *XTA*. "I think it was Yma Sumac."

"God rest her soul," Gary said, and I chuckled at his bleak humor. He gave me a lost-puppy look, and then he laughed, too. "Let's get out of here. This is hopeless." He raised a hand over the mess and made a sign of the cross. "I consign thee to the deep," he intoned.

I helped him carry the few rescued items back to his van.

"You going to be OK?" I asked once we were under way.

"Yeah," he said, though he wasn't his usual chipper self. "It's just stuff, though it'll be a pain to replace a few of the things. The bike wasn't cheap, and I need that for therapy, you know?" He shot me a sad smile. "I'll stay at my mom's for a while, save up and get another apartment."

"Not to offer a cliché, but you know the most important thing."

"I know," he said. "I survived."

"No," I said. "You saved the cat."

He laughed. "No, *you* saved the cat. Thank you."

"I have a feeling she'll be living high on the hog at your mom's house."

"Literally. Bacon," Gary said. "That reminds me, I have to pick up food for her and the fish. How about I drop you off, and I can pick you up later?"

"Later? Oh, that's right. Dinner. I'd almost forgotten amid the apocalypse."

"At least it's not the zombie apocalypse."

"Stop it! I hate zombies!" I said. "And I'll pick *you* up." *That way I can escape whenever I want,* I thought. I wasn't sure that I was ready for Dinner with a capital "D" with Gary, but I had a feeling the past several hours would have been hell without him.

He grinned as he pulled up to the curb outside my place. "Seven?"

"Sure," I said. "I'll be wearing my best ketchup outfit."

"Ketchup — and nothing else?"

I stepped out and held open my door for one more second, flashing him my rock-and-roll smile. "Only if you like to lick."

His mouth dropped open. I slammed the door shut, turned and sashayed in my shorts to my front door.

THE IDEA of wearing ketchup was a lot less glamorous than it had sounded at the end of our morning expedition. I used the laundry machines on the first floor of our building to try to rescue the "maybe" garments from permanent destruction, and maybe half of them turned out to be worth keeping.

Julio, the spiky-haired eight-year-old who lived on the first floor, found me pulling them out of the dryer in disgust.

"Why do you look so angry, Ms. Falcon?" He said my last name the way they'd said it in Miami, the Cuban way, *Fall-CONE,* with the accent over the "O." That had been too much for my Bohemia teachers to handle, and I became Esme Falcon, the bird of prey.

"Because that guy who was rooming with me for a while

ruined a bunch of my clothes," I told him. I always told Julio the truth. He needed to know what a crappy world this was.

"Why?"

"Because he was a jerk." I started folding the clothes worth keeping. "Don't be a jerk to girls, Julio. Be a good man."

"I will, Ms. Falcon. When are you going to give me another lesson?"

"Our schedules never seem to match up." Which was true, though they might match up better if his mom paid me. She had her own issues, doing it all herself, and I understood.

"You could come when I get home from school," he said.

"I'm still at work then," I said. He looked so disappointed, I made a counteroffer. "How about Monday at 6? A quick lesson before your dinnertime. But only if it's OK with your mom."

"It will be! Thank you! I'll ask her right now!"

"OK," I said to his fleeing back as he ran to his apartment. He was back in moments. "She says yes!"

"I want you to practice that song we picked out last time, OK?"

"I've been practicing, and I have a new one, too! And I do my scales every day," Julio said, beyond excited. I'd never seen a kid who loved piano so much. He had a cheap electronic keyboard his mom had somehow saved up for and bought him at Christmas. He'd used Internet videos to teach himself the basics, though he had a lot of bad habits.

"Great." I hoisted my basket and headed for the stairs, leaving him at his apartment door. "See you then."

A two-hour nap and a shower later, I picked out an outfit that I thought might make Gary just a little bit crazy. I knew I could be a provocateur with men, but with Gary, oh-so-easily-interested Gary, I felt a need to exercise my power to a wicked degree. It was that innate thing I had, that desire to perform, that thing I knew wasn't entirely healthy, given my past. But Gary was such a perfect audience to feed my compulsion.

I donned my favorite sheer, black sleeveless top over a not-quite-sheer bra, a combination that invited stares. I squeezed into a pair of freshly washed jeans that were so weathered, the subtle new stains fit right in. Smoky makeup brought out my almond-shaped eyes. Dangly silver earrings added sparkle. I checked myself out in the bathroom mirror, flipping my long, dark bangs over my face, then back. *Saucy.* Red lipstick completed the look.

But it also stopped me, just for a minute. I remembered seeing my face, my much younger face, thin and nervous and starkly made up with crimson lipstick, caught in a photograph — one of *those* photographs — and for a second, I hated myself.

I shook the feeling and headed for my car, a 1997 red del Sol I'd purchased from a guy in Bohemia Beach who'd let it sit in a garage for a decade. It had 180,000 miles on it, and the seals around the removable roof leaked, but when it was convertible weather, there was nothing like it. My keyboard, when I needed it, just fit in the trunk. Beyond that, what else mattered?

The gate was open when I arrived at Gary's mom's house. The sun sank in the western sky, casting a mellow glow and long shadows, picking out the home's weathered wood trim. The whole thing looked like it needed a coat of paint and a going-over with a nail gun. Maintenance must be hell with the sun and salty wind battering it all the time and money thinner than it appeared.

Gary walked out the front door as I pulled up, his curls blowing in the breeze. I was pleased to see him in khakis and a loose, white linen shirt that echoed the gleam in his smile. His tan glowed subtly through the fabric, and I flashed back on the memory of his naked chest.

I cleared my throat as he got in the car. "You dressed up for me."

"I just went out and bought a few things. Wow, and you dressed up for me," he said, his roving stare lingering on my breasts. They might only be a handful, but I knew the sheer top and bra made them magnetic. He dragged his eyes up to my face. "I'm so glad you could go out with me tonight."

I smiled. He really was cute. He caught my eye, and looking into those deep amber and emerald irises, I was struck mute for a minute, too.

I tore my gaze away from his, put the car in gear and whirled back through the gate, which closed behind us. "So where should we go, tiger? You know the beach better than I do."

"There's an exotic new restaurant not far north," Gary said.

"Exotic? How so?" I asked, turning right on A1A.

"It's a hotel restaurant that's actually good, with a pretty cool bar. So I'm told."

"What kind of food?"

"American with a touch of adventure. Seafood and the occasional wild game."

"Really? I wonder if they have venison." I glanced over at him, then back to the road and the sky, turning orange and purple now. "Sometimes I feel like the last carnivore of our generation."

He laughed. "There are a few of us left."

The hotel was unusual — boutique, a 1970s property renovated to look more Polynesian than polyester, with tiki torches burning out front and a lushly landscaped courtyard we had to walk through to get to the oceanfront restaurant, Bohemia Key.

"Going for the Key West theme, looks like," I said as we entered. Hemingway memorabilia, photos from the Keys, big fiberglass fish and a scaled-down mockup of the red, black and yellow "Southernmost Point" buoy decorated the lobby. Weathered wood and corrugated metal were everywhere, adding to the ambience, and the door to the left led out to a large oceanfront deck and an outdoor bar.

Gary gave the hostess his name, and she led us to the right, to a table by windows that overlooked the ocean, now turquoise under a deep pink sky. Palm trees and bougainvillea with hot-pink blooms framed the deck outside.

The restaurant was packed. It was spring break, after all, and while Bohemia Beach didn't get that many drunken college students, a lot of people still vacationed here.

"You requested this table?" I asked him after the hostess had handed us menus, got a waitress to take our drink orders and left.

"Yeah. You like it?"

"Very nice. Can we afford it?"

"It's a pretty casual menu," he said, opening his. "Plus, I don't have any rent to pay for a while."

"You OK with that?"

He shrugged and smiled. "There are worse things than living on the beach. Hey, look, they do have venison."

"Poor Bambi. You're dead to me," I said.

He laughed out loud. "I'm going for the citrus mahi. I'm glad they don't call it 'dolphin.' It's so confusing for the tourists."

"Flipper and Bambi. It's a bloodbath."

He chuckled. "But it's not Flipper. Just a very tasty fish."

"That's what they *say,*" I said, looking out the window at the pastiche of tropical sunset pastels. "Oh, no. I think I see his friends offshore, squeaking. It's a posse of deadly dolphins. They want revenge."

When I turned back to Gary, he had a hand over his mouth, and our server was standing by the table, giving me a funny look. She set down my Hemingway daiquiri and Gary's beer and took our orders.

Gary grinned after she left. "I needed that."

"I know. The sexual tension was just too much," I joked, and he laughed again.

And then he got quiet, holding my eyes with his. He lifted his beer, and I held up my glass to meet his toast. "To sexual tension," he said softly.

I clinked my glass against his as I held his gaze, took a sip and felt a wave of warmth slosh through me with the rum cocktail, brightly flavored with fresh lime and grapefruit juice. The drink was cool. His look was anything but.

"How's Pumpkin Spice?" I asked, not comfortable with the moment. Gary wasn't supposed to be making *me* melt.

"Oh," he said, blinking, setting down his beer. "She's good. I caught her trying to get to my fish, so I had to make a new screen for the top of the bowl."

"Plucky thing."

"She's down to eight lives, so she's trying to live them to the max, I guess."

"Sounds like a good idea."

"What are the Emeralds going to do about a drummer?" he asked, taking a biscuit from the bread basket the server dropped by.

"We're advertising online. We have a practice Wednesday.

I hope we get somebody by then. Robby and I are actually supposed to be meeting a record label guy on Tuesday, so it's kind of an awkward time."

"That's great, though! I always thought you guys should go national. You are so good."

"Thanks," I said, "but it's not a big label. They're based in Orlando."

"The days of the big label are over," Gary declared. "This might be just what you need to go to the next level, a record deal, a tour, maybe."

"Maybe. Things are so weird now. So much happens online. We can keep playing clubs, put out a music video, put out a couple of songs for free, but you just never know who's going to hear us at the right time and plug us in, you know? And the truth is, sometimes I just want to sit in my room and write music."

"You're great at that, too," Gary gushed. "I mean, not to sound like a fanboy."

Which is exactly what he sounded like. Why did that bother me? I was suspicious of anyone who could like me that much. I knew better.

"What about your pottery? Where do you want to go with that?" I asked him as the food arrived.

"Hoping for a stadium tour," he said, and it was my turn to laugh. "Exactly," he said when I quieted. "It's not that kind of art. I mean, I hope to get into more shows, bigger and better galleries, but at the same time, I'm really happy at the school. I work there, I teach there, I make stuff there. It's pottery all day long, at least when I don't have another gig. I love it."

I heard it, that satisfaction in his voice, and I envied it. I wasn't there yet. I still wasn't sure what path I wanted to take.

"Bambi is delicious," I said after a minute of chewing, and he grinned.

"So is Flipper. Dolphin-tastic! I can almost taste the squeaks and clicks."

"Mommy," a little girl said at the next table, "are they eating a dolphin?"

The woman with her shot us a reproachful look. "No, sweetheart, they're eating a fish that's sometimes called dolphin."

"OK," the girl said, but her voice wavered, and she didn't look convinced.

I raised my eyebrows at Gary, and he didn't say anything, but his dimples showed as he shot me a wink. Eventually, we chatted more quietly about the food and his life on the beach growing up. He surfed, bicycled and learned to love the arts as his mom, once a society doyenne, raised money for the endowment that helped make the Bohemia School of Art and Design what it was.

I grabbed the bill when it arrived and gave the folder back to the waitress with cash.

"Hey!" he said.

"I've got this. You saved me from ketchup man." And I figured I made more than him at my day job, though I'd never admit it.

"But you saved my cat."

"How about you get it next time?" *Oh, crap. I didn't mean to say that.*

"Next time?" Gary was grinning again. "Excellent. But for now, I'm going to buy you a drink at the bar."

I nodded, accepting the fact that I'd just agreed to — no, *instigated* — a second date.

"I never turn down a drink," I said as we walked out the

deck doors and into the breezy evening. "Especially another one of those Hemingway daiquiris. Beats frozen pink stuff any day."

"Though I can't stay out too late," Gary said, gesturing to a table by the railing. The rushing sound of the ocean was mesmerizing. "Have to be at the school early tomorrow."

"I can't either," I said.

"Why not?"

Oh, shit. I never talked about my day job. It ruined the whole musician mystique. "I, uh, have stuff to do. Have to buy clothes and stuff."

"But the stores won't open till 10 or so."

"Yeah," I said vaguely. "Waitress!"

In a few minutes, we were equipped with beer and a cock-tail. "You might have to drive us back to your place. You OK with that?" I asked Gary as I took a healthy sip of the daiquiri.

"Sure. Cute car," he said. "For a cute girl."

"Cute? Gawd, I was going for sexpot."

"Oh." Was he blushing? He slid his chair around so it was next to mine, facing the ocean. For a few minutes, we enjoyed our drinks under the strings of glowing lights, watching the other patrons and listening to the waves. As the water moved, it shimmered in the darkness.

"I apologize for calling you cute," he finally said in a lower voice. "Mere 'cute' would never be enough. My vocabulary is always lacking when it comes to you."

Wow. Now that was — a well beyond *cute* thing to say.

I set a hand on Gary's knee and trailed a finger slowly up his thigh, feeling toned muscle through the fabric of his pants. He sat very still, then jumped as my finger got close to what appeared to be an expanding mound at his crotch, shaking me off.

"You're not what I expected," he said.

I gave him what I hoped was a sultry smile. "You've known me forever."

"Yeah, but not like — I mean, I never got to spend any real time with you. Not like I wanted to."

I leaned in and touched his shoulder, now running my hand down his sleeve, feeling his heat through the thin linen.

"Well, here we are," I whispered in his ear. I clutched his thigh again.

His breathing grew ragged. He looked around. There were plenty of people out on this sweet spring evening, but they were involved in their own merry conversations.

"They don't care about us," I said softly in his ear, sliding my hand a little closer to his bulge. "What do you want to do?"

I touched it.

"Oh, hell!" He jumped up and slammed down his beer. He looked down at me, his thin, dark eyebrows executing a glower, his eyes a beach bonfire of desire and mortification. "Maybe we should have this conversation somewhere else."

I sat back in my chair and drained my cocktail. I set down the glass and blinked at him from under my eyelashes. "Whatever you say, Gary."

He nodded and slapped down some money, stuffing it under his beer bottle, pointing it out to the server as he led me back through the restaurant and the hotel courtyard to my car.

"Too bad," I said when we got to the del Sol. "That's a nice place to sit and watch the beach."

"I have a place where we can sit and watch the beach," he said gruffly, plucking the keys from my hand, opening and closing the passenger door for me and moving quickly to the driver's side. "And maybe talk."

"Is that what you want to do, Gary?" I asked as he drove back toward the beach house. "Talk?"

"Shut up," he said, but his voice was soft, tense. "I just want to really get to know you, Ez. Get to know your soul. What I hear in the music."

"You've heard it all in the music. You have me right here."

"Not all of you. I know it." He shot me a look that seemed full of pain, of fire. "I wanted to do this right."

"I have no idea what 'right' is."

He had to key in the code for the gate. He pulled the car into the driveway and looked at me, motives warring in his eyes. Finally, he turned off the car and spoke, his voice low and intense and not at all the way he usually sounded.

"Let's go look at the beach."

WE WALKED through the house to the den, where I dropped my purse and grabbed the bottle of bourbon from his globe bar without asking. He said nothing, just pulled a thick fleece blanket from the couch and led me out the sliding door.

"Why the blanket?" I teased, keeping my tone innocent. "We can see the beach perfectly well from the deck."

"And every person in this house can see and hear us, too," he said. "We'll walk. There's some advantage to having this much wild land."

"That anyone can walk on at any time."

"The beach, yes, and I'm glad about that," he said, taking off his shoes at the steps. I left my sandals there, too, and we walked south on the sand. "It would suck if all the beaches were closed off to everyone except the rich people who can afford to live here."

"And you." The lights of the house, already minimal for the sake of the sea turtles, seemed to fade away as we headed for the darkest spot on the beach, shadowed by dunes and sea grass on this moonless night.

"We're not rich. I fell in love with the arts when we were. And then reality stepped in."

"But you wouldn't give up pottery."

"Never," he said, spreading the blanket. The wind folded it over at the corners. I sat, keeping it in place, and he sat next to me.

"I feel the same way about music. I could never give it up, no matter if I never get rich from it. It's my passion."

"See," Gary said, and finally, he smiled. "You can talk."

"That's not all I can do." I smiled back, unscrewed the cap on the whiskey and took a swig. I handed it to him.

"I usually prefer beer." He looked uncomfortable again.

"Indulge me."

"I'm pretty sure I would indulge you in just about anything," he said ruefully, and took a swallow.

"I'll remember that." I could hear my voice slipping into sex-kitten mode. I was the slinky cat, sure of her conquest, playing with my prey. *But he's not prey,* came the unbidden thought. *He helped you. He likes you.* "Fuck," I said under my breath.

"What?"

"Just practicing my four-letter words." I had to remember that Gary wanted way more from this, whatever this was, than I did. My only plan had been to blow his mind Saturday night and go home, not engage in a twenty-four-hour adventure.

I took the bottle back and took a longer swallow, then capped it and stuck it in the sand so it wouldn't tip over. I leaned back, supporting myself with my elbows, and looked up, letting the bourbon blunt my sharp edges. It was so dark out here, the stars seemed to go on forever, layers and layers of them.

"This doesn't suck." I glanced over at Gary.

He lay on his side, leaning on one elbow. His curls blew in the wind, and his eyes shone. "No street lights. No barriers. Your imagination can travel. Dreams seem real." But he wasn't looking at the stars. He was looking at me, those eyes as deep as the starry night.

I almost folded with the intensity of his gaze, and a rush of heat buzzed through me, a fevered honeybee carrying sweet, sweet nectar. What was it about this man, this night? Why wasn't I making it clear where I stood? My encounters with men were short, shallow and controlled. Always. I got just enough of what I wanted to relieve my tensions, and if they got tense with me, I moved on.

I turned to my side, leaning on an elbow, mirroring him. Silently, I reached out and touched his shoulder, ran a hand down his arm, squeezed his muscles on the way to his hand. He tried to clutch mine, but I slipped my fingers from his grasp, moved to his chest, circling one nipple through the thin fabric.

I felt him shudder as he closed his eyes.

And I — I was getting wet. I couldn't deny it. Was it my power over him? Or was it Gary?

I moved my hand to his stomach, tracing the muscles, dipping a finger into his belly button through the linen, slipping under the shirt and touching the warm skin. He breathed faster and opened his eyes again, watching me.

This time, when I reached for the button on his pants, he didn't stop me. He lay on his back against the blanket and let me work open the button and the zipper. He wore boxer briefs beneath, with a tent pole that made my eyes pop. I pulled his pants down, then the briefs, eager to get a look. His cock sprung free, long and lean as he was. Did I mention *long?*

"Oh, my," I said, gently grasping it, running my hand up and down its length, just once, before touching the moist tip and looking into his face.

Gary's lips parted slightly. His eyes were hooded, but they were directed at mine.

"Why?" he breathed.

"Why what?"

"Ahhh — " he said as I ran my hand up and down his rock-hard shaft again, then again, falling into a rhythm that made him groan. He shifted. "Stop."

"Are you sure?"

"No."

I laughed.

"Just — for a minute," he eked out.

I withdrew my hand, watching him watch me, and ran my tongue around my lips.

"God." He looked as if he'd catch fire. "Why would you give yourself — why are you — "

"Why am I so easy? Trust me, Gary. I'm hard. Very hard."

"You're not the only one," he muttered.

I let out a low laugh. "Don't forget complicated. I'm just trying to keep things simple. Don't you like it?" I couldn't help myself. I eased my body closer to his, pushed up his shirt and kissed his taut belly.

"Yes. What kind of question is that?"

"Why are you asking questions at all?" I centered myself over him, licked my way down the valley that led to the dark hairs where the V of his figure led me. Clutching those narrow, hard hips, I leaned in and ran my tongue up his shaft.

He let out a guttural sound of pleasure.

I paused. "That's the kind of noise a man makes when he's trying so very, very hard to be good, when he really wants to be bad."

"I'm good," he whispered.

"Delicious," I agreed, and I took him into my mouth. He was so long that I couldn't take all of him. I was wet with imagining what he might feel like inside me, but it's not like I would know, and he wouldn't get that chance. I swirled my tongue around him, using my hand to guide him, to extend his excitement as my cheeks hollowed with suction.

"Ahhh," he groaned, and I did it again, taking him a little deeper. I could taste him, the pre-come, and I took my time, tonguing the steely ridge under his soft skin, working my way up and down. He arched up, meeting me, giving in completely to my ministrations, and, *fuck,* he was coming in my mouth. I swallowed his seed, feeling my own thrill, an ache in my core at pleasuring him. I withdrew as he clasped his cock, squeezed and spurted the rest onto the sand.

I lay back on the blanket next to him, out of breath myself. I unbuttoned my jeans, reached past my slip of silky, damp underwear and touched myself.

And he watched me, as I knew he would. I could tell he wanted to touch me, but he didn't. He was overcome; he propped himself on his elbow like he did before, his impressive cock hanging there as I looked into his eyes and pushed two fingers inside myself and stroked inside my slick passage until I moaned and shuddered, lifting my hips, thumbing my clit until the spasms of ecstasy rolled through me. When I was done, I palmed my own breasts through the blouse, squeezed, looked at Gary and licked my lips.

"Enjoy the show?" I asked.

"Ez," he whispered. His cock twitched as if it might be ready for another round. "You are the most beautiful — "

"I'm not, but I know how to give good head."

He looked shocked. I sat up, grabbed the bourbon bottle and took another drink. I handed it to him. He took one, too.

"Yes, you are," he finally said. "Beautiful."

"Nice of you to say." *Being beautiful is a handicap. It makes people notice you who shouldn't. I'm never going to be beautiful again. Just a sexy bitch who's in one door and out the other.*

The old words, the old thoughts. My mantra.

I wondered what Gary saw in my face. He reached out and gathered me to him, wrapping his strong arms around me, and we lay, body to partially clothed body, against the blanket. I was vaguely aware of his cock pressing against me, growing hard again as we lay together. After a few minutes, he kissed my temple, my cheek. He cupped my chin and lowered his lips to mine.

The kiss was delicate and dangerous, a thin whip of desire that made me want — want more. My body warred with my brain. His hand strayed under my blouse, pushing aside the thin bra, kneading my breasts as he kissed me. And then his hand moved down and slipped into the opening of my already unzipped jeans.

"No." I pushed back immediately, the spell broken.

Gary looked baffled. "What?"

"Not tonight." *Not ever.*

"OK." His voice was uncertain. His cock was hard.

I gestured in that direction. "Would you like me — ?"

"No. No! What the hell, Ez? I wanted to give you the same feelings you gave me. Get — closer to you."

"I think I need to go home. You said it yourself. Can't stay up late tonight."

"I'd stay up all night for you."

I stared at him. He stared back. The wind lifted our hair, rushed through sea grapes and grasses, a hissing sound, and then it was picking up sand, hurling it at us, stinging sand that had us fastening our clothes and grabbing the bottle and blanket.

We stood quickly, wordlessly, and walked back to the house, shielding our faces against the sand. Clouds scudded across the stars, and a few drops of rain spattered my skin.

Inside the den, I handed Gary the bottle.

"I'll see myself out," I said.

"You sure you can drive?" He looked windblown, his eyes cloudy.

"I've never felt more sober."

And it was true, I thought as I hastened to my car. Because Gary was battering at my gates, cracking the hinges, and I thought my fortress was invulnerable.

I DIDN'T SLEEP WELL, so I was less than prepared to face my secret life when Monday morning came, hot and humid. But it was time for the reckoning. It was time to pay the bills.

It was time for my day job.

I walked through the doors of Melodeon Music Manufacturing one minute late, as always dreading my transition from free-wheeling musician to responsible citizen. I didn't tell anyone about this job — an office job, for fuck's sake. The occasional musician friend might stop by the building, but if they saw me, I played it off like a temp gig. Which it should have been, if I'd made my fortune five years earlier, when I was twenty, like any real rock star.

But as my lack of success endured, so did my time in the job. And now, the horrible truth was, I was the office manager.

My bright-eyed, balding boss, Sammy Weller, greeted me as I sat at my desk. It was one of half a dozen in a bullpen of workers, just outside the office he shared with his sister and co-owner. Sarah was usually traveling for the business, so Sammy took care of things in Bohemia.

"Hi, Ez!" Sammy called. "Got a cup of coffee for ya." He set my pre-filled Grumpy Cat mug on the desk. Oh, yes. My boss liked me. My boss made *me* coffee. "Hey, I told you I was trying to schedule a meeting with a web designer, right?" he continued. "She and the photographer are coming in this morning at 10:30. Show them to the conference room, will ya?"

"What's her name?"

"Thea something. Not sure about the photographer."

Could it be my friend Thea, the graphic artist Cali had introduced me to? There weren't many Theas around.

"Sure thing, Sammy, and thanks for the coffee," I said, returning his smile as he nodded and went back into his office. He really was a decent guy. This wasn't such a bad place. And at least the Melodeon company made and imported a lot more instruments than melodeons — though I had nothing against accordions, as my Cuban grandfather often played one at family gatherings when we were still in South Florida.

The biggest thing they did here was exotic drums —

doumbeks, djembes, darbukas, cuicas — the inventory list sounded like a Dr. Seuss story. Plus there were gongs, lutes, bagpipes, flutes, sitars, horns, ocarinas, didgeridoos, harps, even finger cymbals. We had a large belly-dancer clientele. And on a slow day, there was nothing more fun than going back to the warehouse and playing *everything*.

But still. It was a day job. And just on principle, I felt like I had to hate it.

"Hi, Ez. Heard about the meltdown Saturday."

Irene. She was one of the reasons to hate it. Meaner than dirt and unhappy that I had the job she wanted, she never passed up an opportunity to cut me down. Her painted-on red eyebrows and faux-bronze hair, sprayed into a spiky 'do that reminded me of Heat Miser in the ancient Rankin/Bass Christmas special, gave her a constantly angry appearance.

She leaned over my desk, smelling of perfume overdose. "You know how to pick 'em, huh?"

"What, you weren't there yourself? I know how much you love art," I said, unable to withhold snark. Irene's idea of art was free calendars from her insurance agent featuring soft-focus photos of kittens in baskets.

"I grew up with enough crappy art that I know it doesn't mean anything unless it can be sold for money," she said. "And I doubt those pictures at that gallery can be sold for much. I heard about your big night from my son. He's always going to gallery parties. Likes the free wine."

"Who doesn't?" My phone started ringing. "I have to get this."

"Have a great day." Irene, triumphant, returned to her desk on the opposite wall.

"Melodeon Manufacturing. How may I help you?" I asked, then immediately regretted ignoring the caller ID.

"Ez, where have you been?" Oh, great. My mom. I loved my mom. I knew she was on my side. She'd proved it. But her calling me at work was never a good thing.

"I'm busy, Mama. How are you?"

"I hear you lost another boyfriend."

"What? How? Never mind. I don't want to know. Did you call for a reason?"

"I'm calling about Izzy."

That shut me up. Phone calls about Isabel were never good news. "Uh-huh?"

"She's in a new rehab place, and I think she's doing really well. You should go see her."

"Mama, I hate to say it, but you always think she's doing really well." Hope sprang eternal. I looked around. The other workers, all women but one, were deep into business calls.

"But this time she had a real scare. I think maybe it — changed her."

"Change is good."

"Don't be flip." She sounded sad. "She needs you. You need to see her. Go after work. Visiting hours start at 5:30."

"I can't tonight. I have an appointment." Teaching an eight-year-old to play piano, but she didn't need to know that.

"Go tomorrow."

"I'm meeting with a record label tomorrow," I said, waiting and hoping for kudos that didn't come. I paused. "I'll go Wednesday before rehearsal. Will she still be there?"

"Yes," my mom said, relief in her voice. "Definitely."

Unless she runs again, I thought.

I got the address and hung up, never asking about Papa. Papa didn't talk to me unless he had to. Hadn't for years. And he and Mama didn't even share a bedroom anymore. I had no idea why they were still together, especially when the rest of us were so screwed up after Miami. Well, all but Reya, rich, oblivious Reya, who'd missed out on most of the fun.

I worked till I got the call about our visitors and headed to the lobby to pick them up.

Yep, it was Thea, her curly red hair tamed in a ponytail, a briefcase in her hand. She was tall, almost Amazonian. With her was Calista Goode, carrying her photographer's bag. Both were more business-casual than I'd ever seen them.

Of course, so was I. They looked at me as if I had two heads.

"Ez?" Cali asked curiously, her long blond hair pinned up and spiky as usual. "You work here?"

"It's just a temp gig," I said. "You doing a website for us?"

"I am, if Mr. Weller likes my proposal," Thea said. "I'll do the design part, and I've got a contact who can do the sales stuff."

"And I'll take the photos," Cali said.

"Cool," I replied, still feeling their surprise. "The conference room is this way."

I led them through a door and down a gray hallway to a conference room with a long, scarred table and just a few photos on the walls, pictures Sammy's sister Sarah had taken on her expeditions to buy instruments around the world. They weren't technically great, but they amused Cali while we waited for Sammy.

"Want coffee?" I asked them.

"Water, maybe?" Thea asked.

I popped into the kitchenette off the room and grabbed bottles of water for everyone, setting them on the table as Sammy walked in. He took the lead and introduced himself, so I didn't have to say anything. I headed for the door.

"Wait, Ez. Why don't you take notes? Ez is the best damn

office manager I've ever had," he told my friends, whose eyes got a little bigger. "What is it, almost five years now here at Melodeon? And she loves music. Did you know she's a musician, too?"

"You don't say?" Cali's ice-blue eyes twinkled.

"Awesome," Thea answered with a grin.

Just over an hour later, with Sammy thoroughly enthused about the project, I was leading my friends back to the lobby when Cali spoke. "Temp job, huh?"

I gave her a dark look, holding her gaze just until she blinked. And then I snorted. "Everything's temporary when you're waiting for your big break."

Thea and Cali laughed. "Come to lunch," Thea said, "and we can talk about Saturday night."

"I'm so through talking about Saturday night," I said. "Though you probably only know half the story."

And so it was that we headed to my favorite pan-Asian restaurant and, over lunch, I gave them the outline of what had happened — Gary's fire, the ketchup assault on my apartment and spending the night at the Gorski beach house. I left out the sordid details.

"Gary's a good guy," Cali said over her pad thai. She looked pointedly at me. "And he likes you."

"He's too nice," I said, finishing up my curry.

Thea, already done with her sushi, looked at me like I was crazy. "What's 'too nice'?"

I shrugged. "I don't do nice. Anyway, he'll wise up soon enough and lose interest."

"So he *is* interested," Cali said. "And how does he kiss?"

"Surprisingly well." *Damn it.* "I didn't tell you he kissed me."

"Of course he kissed you." Cali looked pleased.

"Actually, I kissed him first, but just to get it over with. And then the house caught fire."

"I bet," Thea said with interest.

"Not like that." *Exactly like that,* I thought.

"Give him a chance, Ez," Cali said. "He was crushing on you all through high school."

"He was always dating somebody else," I said dismissively.

"Because he couldn't have you. You wouldn't let him near you." Cali took a sip of her iced tea and regarded me with the smug happiness of someone who was already in a delightful relationship — exactly what I didn't want.

"Look, it's over," I said. "It never began. I'm single. I'm happy."

"Is that what happy sounds like?" Thea asked.

I shot her a thin smile. "I always sound this way." Dry. Unimpressed. "Have you met Gary's mom?" I asked.

Cali had that knowing look, as if she saw I was trying to change the subject. "She's pretty cool. She spearheaded the fundraising effort for the school's foundation back in the day. Now she works for the museum board, right?"

"Yeah, and due to some personal changes in her life, she's going to have to sell the family beach house," I said. "And it's not just the house — there's all this pristine beach that goes with it. That's what's preoccupying Gary right now. They don't want it all leveled for condos and parking lots, but they may not have a choice."

Cali had perked up. "A beach lot, you say?"

"Multiple lots, all joined together. Developers are drooling for it."

Cali nodded. "I heard something the other day when I was teaching at the school about — well, I don't want to say anything until I look into it. It might just be a rumor, but it could be helpful."

"Aren't you mysterious," Thea said, digging out her wallet as the checks came.

"I just don't want to get anyone's hopes up," Cali said. "I'm like the last person to find out anything at that school, and usually by the time it gets to me, it's wrong. But I could ask Alex. He might know, too." Our friend Alex served on the museum board and was a big donor to the school and museum. He had connections a poor musician could only dream about.

We headed out to the parking lot. "OK, gotta go back to my temp job," I said to them as we exchanged hugs.

They laughed, and I couldn't help but smile. Even if I had to push paperwork all afternoon.

My phone rang as I drove back to the office, and I switched it to speaker and answered.

"Ez! It's Gary."

"Gary. Hi." I hadn't expected to hear from him, well, *ever* after last night. And to my surprise, part of me was just a little bit tingly at the sound of his voice.

"I was wondering if we could talk."

"We're talking now."

"I mean in person."

I made the turn that led me into the industrial area on the south side of town. "I don't think we have anything to say."

"Come on, Ez. Let's be friends."

"Friends, huh?" I made another turn onto my company's street, wanting to play the stereo and pretend this phone call wasn't happening.

"Yes," he said. "I'll drop by tonight, OK? We can watch *La Dolce Vita* if you want."

"I can't tonight. I'm giving a music lesson."

"All night?"

I was silent.

"Ez," Gary said. "I can't leave things like — I need to talk to you. I'll see you tonight."

And he hung up, not giving me a chance to say no.

Though, damn it to hell, I'm not sure I would have.

JULIO WAS PRETTY much bouncing on the folding chair in front of his electronic keyboard. The modestly furnished, two-bedroom apartment on the first floor of our building was quiet except for his mother's movements in the kitchen as she made dinner. All I knew was that I smelled frying meat, and I wanted some. But I tried to focus as Julio played the song he'd been practicing.

"That was really good," I said as he finished, and for a kid with no real training outside of Internet videos, it was. "But let me give you some tips to help you out. First, you shouldn't bounce in your seat while you're playing."

"But it helps me keep the beat!"

"It makes you lose control," I said. "Keep your wrists up. Not that high," I added, suppressing a laugh as he made an exaggerated arch with his fingers pointing down. "Like this. And relax." I played a quick riff that elicited a "wow." Easy audience. "When you relax, you can respond better to the music — what's on the page and what you feel. Make it louder or softer. If it all sounds the same, it's boring."

"It's never boring," he said, playing the opening chords again, this time more responsively. I gave him a few more tips, pointed out a sharp he kept missing and helped him with the new song he was practicing. And then his mom, looking tired and a bit impatient, called him to dinner.

"You want some, Ez?" she asked, kindly but perfunctorily. I was tempted, but I knew their food budget didn't stretch that far. And I had perfectly fine frozen burritos in my freezer.

"I'm good. Practice, Julio. You're doing really well."

"Thanks, Ms. Falcon! I'll have that song ready for next time." He was beaming. He seemed so happy, so innocent, despite what he'd been through — his mom's divorce and multiple moves, from what I'd learned. His innocence is what got me, and I suddenly felt fiercely protective of it, knowing what it was like to lose it. The feeling lit a spark in me, an idea for a song. I wanted to go home and write it.

"OK, we'll go over it next time," I said.

"When?" He was beyond thrilled.

"We'll figure it out."

"Let her go, Julio," his mother said with a grateful smile. He latched his arms around me and gave me an unexpected hug that twisted my heart.

"Bye, you guys," I said, and got out the door as fast as I could.

I went up the stairs to my apartment, pleased to see that Gary hadn't made good on his word. But the apartment felt empty. At least I had my electronic keyboard back; I'd picked it up from Robby on my way home. I stuck a burrito in the microwave and sat on the bench to run my fingers along the smooth black and white keys. It was a much nicer version than Julio's, longer, with almost the heft and feel of a piano, but it still didn't have that resonance I craved from an instrument made of wood and iron and steel strings. I was just into the first few chords that had popped into my head when the microwave beeped and a knock came at the door.

I sat still for a moment, wondering if I should answer it. And the microwave beeped again.

"I hear you in there, Ez. The keyboard and the beeping." *Gary.*

"Just a minute." I retrieved the burrito and put it on a plate before answering the door.

He looked a lot like the Gary I'd always known, cute, of course, with his happy energy back around him, his long curls springy and his baggy cargo shorts and black T-shirt hiding the sinewy physique I knew hid beneath. But there was something different in his eyes, now. Things had changed between us, and that new intensity — or was it pain? — made the little hairs on my arms stand on end.

He was officially fucking with my equilibrium.

"Want a burrito?" I asked. Mundane. That's what this conversation needed to be, and then he would leave and I could write my song.

"OK." I really didn't expect him to say yes, but I handed him the first one and nuked another. I popped a couple of beers and turned on an eclectic Pandora station, music easing the tension between us. We sat on the couch in the living room and ate.

It didn't take long. Frozen burritos were notoriously meager fare.

"Did you have a good day?" he asked.

"Yeah. Met a couple of friends for lunch. Thea and Cali."

"Oh, yeah. They're cool. Well, I don't know Thea well, but Cali's neat, and I see her cousin a lot at the school."

"Sloane. Seems to me you had an eye for her once."

"Passing fancy," he said. "A guy can be distracted when he can't get what he wants."

I wasn't going to touch that one with a ten-foot pole. Like his . . .

I took a sip of beer. "Uh, Gary, let's just be cool and forget last night, OK? I know we run into each other a lot. Nothing has to be different."

He put down his beer and sat sideways on the couch, crossing one long leg over the other. "Why not?"

"What kind of question is that?"

"Because we have a connection. And maybe you didn't notice, but we've been through some shit together now."

"Which I'd care to avoid repeating."

He smiled. "No kidding. But — Ez, we have a connection."

"You said that."

"Damn it." The look in his eyes, those amber-and-emerald eyes, flamed into something akin to anger. He grabbed my face with both hands and slammed his mouth onto mine.

"Mmmm." First the sound I made was a protest, and then it was something else. Pleasure. Desire.

Somehow I put down my beer and twisted so I could meet him square on, slipping my arms around his waist, and his ministrations became more temperate, studied, as he slipped his tongue between my lips and explored my all-too-eager mouth.

And then I awoke from this dream of lust, realizing that with it came an intimacy, emotional and otherwise, that I just didn't want. I didn't want it. *I didn't want him.*

Oh, yes, I wanted him. But I couldn't let this go further. Gary couldn't be more of a distraction than any other boy-toy

I'd entertained. I had to set some boundaries if — if I wanted to play with him.

Play. *This doesn't feel like play.*

I pushed him back with a broken moan and looked into his eyes, both of us breathing hard.

"I'm not in the market for a boyfriend," I told him coolly.

"That's not what you just told me."

"I didn't — oh." I shook my head at his impish smile. "That was a kiss, Gary. I'm pretty good at it. So are you." *Saying too much.*

His smile broadened. "Ez. This is good."

I had a feeling Gary was a *show, don't tell* kind of guy.

So I'd show him. "I think we need to define some parameters," I said, pushing him back against the couch. He still wore a smile as he lay there, reaching for me. I batted his hands away and reached for the buttons on his shorts. The trace of puzzlement in his eyes was soon eclipsed by arousal as I slowly unbuttoned his fly and pulled them down. His erection pushed hard at his boxer briefs, and I pulled those off, too.

"Come here," he said, reaching for me again.

"No." I batted his hands away again. And then I cupped his balls, kneaded them. He groaned. No longer reaching for me, he gripped the couch. I grasped his shaft and ran my fist up and down his generous length, harder and even longer now as I caressed him. Despite myself, I felt my own arousal peaking again, and I breathed faster as I watched myself stroking him, as I watched his face, eyes closed, mouth open as he bucked his hips up, trying to fuck my hand. He came like a volcano, and I milked him until he begged me to stop. And then, as he opened his eyes and looked at me, his face and breathing wrecked by orgasm, I leaned in and licked his cock, just once, swirling my tongue over the sticky tip. I sat up, licked my lips and swallowed.

"God, Ez," he gasped, closing his eyes again.

"Now get out." I stood up and took the plates to the kitchen, trying to ignore the stunned silence in the living room.

"What?"

"Go on, Gary. I'll see you around. Maybe we can do this again sometime."

"Do what? I mean, yeah, this was — good — but what the hell?" I walked back into the living room to see him scrambling to pull his clothes back together. He stood. "I want to be with you, Ez. I'm not just here for whatever you call this — "

"A hand job."

"Damn it. There is more to you than this. Why are you doing this?"

"I didn't see you saying no."

"Because I thought you were saying yes." He was furious. I had never seen Gary furious.

"You need to leave."

We stood there, facing each other, him breathing hard, his face red, his hair more mussed than usual, and me, arms crossed, watching. Gate closed.

He said nothing else. He walked to the door, went out and slammed it behind him.

But his look — that look he gave me before he walked out — that look of anger and agony and reproof cut me deeper than any words could have. I let out a held breath, shaking, feeling the blood leaking from me. And I went into the kitchen to look for a drink.

∼

I GOT out of work an hour early Tuesday and changed into something more rock-and-roll, a sexy black tank top and blue jeans, just in time for Robby to pick me up for the drive to Orlando and our meeting with Crystal Slice Records. We'd assumed the role of co-leaders of the Emeralds organically, booking gigs and such, but this was our most important task so far.

Robby also wore a black T-shirt and jeans and had drawn his long, light brown hair back into a ponytail. I noticed for the first time it was streaked with a few strands of gray. One of these days we weren't going to be young rockers anymore.

"So how did it go with Gary the other night?" Robby asked as he negotiated his truck through a highway interchange on the way into Orlando.

"You are really going to ask after the shit you guys gave me?"

"I hear you burned his house down."

I turned to him, ready to give him a lashing, and saw he was grinning. "Very funny," I said, reacquiring my cool.

"What you do is your biz, Ez, but Gary's a good guy. Go easy."

"Whatever. I'm sure he's through with me now." And that thought made me more sad than I thought it would.

"That's too bad." Robby sounded genuinely sorry.

"Forget it. That was the idea. Let's focus on the meeting. Crystal Slice Records. I did a little Googling. They've launched a few regional bands to success. And Hood Ornament is one of theirs."

"They went No. 1 last year! Grammy nom, too."

"Surprising, isn't it, for a record label whose name sounds like a refreshing diet drink?" We passed through the last toll

— neatly paid for by his E-pass — and exited the highway, the skyscrapers on the horizon lit gold by the setting sun.

"I don't really have a sense of these guys yet," Robby said, "but Terry seemed really high on us when he caught us at The Junction Box."

"I don't even know what a record label is for anymore, anyway," I said as we entered a neighborhood of mostly homes-turned-businesses, well away from the theme park mobs the city was known for. "I mean, if you hit it lucky, or if you're one of the percentage of a percentage who gets the really big treatment, it's got to be great. But who is that anymore?"

"Maybe it'll be us. It's working for Hood Ornament."

"Except this is an indie label," I said, and in case there was any doubt, directed by the GPS, we pulled into the miniature parking lot of a tiny company, housed in what once was a rambling residential bungalow. Its stucco walls were painted yellow, and its thick, clear acrylic sign, bolted into the wall, was labeled only with the black letters "CSR" over what looked like a etched round slice of some kind of citrus fruit.

"Subtle," Robby said.

"Let's rock and roll."

The heavy wood front door led into a narrow lobby with one long couch and a wall full of framed album covers and concert posters. Though I didn't have the vinyl fetish so many of my friends had, I really missed album covers. They just weren't the same on an iPod.

Rock music pumped through invisible speakers. There was no receptionist, just a retro red phone on an otherwise empty coffee table that looked like something Batman would use. I picked it up, and I heard it ringing through.

"Crystal Slice," came the female voice on the other end.

"Ez Falcon and Robby Beringer with Ez and the Emeralds, here for a meeting with Terry."

"Awesome!" The voice got perkier. "I'll send him out."

After a moment, the interior door swung open. A roughly handsome man with startling silver eyes and glossy black hair that just brushed his ears greeted us.

Also wearing jeans and a black T-shirt.

"I see you have the uniform down," he joked in a Scotch-and-cigarettes voice as he shook our hands. "I loved your stuff at The Junction Box. Sorry I didn't get to talk to you then, Ez." His eyes swept over me in a way that seemed on the wrong side of professional, but then again, I was used to it. It's just something men did with me, and I can't say I discouraged them. "Why don't you two come in and look around? You're my last meeting of the day, but you can say hi to everyone."

"Everyone" was about ten employees, staffing a mailroom, a promotion office and several desks with computers doing things like tracking radio play, online sales and social media, according to Terry.

"This is Poppy, another of our producers," Terry introduced a woman with a severe, dark pageboy cut and red lips. She was playing with the panels in the sweet production studio, mixing a track.

"I heard you guys one night in Bohemia. You're great!" she enthused. "I hope I get to work with you here."

"Thanks," Robby and I said in tandem. We swapped embarrassed glances.

"I'm sorry I missed you at the show," I said.

"Oh, I always go incognito when I want to check out a band," Poppy said. She gestured to the equipment. "This studio is at the disposal of our partners, with different levels of involvement from us, depending on the deal. Terry will tell you more."

"So we use the word 'partner' a lot," Terry said a few minutes later, sitting next to me and across from Robby at a small conference table, where we each sipped fresh Cokes he'd pulled from a small fridge. The walls of the room were decorated with more album covers, along with three gold records and one platinum — Hood Ornament's "Pitted Chrome" CD. "But there are partners and there are *partners*. We help a lot of bands with what they need — production, promotion. And sometimes they pay us to do that and keep what they earn. But that's not what we're looking for with you guys. We're looking for the next band to take to the next level and, not to put too fine a point on it, earn a *lot* of money. Your sound is fantastic. We'd like to talk to you about what we can offer."

Robby grinned at the mention of "The Sound." And Terry's knee touched mine.

What the —?

I shifted away. It was inadvertent, surely.

I looked pointedly at him. "We'd like to know what you offer that we can't, frankly, do ourselves. Everything's going pure indie now, and we already have a following on social media."

"Absolutely," Terry said, staring at me with his silver eyes, the irises rimmed with dark blue. Weirdly hypnotic. "We love that you have a following already. But our job will be to make all of that easier so you can focus on the music. I'm guessing you don't do it full time now?"

Robby and I exchanged glances. "We all have day jobs," Robby said. "Well, not sure if Ace has one right now — "

"Your drummer? I liked him."

We exchanged another glance.

"Bass player," I said. "We might as well tell you right now that we're in the process of replacing our drummer. He — had to leave."

Terry nodded thoughtfully, touching my arm as he replied. It would have been rude to pull away, so I stayed still as he spoke. "If you all can retain your strong sound, that should be OK," he said.

I slipped out of Terry's grasp and picked up my Coke, making a big deal of draining it, then sat back with my arms crossed. "We've replaced drummers before. And we're serious about making great music."

"Of course you are," Terry said. Was he being patronizing, or was it just me? "Fill the vacancy, and then we can talk some more, maybe get you in here to do a demo, on us."

Robby was nothing but happy. "We'd love to," he said. "Can you give us an idea of, you know, terms?"

"I'll have Patti send you the standard contract so you can think about it. I still have your email. Sound good? Now I've got to get out of here. I've got a band to see downtown. I'm trying to save them from life as cruise ship entertainers." Terry's laugh jangled in my ears as he stood, and we with him.

OK. I didn't like him. I *really* didn't like him. But if working with him was what it took to make the band happy — to get our break — maybe it would be worth it.

"Where's your bathroom?" Robby asked. "Long drive back."

Terry pointed him down the hall and looked at me. And looked at me some more.

I stared back, impassive.

"You're the soul of the group, you know," Terry said

quietly, crossing his arms over a muscled chest to match mine, which were crossed over my bra-less tank top. "I love your sound as a group, but your songwriting, your playing and, holy shit, your *singing* — they're all sensational, Ez. You could go solo anytime. I could help you."

I sucked in a breath. I hadn't expected this. I was here for the band, but it never hurt to listen, right? I uncrossed my arms, and his eyes slid to my breasts and back to my face.

"I'm also dabbling in television production," he said, moving closer, his voice lower. "I'm working with a new show that's going to follow young musicians as they try to make it in the biz. Everything they do is paid for — the camera just follows them and documents their lives. It's something to think about."

"Could the whole band do it?" I asked. I hated reality shows, but if it helped the Emeralds . . .

"It's for solo artists. Group house for a year here in Orlando, but I swear, it wouldn't be a soap opera. It would be quality television."

"Sounds like an oxymoron."

He laughed. "I like you, Ez." He moved a step closer, into my space, and my brain flipped to a static channel at the sensory and information overload, looking for a safe place.

Robby walked back into the room. "Ready, Ez?"

"Let's rock and roll," I said, repeating myself. Terry laughed again and put a hand on the small of my back, warm and persistent and invasive, as he guided us down the hallway and out to the lobby. He shook both our hands and told us he hoped he'd hear from us soon.

Robby could barely contain himself as we got into the truck. He kept quiet until we reached the stop sign at the end of the street.

"This could be fucking *awesome,*" he enthused.

"We don't even know the fine print yet." And Robby didn't know that creepy Terry was working whatever deal he could get. And he didn't need to know. My plan was to stick with the band.

"We'll book a drummer tomorrow night," he said. "I know we'll get a good response with the Craig's List ad."

"Oh, about that. I might be a few minutes late. I have a family thing."

"Ez, this is important."

"Chill. I'll be there. Anyway, maybe you shouldn't put too much stock in what this Terry says."

"Well, he's all about how much he loves you," Robby said. "I told him after that gig — not sure where you were, maybe under the table." He laughed. "Anyway, I told him you wrote most of the songs, and he was really interested. He said he's always looking for a new voice. And, of course, The Sound."

" 'The Sound of Music,' " I sang from the Broadway tune.

"Not that. *Our* sound, Ez. He loves our sound!"

I didn't say anything as he turned the radio on. As it happened, a high-volume hit of Hood Ornament's had just started. We hit the highway, and I listened closely to the slick sound, the sound of success, and wondered if it was worth it.

THE SEA DUNES Center in Bohemia Beach was probably the nicest rehab Izzy had been in to date, and I'd seen them all. Generally, she disappeared for a while, showed up wasted at my parents' or had a friend call on her behalf or, once, got arrested, and she'd take a stab at a thirty-day program. Sometimes she stayed on the wagon for a while, but always, she slipped off. Pills were her drug of choice. She'd started with Ecstasy, supplemented by pot, and graduated to prescription painkillers with the occasional hit of cocaine.

Three years younger than I was, the adored baby of the family, she had broken all of our hearts. Still, I couldn't forget that hers had been broken first.

Because of me.

"Isabel Falcon?" I asked at the front desk. "I'm her sister."

"Oh, yes, your mother said you were coming," said the receptionist, an angelic blonde who looked like a college intern. "Visiting hour starts in ten minutes. Do you mind waiting?"

"Fine." I glanced at my watch. I had to get to rehearsal, but they could wait for me. They were auditioning drummers, anyway, and I had a feeling the guys wouldn't value my input this time, given how much I had pushed for them to take Stuart. I'd liked the look in his eye at the time. The weaselly, ravenous look.

I sat in the waiting room and read an article in a magazine about how to find your man's hot spots. I got a pen out of my purse, scratched out some of the advice and added some of my own. I left it for the next visitor in need of enlightenment when the receptionist called my name. She escorted me to the common room, which had a handful of tables with hard chairs, a few comfy chairs in clusters, and a view of the ocean. *Definitely* the nicest rehab Izzy had ever stayed in.

I sat in one of the comfy chairs by a big window and watched the waves, waiting.

"Esme?"

I turned at the voice, familiar and yet smaller than I remembered. Thin and pale, Isabel wore yoga pants and a T-shirt, and her long, dark hair was doubled up in a loose bun.

Her pretty features were careworn. "Izzy," I said, standing and hugging her tenuously. She hugged me hard.

We sat after a moment in the soft chairs and gazed at the ocean for a minute before turning to each other.

"Pretty view here," I said.

"I like the sound of the ocean. It helps me sleep at night. I have trouble sleeping."

"Is it getting better?" *It* meant a lot of things when I was talking to Isabel.

"Yeah, I really think it is. There's a counselor here — mental health, not just addiction — who's helped me a lot." She paused. "I know you won't believe me, but I'm ready this time."

"Why are you here, Izzy?" What I meant was, *why are you here this time?*

"I woke up with my boyfriend one day and he didn't. Wake up, I mean."

"Shit."

"Yeah. I'm tired of my own fuckups. I'm ready to get better."

"And are you getting better?"

"I am." Her voice was stronger now, and she looked at me directly with her golden eyes. I'd always envied those eyes; mine were so dark, caves of obsidian. Hers were caramel-dipped sunshine. "What about you? Are you getting better?"

"I'm fine."

"Still drinking?"

"Only medicinally." I squeezed my hands together automatically, though they weren't trembling just then.

She gave me a wry smile. "Did you ever try a counselor yourself?"

"I'm not the one — I don't need a counselor."

"Oh, yes, you fucking do," she said.

"When did you start using that word all the time? Don't get me wrong, it's one of my favorites, but you never cursed much."

"It's my new, healthy, unvarnished self-expression."

"Ah, there's the writer coming out," I joked. I remembered her making up fantastical stories when we shared a bedroom as kids, back in Miami, after Mama had turned out the light. Izzy always had stories, then.

"Ez, you should talk to someone."

"I'm fine. The time to change things was twelve years ago. If I had, you might not be here now."

"You were as much a victim as I was."

"That's big of you," I said bitterly. "But if I'd acted sooner —"

"I've accepted it now. I'm moving on. I'm getting better. Please, Ez, don't be angry."

"I'm not angry at you!" I stood and turned to the ocean as the twilight burnished the turquoise waves with gold, deceptively pretty, hiding so much darkness.

"You sound like you're angry at me."

I turned back to her, curled up in her chair, little Izzy with her big heart. "I love you, Izzy, and I'm glad you're getting better. And I'm sorry. *I'm sorry.*"

I whirled and got the hell out of there.

In the parking lot, I brushed past Reya, who was getting out of her big white Escalade, a sheaf of magazines in her arms. "Esme! Esmerelda!" she called. I shot an angry glance at my older sister, with her perfectly styled blond-streaked hair and heavily made-up face, as I got in my car. She looked baffled and, as always, disapproving.

I slammed the door, started the engine and peeled out of Bohemia Beach.

RONNY HAD LEFT the front door of the music store in downtown Bohemia unlocked, though the sign was flipped to "closed" and the lights in the high-ceilinged showroom up front were dim. It's where he worked as assistant manager, and he loved the rows of shiny guitars on the walls. I envied him his proximity to the beautiful pianos on display here.

Oh. There was a new one. *Holy shit.* It was a mid-size Fazioli grand, a special one, I could tell — a beautiful white presence in the center of the room, one spotlight shining down on its gleaming surface. I put it at a hundred and fifty grand, gold hinges and all. I slipped the flask out of my purse, took a gulp of the whiskey, put it back and let the glow fill me as I beheld the elegant instrument.

Robby really should lock the front door.

I reached for the piano, momentarily forgetting my encounter with my sisters, and caressed the glossy, cool case. How I wanted to play it. Maybe just a few notes . . .

I heard the muted sounds of the band kicking into a Beatles song in the back room, standard audition fare. The drummer gamely kept up, even kicked it. Pretty good, but they still needed my opinion.

I couldn't play the piano. Not yet.

I squared my shoulders and headed through a door that opened into a big practice room. A hallway to my right led to smaller rooms where the store staff gave guitar and piano lessons; offices were to the left. And in front of me was the band, the much less glamorous console piano waiting for me.

"You've got to be shitting me," I muttered as I saw who was playing the drums, rocking to the end of "Revolution" with a crash of cymbals.

"Hi, Ez," Gary said, twirling a drumstick and looking at me with a new, wiser expression. Maybe even a wise-ass expression.

Well, I said he'd wise up. But playing drums with the Emeralds was not wise.

"What are you doing here?" I asked.

"I'm auditioning."

"You want to be our drummer?"

Robby looked as if he was trying not to laugh. "He says he's auditioning to be our backup drummer. But since the only other person who showed up tonight was a thirteen-year-old who can't go to bars, Gary might be it for another week or so. I've got another friend I've almost talked into it, and he's really good, but he won't be available till he delivers a freelance project he's working on. He's a software guy."

I narrowed my eyes. "Are you sure we can't get a fake ID for the thirteen-year-old?"

"He really wasn't bad," Ace the Bass mused.

Banjo Brian, who'd been playing a tambourine for the Beatles song, shrugged. "Gary's good. He could do it full-time."

"No, I can't," Gary said. "I have another avocation. But I'd be glad to fill in if you need me."

"You available Friday?" Robby asked.

"Now, wait a minute," I interrupted. "Don't I have a say here?"

"No," my bandmates said in unison.

I couldn't narrow my eyes any more without closing them, so I closed them and inhaled a few enraged breaths. My hands were trembling again. I resisted the urge to get out the flask, opened my eyes and flipped them the bird.

"So we're just going to run through a few numbers . . . " Robby called after me as I headed back toward the showroom.

"I've got to work on a song," I shouted back, slamming the door behind me.

I stopped, took a drink, calmed down. Then I walked to the Fazioli, set down my purse and sat on the white leather tufted bench. *Ah.*

I took another sip from the flask, then another.

There. Steady. Easy. Half gone.

I set it on the floor and lowered my fingers to the keyboard, channeling the muse.

The keys responded to my touch like a lover, or how I imagined a real lover would, one responsive and giving and everything I knew I could never have. The instrument gave generously — it gave me its supple dynamics, its pure tone, its soft resonance, its *feeling,* sensual and light and dark and wrenching as I swept into a minor key. The melody had been haunting me for days, a note here, a note there, and now it emerged, almost whole, digging into the bass notes with a slow, agonizing rhythm, then soaring into the heights, the plaintive, melancholy theme so ecstatic in its sadness.

"*Lacrimosa,*" I whispered as I played, tears in my eyes. My melody was nothing like the one in Mozart's Requiem, but it had the same heaviness, the same ethereal counterpoint. Ha, was I comparing myself to Mozart now?

No. I was only me. The lyrics began to flow, words I'd been jotting in the little notebook I carried around.

I thought the door could save me

if I locked it tight
I thought the door could save you
if you were out of sight

I thought the shots would freeze me
if I closed my eyes
I thought he couldn't see me
if I maintained the lies

I shifted into a chorus, more strident, imagining the rock beat:

His glass gaze broke us both
and now we're on the run
His glass gaze snapped us both
and now our hearts are done

And then back to a verse:

I thought that I could make a break
and you'd be safe alone
But you walked through that iron door
and no one heard your moan . . .

"Singing about sex again, Ez?" The low voice interrupted me. I looked up and sucked in a breath. And made a mental note to change the lyric.

"Anything but," I said to Stuart, my fingers frozen in place, my foot on the pedal, the last notes fading into oblivion as our ex-drummer slowly circled the piano. I hadn't even heard the door open.

"Sounds about right," he replied. He stood still, watching

me, his gaze possessive and cold, one statue to another. He was still good-looking, with his blue eyes, shaggy, sandy hair and goatee, a decent body that had done little more than distract me. He didn't look so evil from here, from inside my miserable, inebriated mind, not when I'd been singing about real evil.

"I'm sorry about the other night," he said, turning on a pretense of warmth. He always was a charmer, before he went psycho, that is. He stepped closer, then behind me, setting his hands on my shoulders, rubbing them slowly.

I need to tell him to go to hell, I thought, but I closed my eyes and let his hands work me over. They felt so good. But then again, he'd done something bad, right? *Oh, shit.* My clothes. My apartment. I couldn't forgive him that.

I shrugged my shoulders to get rid of him, about to tell him off, and his hands eased to my throat, tightening slightly. I tensed, registering a prickle of fear.

And then I heard another voice.

"What the fuck are you doing here? Leave her alone."

Gary?

My eyes snapped open, and I looked up to see Gary walking toward us the way a lion walks toward a wildebeest. I slipped away from the distracted Stuart, putting the piano between us, still feeling the pressure of his hands on my neck.

"Are you her next stooge?" Stuart said to Gary, his tone snide. "Run now, man. She's sexy as hell, but she's not worth it."

"Fuck off," I said, feeling dizzy from the alcohol, from the confrontation.

Gary continued toward him. "Get — the — fuck — *out.*" I'd never heard Gary talk that way, forceful, absolutely in control, his voice a steel hammer. *Whoa. Alpha Gary.*

He stopped less than two feet from Stuart, his mouth set, his eyes sparking, his fists bunched, the muscles in his arms sharp and defined and *hot* —

Should I be thinking that right now?

Gary's hand shot out, and he grabbed Stuart by the collar of his T-shirt.

Stuart staggered and threw his hands in the air. "Easy, man! I guess it's too late. Bitten by the vixen, huh?" He pushed Gary away and stepped back, way back, half stumbling toward the door, as Gary advanced again. "I'm going." Stuart looked at me as he left, his expression ugly, and I wondered what I ever saw in him, why I'd ever, even for a moment, let him touch me.

When the door closed behind him, Gary turned to me, his eyes cooled to green-flecked amber. "I don't understand you."

"What?" My body flushed hot with booze and a new sensation, a screaming need, as I eyed this new and powerful Gary.

"I don't get you entertaining *him*. After what he did to you."

"I was just about to tell him to go to hell."

"With his hands all over you? I guess you can let in somebody like that, but not me, right? Too *nice* for you?"

Ouch. "Gary." I walked to him, put my hands on his chest. "You're not too nice."

"And you're drunk. Perfect." But despite his angry words, something else was going on in his face, in his eyes. Suffering. Desire.

"Come on, Gary," I whispered. I *was* drunk. All rational thought had fled. I kissed his neck, tonguing his salty skin below his ear, mouthing him as if he were something so savory I couldn't stop. I didn't want to stop. I wanted to devour him. I ran my hands down his chest as he huffed into my hair; I reached lower and cupped him through his shorts. Oh, he was hard and getting harder. I fingered his length straining against the fabric; I squeezed and rubbed and pressed against him, feeling his bulge against my body. He grasped my shoulders and thrust against my hand, once, twice, thrice, in the semi-darkness among the pianos, and a low moan arose from his throat.

And then his whole body stiffened and stilled.

"No." His voice was hoarse. He grabbed my wrists and firmly pushed me away, his face filled with anguish. "I don't want to be your B-side."

"You're not."

"I'm not your A-side. I'm not your anything. But I can't stay away from you, and you aren't good for me."

"You're right," I said with a bitter chuckle. "I don't deserve you."

"Bullshit, Ez." His voice softened. "You deserve the world, but you won't take it."

"You just don't know."

"Know what?"

I said nothing.

"Tell me." The look in his eyes was killing me.

"Hey, guys." Robby had appeared in the doorway to the practice room. "Want to run through a couple of songs together?"

"I have to go," Ez said. "I'll see you Friday."

"But you haven't played with Gary yet," Robby said as I slipped the flask into my purse, slung the bag over my shoulder and headed for the door, avoiding Gary's eyes as my body crackled with unquenched fire.

Oh, yes, I had played with Gary. And look where it had gotten me.

My hands shook as I closed the door behind me and started my dark walk home.

ANOTHER FRIDAY, another gig at the Junction Box — a hip bar by the railroad tracks in downtown Bohemia with Victorian decor, excellent cocktails and a real piano. Only this time, Gary was our drummer, and he wasn't talking to me.

All of our friends had come out tonight, it seemed, perhaps for the novelty of hearing Gary on drums. Cali and Wyatt hung out with Cali's brother Damien, dressed in black as usual and making faces at Gary with eyeliner-ringed blue eyes. Ever-casual Thea was nearby, her red hair wild and curly, along with Penelope, a fabric artist with a pink and yellow 'do who wore one of her pinup dresses, far outclassing anyone else in the joint. Cali and Damien's cousin Sloane sat with Alex at a table. The couple listened to us, but they were constantly talking to each other, almost always touching, exchanging God knows what intimacies. I wasn't sure what was up with those two, but they stuck together like hot glue.

Sloane, a potter studying at the school, also worked with Gary. Maybe I should ask her what was up with him, because, I had to admit, I was more curious about him than ever. He'd turned me down, all the while indicating he wanted more from me. And guys didn't turn me down.

We didn't try out any new material, since it was all new to Gary, but I was surprised at just how well he picked up the tunes. Maybe all that time watching us play at every gig paid off.

Robby's drummer friend Wilson came to watch, too. About ten years older than me and married, with a gray-streaked black beard and a somber expression, he was clearly a solid guy with a lot of experience. It looked as if he would take the gig. So tonight was the first and last time Gary would be an Emerald.

I wasn't sure how I felt about that. Especially since he wouldn't talk to me.

One thing I'd figured out in the past couple of days of going over what had happened at the music store, and everything that had happened with Gary: I could trust him. I had never been this close to any man I could trust.

Maybe we weren't close, not really, not by the definition of so many of my girlfriends who were seeking and finding love. But for me, my encounters with Gary set a new standard. We'd escaped a fire. He'd helped me through the mess in my apartment and kicked out Stuart when he got too scary. He knew me, at least as much as anyone ever did.

So yeah, I had new thoughts about Gary. I just might need someone trustworthy like him to help me get past my little problem, the one that had become almost embarrassing, given my rep. Would I be using him? Maybe. But I was pretty sure he would enjoy it.

We got deeper into the first set, an eclectic mix of rockers and folky anthems and one or two of my agonized ballads, and the music began to subsume all my thoughts and worries. The music was like a drug, a drug I had to have, a drug I created even as I shot it up. I knew I could perform, but performing wasn't what jazzed me. It was actually making the sounds, making them more than their individual parts. And even better, writing the sounds, writing the songs and singing them. I was never more alive than during that act of creativity.

Some of those songs stripped me open, flaying my heart, leaving me naked on stage, but at the same time, they were sung by a persona — that other me, the performer, the woman who told the truth only in lyric and melody.

And then the set was over, and I was emotionally exhausted, and I needed a drink.

We had a routine at break time. The rest of the band went outside to smoke, and I headed over to the bar, where Neil, the mustachioed, suspender-wearing barman, set up two of his concoctions for my imbibing pleasure. Gary didn't go out back with the others. He came over to the bar, too — not looking at me at all — and ordered a beer while I picked up the first of Neil's ruby-red cocktails, each glistening in a rocks glass with a huge ice cube at its heart.

"What is it tonight, my dear?" I asked him. It always paid to flirt with the bartender.

"Sazerac. I was feeling a little New Orleans."

I took a sip. "Mmm. You've been holding out on me with the rye whiskey. And you know I love that hint of absinthe."

"It'll give you dreams," Neil said, his smile turning up the curled ends of his mustache. His facial hair was absurd, but it was *so* Neil.

I sucked down the rest of Drink No. 1 and looked around. Another bartender had given a beer to Gary, who'd gone over to Alex and Sloane's table to avoid me.

He couldn't very well ignore me if I went over there, too.

So, I thought, *am I pursuing him now?*

And then, I knew I was.

I wouldn't call the feeling that tripped through me the thrill of the hunt. If anything, it was sick. It was scary. I didn't chase *anybody*. I feared what might happen if I caught them. But I told myself again what I'd already figured out: I could trust Gary. Gary wouldn't hurt me.

I took my second drink, followed him to their table and sat down without being asked, as Gary loomed, beanpole that he was.

"Hey, Ez. You sound incredible tonight," said Sloane, her reddish-brown hair long and pretty against her short green tunic dress, which shifted her changeable eyes to dusky green. "Gary's doing great, too, don't you think?"

"He's fabulous," I said in a not-quite-ironic manner, taking a long sip of my Sazerac, not looking at him. Not yet.

"Why don't you sit down, Gary?" Alex asked with dry humor. "You're making me feel short."

Alex wasn't quite as tall as Gary, true, but he had nothing to worry about, with his toned physique, dark-honey hair and gray eyes that were always, always studying Sloane. I'd heard she'd moved into his ritzy Bohemia Beach condo. Something crackled between them, a connection I wondered if I could ever find — or handle.

Gary sat and sipped his beer, silent.

"Do you like playing in the band?" Sloane asked him, filling the silence.

"It's great, but I don't love it as much as pottery," he said. "I love music, but it's not my obsession, you know."

"Would you call pottery your obsession?" Alex asked.

"One of them," Gary said, picking at the label through the condensation on his bottle. And then, ever so briefly, he glanced at me.

A slow, warm tide rose through me. I — I *wanted* to be Gary's obsession.

Another random, annoying thought passed through my brain: I wanted to deserve him.

Was I going crazy?

"I heard something about your family's beach house," Alex said. "Your mom is selling it?"

"How'd you hear about that?" Gary asked sharply.

"I told him," Sloane said, her tone appeasing. "Cali said something."

"How did she know?" Gary asked, and then he slowly turned his head to look at me.

"I was wondering if there was any way to save it. You know, save the wild land. It's beautiful," I said to no one in particular, wondering how pissed Gary was. "So I kind of mentioned it to Cali and Thea."

"And Thea," Gary echoed, sipping his beer.

I shifted uncomfortably.

"It's odd and rather unfortunate this should be coming up for sale now," Alex said, "assuming she's going to sell. I wish it had happened a few months earlier. We, I mean, the school, whose leadership I've taken a special interest in lately" — he shot a warm glance at Sloane — "is in the final stages of negotiating the purchase of a riverfront property for a new outreach effort. We got a substantial grant to help fund it, and we're told zoning won't be a problem for what we intend. It'll be a retreat for artists of all kinds, a place where they can focus on their work, hold a seminar as part of their stay, but really just devote themselves to their art in a place where their imaginations can be at play with nature."

"Really?" Gary perked up. "But the beach property would be perfect for that. You have to see this land, Alex. There are so many different critters using it as a haven. And it's beautiful. It's an island, really, an island within the barrier island. Bohemia Beach doesn't need another half-dozen condos."

Alex sighed. "I'm just advising the board of trustees, but I understand they've made an offer on the riverfront property. It's a rambling mansion and about five acres owned by Greer Allighant. She's offering it at a tremendous deal. You know her?"

"I know of her," Gary said.

"Isn't she the lady with the enormous private art collection in her house?" I asked. "Kind of eccentric?"

"That's putting it mildly," Alex said. "Her three grown kids have been trying to get her to move out and sell the property and everything in it for years. Of course, I hear they're none too happy that she's selling it for a song and donating her art to the museum."

"Wow," Sloane said. "I didn't know about that part. That's a ton of art."

"Not all of it's good, but there are some extremely valuable pieces in the collection," Alex said. "We know there's a Picasso and some minor Warhols."

"Who are her kids?" I asked.

"One is a land developer. No surprise he's pissed, given the value of the land," Alex said. "One of her daughters runs a boutique in downtown Bohemia."

"You may have been there — it's called Sweet Alley," Sloane said. "Really cute dresses, if a little beyond my budget."

"I'll get you whatever dress you want," Alex whispered in her ear.

I rolled my eyes.

"The other works for a music company in Bohemia," Alex said. "Mrs. Allighant let me listen to her voicemails complaining about the sale. Apparently her kids love to nag her but never actually visit."

"What's the name of that daughter?" I asked, my interest piqued. "I know a lot of people who work in the music biz around here."

"Irene something. Definitely not Irene the Serene."

I nodded. If this was the Irene I knew, she sure wasn't. "What's Mrs. Allighant going to do now?"

"Live on cruise ships," Alex said with a smile.

"Hard to argue with that," Gary said, sounding depressed.

I noticed the rest of the band coming back inside and knocked back my second drink. Now I was loose. My wheels were spinning with the news of Mrs. Allighant and the school's plan for a retreat. And I was ready to get Gary back on my side.

"Time to play," I said to him in a flirtatious tone.

He turned to me, and the corner of his mouth quirked up, manifesting, however briefly, an puckish dimple. Then the hint of a smile went away.

"I'm ready," he said neutrally.

I nodded and waved at Alex and Sloane and grabbed Gary's arm, heading back toward the band.

"Are you drunk again?" he asked.

"Only a little. But you know how much fun I am when I'm drunk."

"I'm not sure 'fun' is the word for it."

"Then maybe I'll have to demonstrate later," I said. Flirting might not be the way to win Gary over, but I hoped it might break the ice.

His face was unreadable, but his eyes shone with reflexive interest as he took a seat behind his drum set. I smiled at him and slid onto the piano bench; I loved that this place had a baby grand. It made my job, such as it was, that much more of a pleasure. And now that I had an idea of what I wanted, I relaxed into my songs with renewed verve, and we had a really great set. It almost made me wish we could play with Gary again. But Gary had other passions, and I wanted to be one of them, even if only for just long enough to get what I needed.

"Need a hand?" I asked Gary.

It was 1 a.m. The bar was open for another hour, but we were done playing, and the crowd at The Junction Box had thinned as the nomadic youth of Bohemia sought out fresh diversions on their drunken rounds. Robby and the other guys had finished stowing their instruments and mikes and speakers and were taking Robby's friend Wilson, our drummer-to-be, out for a late-night grease fest at The Diamond. Gary, who'd declined to join them, was packing up his drums. And ignoring me.

"Sure I can't help?" I inquired again.

"I've got it," he said, bass drum in one hand, snare in the other, muscles popping on his sinewy arms as he carried them easily. *Nice.* I picked up the ride and splash cymbals on their stands and followed him to the back parking lot. At least I didn't have to haul the piano.

"Thank you." Gary put his drums in the van and reluctantly took the cymbals from me and set them down. He pushed his drums farther into the hold, next to his tools and buckets, not looking at me.

"You were really good tonight," I said. He was. He might

not have the finesse of a guy who played every weekend, but he had talent.

"I was inspired." He climbed into the van. "Can you hand me those one at a time?"

"Nice gear." I passed the first cymbal to him.

"I love the Zildjian sound." He paused as he found a stable place for it. "And the look of them — it reminds me of throwing pots."

"How so?"

"Bring that one in here and I'll show you."

"This could work much better than a puppy," I joked, climbing inside the back of the van. I grabbed the cymbal stand and passed it back to him.

"Very funny." He took it from me, and I moved closer, kneeling next to him in the semi-darkness. He leaned the stand so the cymbal caught the dim light coming in the back door. "See?"

"The bell shape?" The cymbal, its gold-colored alloy dulled by use and time, had a dome at its center, then spread out in a shallow, dish-like circle.

"That, but also the grooves. The cast cymbals all meet strict factory standards, but there are always subtle differences when it comes to lathing and hammering. It reminds me of the patterns I make in spinning clay — a perfectly round bowl becomes more interesting with delicate grooves and lines made by pressing tools or fingers in the surface when it's soft, when I'm still shaping it. I love the feel of that, the speed as it spins under my hands. Anything I do when I touch a perfectly centered piece of clay makes a thing of symmetry, and therefore a thing of beauty."

"But you probably wouldn't want to hit it with a drumstick."

He laughed. It was so nice to hear him laugh again. "Probably not."

"So do you make the patterns from your notebook?"

"My what?"

"The notebook you saved from the fire."

"Oh, that," he said, his voice a little strange, as if he didn't want to talk about it. "That's — different drawings. For carvings, mostly. Not for the concentric grooves. Those I do mostly by feel. It's almost instinct at this point. I just know what will work, what makes the most graceful lines." He avoided my eyes. "I'd better go get the rest."

"Wait a minute." I put a hand on his arm, felt a prickle of warmth.

"I need to get my high-hat and stuff," Gary said, but his voice was soft and hesitant.

"I just wanted to say thank you for defending me the other night."

"I thought you thanked me then," he said, a touch sarcastic, and I remembered my drunken groping, my sudden desire for him.

"Should I apologize for that?"

"What self-respecting guy would ask a girl to apologize for the laying on of hands?" he said, even more sarcastic, as he scooted past me.

"I think you would," I called through the bushes as he went through the bar's back door. Gary seemed to have a lot of self-respect. I wondered what that was like.

I scrambled out of the van and leaned against it as he brought out the high-hat and the tom-toms. I handed them in as he packed them, neither of us talking. Next came the floor tom, an accessory stand, a rolled-up rug that kept the drums from slipping during performances and a bag with sticks and extras. Gary threw a blanket over everything and looped a strap around it. "Beats dealing with cases," he explained. Then he got out, closed the doors and stood there looking at me, rocking back and forth on his heels for a second.

"Well, it was nice playing with you, Ez. I always wondered what that would be like. You'll go far."

"That remains to be seen. I really enjoyed playing with you."

"Really?" His face lightened for a moment, a flash of the carefree Gary. And then it shuttered again. "I've gotta go."

"Home to mom?"

He stopped rocking, crossed his arms and glowered at me. "Are you giving me shit? Would it be better if I was homeless?"

"I'm giving you shit." I grinned at him, trying to elicit a smile. Damn, he was tough to crack.

"Don't. I've had enough."

"Gary, don't be that way. I'm trying to make nice."

"Don't 'make nice.' Nice guys don't like it."

I wanted so badly to touch him again, and not, I realized, just for nefarious purposes. Instead, I stood still, feeling the breeze ruffle my hair, my silky sleeveless top. "You seemed pretty tough to me the other night. Not nice at all."

"So that's what you like?" His voice was lower, simmering. Was he angry? Or, like me, aroused? "Rough and tough? That sounds healthy."

"Oh, I'm anything but healthy, at least in the mental health department," I agreed. "But we're talking about you. I like you however you want to be. Nice" — I took a step closer, placed a hand lightly on his chest — "or naughty."

"Ez, maybe you've had too much to drink. Maybe we

played amazing music together. But I know you too well to be your one-night stand."

My eyes widened. "I suppose I should be stung by that." And, to tell the truth, I was. "But I want to be real with you, Gary, so I guess I should start by telling you something about me. I've never had a one-night stand in my life."

The look on his face was priceless.

"I see you're confused," I continued, running my hand up to his shoulder. I looked into his eyes. "I don't give a damn about my reputation."

"Isn't that a song?"

"And you shouldn't give a damn, either."

"Even if it's true?"

"Not very *nice* of you to say so." I dropped my hand, took a step back. I felt a twinge of real hurt this time, started to doubt this foolish quest. My bad reputation was all I had to hide behind. I wavered. Fuck this. I'd go home and drink some beer and put on my earphones. "I guess I'll see you around."

I turned and took the circuitous route through the parking lot and alley to get back to the street and my walk home. My eyes blurred. That wasn't how this was supposed to go. I was supposed to lead Gary down a path to my door, where he would be nice, and he would trust me, and because I knew I could trust him, maybe, just maybe —

Oh, fuck fuck fuck.

"Ez." I heard Gary behind me, looked back to see him catching up with his long strides just as I hit the sidewalk. Scattered clusters of inebriated hipsters shifted and staggered around us, between bars. I tried not to look at him, but a goddamned tear slipped from the corner of my eye and trickled down my cheek. "Are you *crying?*" he asked, incredulous, as he walked next to me.

"Of course not. It's — spring allergies." I rubbed away the unexpected tear and snuck a glance. He was almost smiling. "You think this is funny?"

"Allergies? Allergies are hysterical."

"Right." We split as a drunken frat-boy type ran between us, uttering a caveman roar.

"Were you being straight with me back there?" Gary asked, this time moving closer to me, perhaps to fend off more drunken sprinters.

"That was the idea."

"You know, I've been walking around in a terrible temper," Gary said. "Moping. Growling at everyone. I'm a happy person, generally. I've always been a happy person. You're doing this to me."

"Then maybe you should leave me alone."

"I can't!"

"You were about to," I pointed out as we walked around a Volkswagen parked in the middle of an intersection, blocked by a police car with flashing blue lights. The Bug's presumed and probably soused driver, a barely legal girl with a tiny dress and hooker heels, was being interrogated about a bottle in a paper bag the cop held in her hand. I recognized the officer as the one who'd talked to me after the ketchup incident.

"You're right," Gary said. "I'm about to leave you alone because — "

"I'm bad for you. You said that before."

"Because I care so much for you, I can't stand watching you tear yourself apart."

I stopped dead, and he did, too, forcing the cluster of

partiers walking behind us to split around us, a river of drunkards.

I turned to face him. "My place is a block away. Come talk to me."

"Talk?"

"Maybe," I confessed, thinking I'd like to do more than talk.

"I don't know if I trust you."

I laughed bitterly. "You don't trust me not to ravish you?"

"I wouldn't mind so much being ravished," Gary said with dry humor. "I just don't know if you can ever be straight with me, really."

"How about this." I stepped closer, spoke softly. "I will not lie to you. I may not tell you everything, not right now, maybe not ever. Some things you may not want to hear. But I will not lie to you. I just need you to be a little — patient with me."

He gazed at me for a moment, those luminous hazel eyes thoughtful, and nodded slowly. And then he reached down and took my hand, shooting a strange new thrill through my veins. He walked toward my place, keeping me close by his side.

PART 2

"Just so you know," Gary said as we got to my building and I let us inside my apartment, "you can tell me anything."

"That's what you think now." I tossed my purse on the kitchen counter. "Want something to drink?"

"That's another thing . . . "

"Gary. Sweetie," I said drily, opening the fridge and glancing his way. "I'm not an alcoholic. I just really like alcohol."

"Yes, you do." He looked at me with concern as I stood there with the refrigerator door open.

"I'm air-conditioning the neighborhood, as my mom likes to say. You want a beer or not?"

"OK."

I pulled out two bottles, popped the tops and handed him one. "Want to get comfortable?"

"The couch?"

"I was thinking the bedroom."

"You're unbelievable," he said, but an ember sparked in

his eyes.

"I'm totally believable. I promised. We'll talk if you want. But I need to get comfortable, and the couch isn't going to do it."

Without waiting for an answer, I walked to the bedroom and set the bottle on my nightstand. I switched on the lava lamp and set the iPod dock to a low-key rock playlist as Gary arrived at the doorway, watching me. He almost choked as I kicked off my sandals and wriggled out of my tight jeans, leaving me in my silky black tank and black satin bikinis.

"Just getting comfortable. Come on, Gary. You've seen me in less than this."

"That blanket covered up a lot," he said of our encounter at his house.

I flopped on the bed and my new black-and-white checkerboard comforter, leaned up against the fluffy white pillows and sipped my beer. "At least I'm not wearing a thong."

His eyes grew wider. "You have a thong?"

"Of course I do, Gary. Come here." I patted the bed, and after a moment, he walked to the other side, slowly, as if it might burst into flames. He toed off his sneakers and eased himself onto the mattress, keeping a foot of space between us.

I nudged myself closer until we were hip to hip, and he sighed as I leaned my head on his shoulder.

After a moment, he wrapped an arm around me, and we sank a little deeper into the pillows. "Ez, I want to ask you something. A couple of things."

"OK."

"Why did you tell your friends about our house — my mom's house?"

I nuzzled against his warmth. "I thought maybe they'd

have an idea of how to help."

"Huh." He took a sip of his beer. "At least you were thinking about me."

Actually, I'd been thinking about him a lot more than I ever thought I would.

"Also," he continued, "why did you let Stuart touch you the other night after what he did to you?"

"I was drunk and stupid. But your timing was perfect. He was getting a little scary."

"I was on the other side of the door, listening to you sing. When you stopped, I wanted to know why."

"Oh." I took another sip of beer. "You heard the song?"

"Most of it. What's it about?"

"Shit from the past. What most songs are about."

"Tell me."

"I can't," I said, squeezing my beer bottle as I felt the first hint of a tremor. I looked over at the lava lamp. It had started to heat up, and the globs inside were moving slowly around one another like shapes from a nightmare.

"You said you would be honest with me," Gary said.

"I honestly can't tell you."

"Can't or won't?" he asked.

"I will not tell you."

"Ever?"

"Ever is a long time," I said, putting down the beer bottle and turning onto my side so I faced him. It was nice being nestled in his arm.

"So you might tell me?"

"I'd like to be able to tell you. It's not something I've ever told a guy." I laid a hand on his belly. I loved the feel of it, firm and warm. I slipped my hand under his shirt.

"You're trying to distract me."

"Is it working?" I grinned up at him as his breathing increased ever so slightly.

"I'll leave it alone for now," he said, trying to ignore my caress. "I don't want to upset you. But that melody, I wanted to tell you — it haunted me. I want to know where it came from."

"Be careful what you wish for," I whispered, pulling up his shirt and kissing him right above his belly button.

He let out a long, slow breath and set down his beer bottle. "Ez . . . "

"Yes?" I kissed him again and then again, moving up his torso slowly, deliberately, pushing up his shirt as I went.

"Are you doing this because it's easier than talking?"

I stopped and looked into his face, searched his eyes, finding more in them every time I dove into the swirls of amber and emerald: Concern. Admiration. Intelligence. Lust.

I pulled his T-shirt up over his head. "I'm doing this because I want to do this. Because I want to be with you."

He closed his eyes as I licked one nipple, teasing it lightly with my teeth.

"I can't help but think," he whispered hoarsely, "that I'm one in a long line of . . . "

I paused on my precipice, one I'd built up for years, making it so tall, leaping off it never seemed possible. "You're not the first guy I've kissed," I said lightly. "But you're here, now, and you're the only one I want."

"For now."

"There is only now." I slid over him, covering him with my body, and slanted my lips over his.

"Mmmm," he murmured into my mouth, and then reluctant Gary wasn't so reluctant anymore. His hands found my back, slipped under the tank, and he made another sound as he confirmed that no bra stood in his way. He broke the kiss and pulled the shirt over my head and marveled at me from the pillows, a small smile playing about his lips. He slipped his fingers over my breasts — mine weren't large, but they just fit into his big potter's hands, and he squeezed me like clay.

"*Ohhh.*" The sound escaped me despite myself. There was such proprietary strength in his grasp as he manipulated me, thumbed my pebbled nipples, pushed my breasts together, then up so he could reach them with his long tongue, with his mouth. He sucked lovingly on one, and the other almost begged for attention; he caressed the first as he laved the second.

I wriggled against him, against the hard-on I felt through his jeans, and then, I thought, *I'm really going to do this.*

We're really going to do this.

It was about time. And then I was nervous and anxious and felt like an innocent in one of those old novels, even though I'd done plenty with plenty of guys.

But this was Gary, and this was now, and it was time. *And I can trust him,* I told myself.

I reached for his jeans, unfastened them. He lay back on the pillows as I pulled them and his briefs off and dropped them to the floor with his socks. His length, hard and erect, was almost frightening. And enticing and wonderful. I grasped him with one hand and slowly worked it up and down and up and down —

"Stop," he said.

"Really?"

"No, I just need something. I mean, if you — "

"Yes, Gary," I whispered, feeling weirdly meek. I slipped off him and let him reach for his jeans, grab the condom from his wallet. I watched him roll it on, fascinated by the way it hugged him, all of him. *Oh, my God.*

He lay next to me for a moment, on his side, tracing a finger along my shoulder, my breasts, down my belly to my little satin underpants. He ran his hand over the damp fabric, cupping me, rubbing my clit through the satin, and my breath hitched. He placed his hand on my hip and kissed me.

"I've wanted you forever," he said, his voice low and electric.

"You have me," I whispered back, not sure how to feel. I wasn't equipped to feel.

He felt enough for both of us, kissing me harder this time, urgently, deftly, his tongue claiming my mouth, and a dam broke inside me. Was this what it felt like to really want a man, to want all of him, to feel him fit inside you and possess you?

Because, oh miracle of miracles, *I wanted him.*

What a liberating feeling, to want a man, really *want* a man, and be wanted in return — and to have it be Gary, the guy I never used to see, the strong, hot man who now rolled me onto my back. The man who devoured my mouth and reached for my underpants, stripping them off in a heartbeat. I was completely naked before him, naked in more ways than one, in more ways than he realized.

He ran a finger through my folds, slick and ready, and *yes,* I was ready —

"Are you ready?" he asked, intense, gorgeous, really, his dark curls falling around his face. His luscious lips. How had I never noticed before?

I could only nod. He seemed to sense my hesitance, and he kissed me again, a beautiful, searing kiss, and again, I tasted that longing of his, that heartbreaking longing.

He slipped a finger into my pussy.

"Oh, yes," I whispered, rising to meet him as he fingered me, pushing deeper.

"You like?" he asked, a devilish twinkle in his eyes.

"I like." I licked my lips.

"That drives me crazy when you do that."

"This?" I licked my lips again.

"I'm going to fuck you now, Esmerelda Falcon," he said, his voice now urgent, humming with a hunger that sent a thrill up my spine.

I spread my legs, bit my lip and tried to prepare myself as he rubbed my clit with his cock — *so good* — and as he slid in the first few inches, teasing my opening, dipping into my honey. And then he pushed in — and *in* — and through.

"Ah," I whimpered, a little cry of pain. So this is what it felt like.

"Ez?" Feelings, realizations tumbled over his face. He froze. "Did I? You?"

"You said you were going to fuck me, Gary," I bit out. "Fuck me."

My words stoked his conflagration, and he gave in to his lust, questions moot, his face shadowed with desire. He pulled back and thrust again, this time seating himself in me so deeply, I moaned, forgetting for a moment the sting and burn and just feeling everything, his hips against mine, his chest and its dusting of hair brushing my breasts as he used his muscular arms to support himself over me, the hot scent of him, his eyes.

Oh, his eyes, boring into mine — they were a beacon, the light I held onto as he thrust inside me, turning my pain into pleasure, a ripple at first and then a rising tide of anxious desire, then a tsunami, an imperative, and I bucked up against his deep penetrations, wanting him to pierce me through.

He gasped as he came, holding himself there as he quivered and thrust again, hard, and I cried out in delicious agony, the waves of response excruciating as I grabbed his ass and wrapped my legs around him, shaking with my release.

I collapsed back on the bed, and he lifted his body, easing out of me, concern back in his eyes. "Did I hurt you?"

"No." It wasn't quite a lie. It wasn't all pain. Far from it. But I saw it at the same time he did: the blood on the condom.

A swallow traveled down his long throat as he rolled it off, tossed it in the trash can in the corner. And then he sat up next to me, not touching me, a crease in his brow, looking at me in disbelief, regarding me as if I were a stranger.

I sat up and slipped out of bed, headed for the bathroom. I used the toilet and washed up. There was blood, but it wasn't too bad. When I came back out, Gary had the same expression, only now he held a pillow over his middle.

I deliberately climbed over him and sat cross-legged in front of him, all of me on view. And why not?

"What is it, Gary?" I asked. "You've never heard of a promiscuous virgin?"

He shook his head. "Maybe as a creature of legend, like a unicorn," he finally said, and I laughed. "Are you kidding me, Ez?"

"That you should doubt me at this tender moment is somewhat depressing." I shifted, feeling the needling ache between my legs. I spread them and leaned back, supporting myself with my arms, so he could see all of me. This felt good. I wanted him to see me, really see me. I liked the way he looked at me, even now, burning me with his eyes as they roved from my mouth to my breasts to my exposed pussy. It tripped my trigger, the way he looked at me, speaking to my inner kink, the one twisted into me, the one that made me want to perform in more ways than one.

Like a man in a trance, he reached out and touched one of my nipples, running his finger around the dark areola. I closed my eyes for a moment, lost in the sensation, then opened them and looked at him again.

He dropped his hand and held my gaze. "I really was —?"

"My first. Well, first *you know*. Don't freak out on me, Gary."

"Oh, Ez." Emotion swept across his face as he threw away the pillow and grabbed me, knocking me into the mattress. He kissed me, a hungry, open-mouthed kiss, and then he embraced me, holding me tight.

I tentatively wrapped my arms around his back and let his heat envelop me.

That was over with. Now what was I going to do with him?

As ready as I was to finally bust my cherry, I wasn't all that ready to keep fucking Gary. If I did, that might mean more commitment than I was ready for, and it was clear he thought I'd crossed some bridge into relationship-land by giving it up to him.

At the same time, I found myself looking at him differently — especially as he slept in my bed the morning after, lanky and handsome and sweetly at peace, his hair spread out on the pillows. Because even though I'd planned to push him out of there pretty much as soon as the deed was done, there was something so damn — oh, hell, there was that word again — *nice* about being with him that I wasn't ready to give him up just yet. I mean, I *did* trust him. Me trusting anyone was a miracle in itself. And it's not like I had any asshole boy-toys lined up.

It's not like I really wanted one, either.

Gary — could he be that elusive creature, the friend with benefits?

Not the way he was looking at me. Not just friends. And the idea of more than friends was terrifying.

Awake now, he smiled at me with an adoring gaze as I lay on my side next to him, contemplating my options. And his lithe, strong body.

"Good morning," he said.

"Good morning, Gary." My cool tone must have thrown him, because concern furrowed his brow.

"You feel OK this morning?"

"Pretty much. Although I'm a little sore. It's almost like I went horseback riding or something. I can't imagine what it could be," I said drily.

"Hmm," he said, playing along. "What *were* you doing last night?"

"Oh, wait, I think I remember. Some guy with the longest schlong I've ever seen fucked me senseless. Me, a poor innocent. I'll have to wear a scarlet 'A' now."

His grin broadened and shone like the morning sun itself. " 'A' for Amazing," he said, reaching for me, but I slipped out of his grip and stood, nude, of course. His eyes raked me with a growing heat that made nerves tingle at the base of my spine.

"Don't you have somewhere to be?" I asked.

"Not when I have a goddess standing before me." Before I knew it, he'd practically leaped out of the bed and grabbed me from behind, sweeping me up against his hard body, his harder cock. *Ready to rock,* I thought, starting to wriggle, but he held me tighter, cupping one breast with his wide palm, squeezing it as he kissed my neck, licking the skin there, shooting electricity through my body.

Whoa. Is this what it felt like to be past all that virginal nonsense? I'd had men touch me, even bring me to orgasm, but it was never like this. I never let them get this close.

My wriggling changed; now, I rubbed my ass against his cock. He moaned into my neck, squeezing both breasts now, holding me tightly to him, bucking subtly against me.

"Do you feel well enough to — "

"Hell, yes," I said, suddenly wanting more of this, more of him.

He let go of me and I almost fell, wondering what happened. Oh, yeah. He was grabbing something out of his jeans, another condom, ripping open the packet, rolling it on.

"I want you now, Ez," he whispered, coming up behind me again, slipping an arm around my waist. "I want to be inside you. I want to fuck you deep, baby."

Oh, and Gary did dirty talk, did he?

I liked it.

"I don't think you can do it any other way but deep," I said, my voice husky. He chuckled.

I stepped forward and knelt on the bed, on all fours. I realized I could see him standing behind me in the mirror on my closet door. "Do me this way, Gary. I want to feel you from behind. I want you to watch me. Us."

I wanted to do it all the ways I could, now. I wanted to understand what I'd been missing.

He caught my glance in the mirror and a look crossed his face, some understanding that he was moving from simple body worship into something more wanton. He was going to fuck me, and we were both going to watch ourselves do it.

He stepped up to me and ran a hand along my back, along my spine. I arched, purring like a cat, watching him. He reached under me and cupped my breasts; I watched him again as he pinched the nipples and stretched them and made me moan. His mouth opened; his breathing accelerated. He was caught up in the lust. As someone who had grown used to being watched, was turned on by it, I reached a new level of want in watching Gary watch me.

He laid his big palms on my buttocks and squeezed, then slid one hand between my legs and fingered my clit, swirling, rubbing until I was moving against his hand, groaning, pleading.

"Please fuck me, Gary."

"In good time," he whispered, slipping a finger inside my slit. I was so slick for him, he easily slipped a second finger inside me. Those long, deft fingers that had sculpted exquisite pieces of art found places in me I didn't know I had. The firecrackers started to pop in my pussy, and my cries grew louder as I shut my eyes, pushing against him.

He paused. "Does it hurt?"

"No — yes, it hurts so good, Gary. Please fuck me now."

I opened my eyes as I moved and met his striking gaze in the mirror.

"I never thought I'd hear you beg me for it," he murmured, his voice low and sexy.

I almost came right then.

He slipped his fingers out, dragged his cock through my folds and plunged inside me.

I cried out, louder now, as his magnificent length burrowed deeply into my wet, slightly sore passage. The pleasure soon far outraced the pain as he grunted and thrust, pulling me against him, faster, harder. I watched him in the mirror, his hair flying around his face, his features focused on the sensuality of it; he would look down, then up, meeting my eyes, searing, commanding, sending my desire spiraling higher. Our naked bodies moved in percussive poetry, beating out a primal rhythm, his tall and muscular, mine small and slight, submitting eagerly to his pleasure. I watched him take me, watched my body writhe against him, watched my breasts swinging, and wanted to give him everything.

He shifted, going deeper, and in ecstatic agony, I came, moaning his name. This was so much better than last night.

My cries seemed to send him over the edge. He groaned as he climaxed and caught my eyes in the mirror again as he banged hard against me, filling me with his need, and then he closed them, lost in the moment and perhaps respecting it, too.

Sweet Gary. Sweet, sinful Gary. *Oh, my.*

He held on for another long, luscious minute, and then he withdrew. I collapsed on the bed, on the soft comforter, and he fell almost on top of me, turning me gently to face him, kissing me with an alien feeling that I had to take a moment to identify: passion. Pure passion. Passion that inspired my own kisses, more playful, even as I was tempted to drown in his. I slipped my fingers into his unruly long hair, clasping it, wrapping the curls around my fingers, making love to his mouth.

Love? No, sex.

So *that's* what sex could be. Why did I wait so fucking long?

I knew why. But with Gary, I realized, I could almost forget.

"WHY DON'T you come over to the beach later?" Gary asked me over breakfast at The Double Diamond Diner, not far from my place in Bohemia. The Diamond was a hangover tradition. He was inhaling a big breakfast with eggs and sausages and bacon; I was savoring the steel-cut oatmeal, fresh fruit and thick raisin bread with butter, all with fresh-squeezed orange juice and high-test coffee.

"What, you don't want to come back to my place again?" I teased.

He looked sheepish and glanced around at the other patrons in this mid-century classic, with its mini-jukeboxes on the tables and chrome trim everywhere. "I'm out of condoms," he whispered.

I laughed. "And it's not like I have any. Though I guess I'll have to start thinking about that now." This was so silly. I was like an eager student starting a new class. I'd do what I needed to do this week to get on the pill.

"So come to the beach this afternoon."

"I should work on some songs I'm writing." I didn't want to get too involved with Gary. But those river-light eyes sparkled at me, softening my resolve.

"You can take a break. Come over and we'll play some music."

"Piano and drums?"

"Your keyboard and my ukulele, unless you play guitar."

"Not anymore. I forgot you told me you play ukulele."

"Every beach boy should play ukulele." He drained his coffee cup.

"So this wouldn't be some lurid assignation, would it?"

"Only if you want it to be." He flashed his dimples.

"Yeah, with your grandma and mom and aunt and cousin all hanging around. And that bohemian Jay."

"My cousin went back to school. I think my aunt was taking my grandma shopping. And Jay and Mom will probably be golfing."

"Ah-ha!" I said. "I knew he was a golfer."

"She's going to marry him, I think." Gary frowned slightly. "Don't you like him?"

"Actually, yeah. He's really low-key. The opposite of my dad."

"Do you ever see your dad?" I bit into the raisin toast. Oh, the butter was good here.

"Not if I can help it. Though he shows up sometimes at the same events. I saw him and his wife briefly at the regional show opening at the museum."

"Was he nice to you?"

"He asked if he could buy my vase. I told him it wasn't for sale. He told me everything was for sale."

"What a philosopher." I sat back against the leather booth bench with my coffee. "Does he know about your mom and Jay?"

"I don't know. But he's probably salivating to stop the alimony payments. It was a generous settlement at the time."

"Probably because he cared about what happened to you."

Gary looked surprised. "I think it's because Mom had a better lawyer."

I chuckled. "Maybe not. I'm sure he thinks about you."

"He's always out to make a buck," Gary continued. "He puts his profits into real estate and makes even more. I know it killed him to give up that beachfront property in the first place, but since Mom brought it to the marriage, she hung onto it in the settlement. And she only had the title because Grandma signed it over to her — which is a good thing, because I wouldn't have put it past my dad to try to get Grandma declared incompetent."

"He could do that?"

"I've heard of such things. Temporary restraining order, then someone in the family gets a court to award guardianship."

"Disgusting," I said. "Why do people get married anyway?"

He smiled and shrugged. "Love conquers all."

"You still believe that?"

"If I didn't, I'd go crazy," he said quietly, avoiding my eyes.

"Gary, the eternal optimist."

"You should try it sometime."

I looked at him with alarm. "Love?"

"Optimism," he said, pushing away his empty plate and patting his belly. "I never would have dropped out of Florida State and committed myself to pottery unless I was an optimist. And I'm a lot happier now."

"What were you studying?"

"That was the problem. I never really decided."

I nodded. "I took some classes at Full Sail, but I realized that I wasn't into music production enough to pay for all the courses. I just wanted to write and perform. So I got a job and started gigging."

Gary looked at me curiously. "Where do you work, anyway?"

"A girl has to retain some sense of mystery, you know."

"You're full of mystery."

I smiled at him and licked my lips. "You've already probed some of my mysteries, Gary Gorski."

His eyes grew cloudy, his face serious. "Don't tease me, Ez. Come over this afternoon."

I was enjoying his discomfiture so much, I couldn't help but say yes. "Three o'clock?"

He sighed, looking relieved and pained at the same time. I wondered if he had a hard-on. I slipped off a sandal and lifted my foot under the table, sliding it between his legs. *Oh, yeah.*

He inhaled sharply as I kneaded him with my toes.

"Anything else?" The chipper, brunette waitress — Millie, I think, one of Cali's photography students — was at the table, pad in hand.

"I think we're fine," I said. "Checks are good."

"One check," Gary said with difficulty, and Millie, oblivious to his struggle, ripped the bill out of her pad and left it on his side of the table.

I withdrew my foot. Gary let out a long breath.

"Too bad about the condoms," I whispered, snatching the check away from him and laying down some cash.

He swallowed, looking at me helplessly. "I can buy more."

"That's the beauty of America. You can always buy more," I said with a wink. "I'll see you this afternoon."

And I strutted out of The Diamond, leaving Gary with his optimism.

IT WAS a top-down kind of Saturday, at least for my car. I had a top on, myself, even if it wasn't much of one — a negligible thin knit in dark purple with a halter neck and a low back. I wore it with a short, black skirt and sandals with a low heel. It might've been a little dressy for hanging out with Gary, but for some reason, I wanted to look less casual than I felt.

Maybe I wanted to test the boundaries of my first sexual relationship with *actual* sex. Or maybe I just wanted to feel Gary looking at me with those worshipful eyes, those eyes that made me feel like I had a chance at being special.

What a joke. I was in the mood to laugh at myself as I took the causeway about ten miles over the speed limit, letting the sultry wind of early spring whip through my hair, my rippling top. The lagoon, or the river, depending on who was talking, sparkled in the afternoon light. The breeze smelled of salt and flowers, a temperate caress on my face and shoulders before the serious heat of summer kicked in. It wouldn't be long now.

Bohemia Beach was crazy busy. The snowbirds had started to head back north, but visitors and residents alike were taking advantage of the best beach day in months.

As I rolled up to Gary's family home — a vast oasis of sea grapes, palms and grasses plunked in the middle of a row of mansions and condos — I saw a few surfers clambering through a skinny path amid the vegetation and over the dunes. I supposed they qualified as native wildlife, too.

I used the button at the gate to ring the house, and Gary's voice came over the speaker almost immediately.

"Ez?"

"I'm selling magazines, sir. We have a new title you may enjoy: *Incorrigible Slut,*" I called into the panel.

"Well, then, you better get in here right away," Gary's voice came back. I laughed as the gate slid open, then closed behind me.

He greeted me on the front step with a chaste kiss and scanned me from head to toe as if he were starved, not stuffed with the massive breakfast I knew he'd had. "I see you brought your keyboard."

I had the bulky thing and its folding stand under my arm. "Yeah. Hard to play without it. Unless you have a glockenspiel."

"Not yet." He grinned. "Come on in. I want to learn more about that magazine. *Incredible Slut,* was it?"

"Incorrigible Slut." I shook my head as I followed him through the door. "I suppose that's not the one you're looking for."

"I'm buying whatever you're selling," he said in a flirtatious tone that sent little sparks running up and down my body.

I still wasn't used to Gary doing that to me. But this morning, seeing him behind me in the mirror, pumping into me — I got wet just thinking about it. And a little confused. I shouldn't be here. I didn't want to be, didn't deserve to be. Why was I walking toward the trap instead of running away?

"My music room is this way," Gary said, taking the keyboard from me — nice, again — and leading me through the foyer and down a hallway. "It's more of a hobby room, really."

He opened the door on a room even bigger than the den on the other side of the house. It had a tile floor dotted with mismatched rugs, sliding glass doors that looked out on the ocean and its own powder room. It held the drum set he'd used the other night, a couple of guitars and a ukulele hanging on the wall, and bookcases crowded with tomes on pottery and music and drawing and a smattering of novels. Another ukulele rested on a wooden chair; there were a couple of wide, worn comfy chairs, too. On the other side of the room were more shelves that held clay pots in various stages of production, and an electric pottery wheel sat in the corner. Two mobiles hung from the ceiling, one slowly spinning with whimsical ceramic birds, another made of colorful ceramic shapes. Posters for gallery shows and art fairs, a bulletin board of old concert tickets and a Velvet Elvis filled every available wall space. The place had an air of messy, busy creativity.

"And here I thought you liked living small," I said, setting up the folding stand. Gary placed the keyboard on top of it. "You have three times as much stuff here as you had in your shack."

"Yeah, but it's just stuff, you know. I could live without it. Still, sometimes it's really nice to come in here and open the doors and listen to the waves while I lose myself in making pots."

"You have a kiln here, too?"

"No, that's where Mom draws the line," he said. "But that's one reason I work at the school. Maybe I'll have my own studio someday."

"Speaking of Mom — "

"Nobody's home but us," he said with a smile.

I smirked and raised an eyebrow. "And you play guitar?" I walked over to check them out — decent brands, one acoustic, one electric.

"I dabble. That's kind of the story of my life. I'm a dilettante, I guess."

I turned to look at him. "You're, like, the resident genius potter at the school, aren't you?"

"No, we have an artist-in-residence right now who is the presumed genius, Montrose King."

"I hear he's kind of an asshole," I said, and Gary laughed, conceding a nod. "But I hear great things about you," I continued. "And, I mean, I've seen your work."

I walked over to the shelves with the pots. A dozen were

draped with plastic or were drying, but I recognized the first vase he'd saved from the fire alongside other glazed pots, many with a similar mottled green and gold finish. He'd cleaned up the lucky vase; I picked it up and caressed its surface — smooth, but etched with swirling patterns. For a moment I got lost in fingering the spirals, perfect whorls like those of a seashell, and the seemingly shifting colors.

They reminded me of Gary's eyes.

I looked up at him, startled, catching that gaze, catching my breath. He was watching me with interest — with more than interest. With rapt attention.

"I'm glad you saved this one," I murmured. I caressed it one more time and placed it back on the shelf. "It's beautiful."

I stepped back toward him and saw him visibly straighten, getting ahold of whatever reason had deserted him when he looked at me. "Thanks," he said, his voice tenuous, as if he were still grappling with the feeling. "It's part of an evolution. I'm trying to get the glaze right. It's not perfect yet."

"I think that's what makes it beautiful. The imperfections. Or maybe I should say the variations." *That, and it reminds me of your eyes.* "The way the form stays perfect but the colors and textures change with the light, when I turn it and feel it in my hands. It's like jazz."

"I like that." He shot me a warm smile that lit up the room. "Want to play something?"

"OK," I said, striving to focus on anything except Gary and his magnetic awareness of me. "What did you have in mind?" I looked around, grabbed the stool from behind his pottery wheel and set it up in front of the keyboard. I found an outlet, plugged it in and played a few chords.

He picked up his ukulele from the wooden chair, which

he dragged closer to me, and sat down, plucking a few notes, tweaking the tuning. The sound was bright and happy, complementing the ocean's muted sighs through the glass.

"We could warm up with something we both know," he said. "How about 'Piano Man'?"

"You know 'Piano Man' for ukulele?" I asked, laughing.

"It's only vaguely ridiculous when I sing the chorus. 'You're the ukulele man' just doesn't have the same ring to it."

Still smiling, I shrugged. "It's sentimental claptrap, but it's perfect sentimental claptrap. Let's do it."

I started in on the opening chords, and Gary soon joined me, playing a nice counterpoint to the boisterous rhythm I hammered out on the keys. I sang melody, and he joined me on the chorus with his warm tenor, at first with me, then in harmony. My ears filled with the pure joy of it, the fresh take on such a familiar song. We exchanged smiles as we got into rhymes that were meant for sing-alongs. When we finished, I sighed with contentment.

"One thing I don't understand is, if he spends all his time in this bar, why is Davy still in the Navy?" Gary asked, and I laughed again. He grinned back. "Want to do another one?"

"What do you want to play?"

"Why don't you do one of yours? One of the slow ones, so I can keep up."

"I've been fooling around with a couple." I thought for a moment, wondering how personal I wanted to get. All of my songs were personal, yet the person singing them wasn't me, it was the Other Me, the performer. I got myself into the right headspace and lassoed the lyrics in my brain, hoping Gary wouldn't see them too personally, either. "Try this one. Key of G."

I played a bright chord followed by single high notes,

sharp like drops of rain, then low notes skipping to keep up, high, low, high, low, a hypnotic, loping rhythm, not in minor key, but still contemplative. The tune hovered on the edge of melancholy as the melody climbed in chords up the keyboard, *one two three four, one two three four,* as Gary picked up the changes and added the plaintive twang of the ukulele.

And then I sang:

I met you in the rain
It seems like I always meet you in the rain
The drops roll down my cheeks
and then you bring the sun

I dress to hide the pain
It seems like my skin can reflect the pain
The flash is lightning fast
and then I'm on the run

You bring the elements to me
earth and wind and rain and fire
You kiss the girl who hides inside
and fan the hot flames higher

Each day feels the same
Or it seems they did till you called
    my name
The smoke obscured the sky
And in the dark I'm done

You bring the elements to me
earth and wind and rain and fire
You kiss the girl who hides inside

and fan the hot flames higher

The thunder rolls and rolls and rolls
but it's only an echo of the light . . .

I stopped. "That's the bridge. Still kind of working on it." I looked up at Gary. He was frozen in place, his face, his eyes — my God, the *intensity* . . . "What is it?"

"Is that about us?"

"What?" I asked, startled by his demanding question. "No, nothing's ever really about me. Not really. It's not about us. There is no *us.*"

He stood slowly, tall and fuming. "Ez, everything you sing is about you. Christ, it's the only time you ever show your heart. And to say there's nothing of us in there, that there is no *us* — "

Gary tossed the ukulele on the chair with a clatter and whirled toward the sliding glass doors that looked out over the deck and onto the beach. The room seemed dimmer now, the sun on the other side of the house, but still he was backlit, his curly hair set aglow by the afternoon light, the blue reflections beyond. His shoulders were rigid, and his tall body radiated tension and power. I almost recoiled from it.

"Gary, it's just a song."

He turned again to look at me. *Shit,* he was furious. "Nothing is just a song. No piece of art is just a piece of art, not if it's real. And this, *this* is where you get real," he said, gesturing to the piano. "Are you going to lie about that? Because if you are, there's no hope for you."

I stood so fast I knocked over the stool as I stomped toward him. "Don't lecture me about what my music means to me. You have no idea."

His laugh was dark as he spread his arms and shook his head. "Look around, Ez. I have some idea. I may act like I'm just living *la dolce vita,* but I'm not the goofy beach bum you seem to think I am."

La Dolce Vita. The sweet life. "But your life *is* sweet, Gary, and all I can do is make it more bitter."

He stepped closer to me, invading my space, his hazel eyes snapping with green lightning. "There is no sweet life, Ez. The trick is knowing that the bitter makes the rest that much sweeter."

He grabbed my arms and crushed me to him, his mouth on mine, angry and hard and hungry, and my lyrics came back to me, *You kiss the girl who hides inside.*

A switch flipped in my brain, my body, setting the moment on fire. I wanted him, his ferocity, his certainty, his need. I grasped his waist and opened to him, to his tongue, sucking his, moaning into his mouth as he clutched my body closer to his, the urgency between us multiplied. His fingers were on my back under the loose shirt, feeling no bra there, and he groaned as he slid his big hands over my skin. I could feel him growing against me through his shorts. He flipped my shirt off, and I fumbled with his zipper. And then his shorts and his boxer briefs were off, on the floor, and he was reaching into the discarded garments for a condom. *Of course,* I thought in a moment of irony, *he bought more.*

He slipped it onto his hard length as I pressed my hands on his chest. I grabbed the hem of his T-shirt and pulled it up; he ducked so I could get it over his head. I licked one of his nipples, tasting the dusting of dark hair there, his salty skin; I lost myself in sucking it.

I paused as I felt his hands sweep under my short skirt and finger the thong there.

He ripped it off.

I gasped, quivered, drowning in desire as he pushed me against the wall, devouring my mouth. He lifted me — *damn,* he was strong. I was beyond turned on; I wrapped my legs around him, eagerly grinding my pussy against his cock. He positioned himself and, after a moment's delirious suspense, plunged inside me. He pulled out slightly and pounded into me again, then again, fucking me against the wall, over and over. I hung onto his shoulders and gripped him with my legs, feeling the hard surface against my back. His shaft stretched my sore passage, but I felt only excruciating plea- sure as he palmed my ass, hoisting me higher, going deeper.

"God, Gary, *yes,*" I whimpered into his shoulder. I shud- dered and cried out, coming hard, and he did the same, grunting and pressing against me and holding me there as his cock pulsed against my womb. I spasmed again in answer, trembling, holding him tightly. We stayed melded together there for a few moments, breathing hard, and then he eased out of me. My feet had barely touched the ground when he scooped me up and carried me to one of the comfy chairs. He gently set me on the cushion and went to the powder room to dispose of the condom. When he returned, he nestled beside me and pulled me into his lap.

I curled up against his naked body, feeling thoroughly used, satisfactorily spent, aching and sexy and high. He lifted my chin with one finger, Mr. Sensitivity again. "You OK?"

"You have to ask?"

"I want to be sure."

I nodded. He wrapped his arms around me tightly and kissed me, so much more slowly this time, so *nice.*

So *hot.*

I tried to fend off a sudden stab of vulnerability. He

supped on my mouth as if I were the sweetest dessert, and his lips said so much more than that fuck had. His lips were more articulate than my lyrics. He cared about me. And my lips, my body wanted to keep having that conversation, even as my defenses fired into the darkness.

> *The flash is lightning fast*
> *and then I'm on the run . . .*

"GARY? GARY, ARE YOU HERE?"

I stirred against his chest at the sound of the voice and looked up at him. We'd been curled up there, listening to the sounds of the ocean, for the better part of an hour, limp and warm and comfortable. I think Gary had dozed off.

But now his eyes were wide open. "Shit. My mom."

I slid off his lap by mutual consent as he stood, and we scrambled to get our clothes on.

"Why do I suddenly feel like a teenager?" I asked wryly as I slipped the shirt over my head. Gary smiled ruefully, watching me cover up. The thong was history, but at least I still had my skirt on. I stuffed the remains of the underwear in my purse and donned the sandals I'd slipped off. Gary got the last of his clothes in place. Too bad, really.

"Gary?" his mom's voice came again, closer now.

I ran a hand through my hair, sifting through the slanted bangs, and stood by the glass doors.

"In here, mom," Gary called.

She opened the door and looked from one of us to the other, then smiled.

There was really no fooling moms, was there?

"Ez, it's so nice to see you again. Gary, could I talk to you for a minute in the kitchen? Ez, would you like something to drink? I made some lemonade."

With vodka? I thought. "That sounds great," I said.

"Why don't you relax on the deck and I'll have Gary bring it out to you."

"OK." I grinned at Gary, whose eyebrows had reached a mournful peak, stretching the elfin angles of his face. He followed his mom out the door.

I took a moment to wander around the room, fingering the random objects that populated the bookshelves — a blown-glass paperweight with exquisite glass flowers inside, a tiny metal airplane worn by years of play, a hurricane glass stuffed with matchbooks, a ceramic dish full of marbles, a tiny Eiffel tower — had Gary been to Paris? I hadn't been anywhere, yet.

Amid the pottery books, a dark leather binding caught my eye. It looked well worn, possibly damaged by water or worse, and I realized it was the small notebook Gary had saved from the fire. I looked around, knowing I was about to invade his privacy, and pulled it from the shelf.

The leather was textured, the raised branches of a tree covering its surface in a random pattern in a lighter brown than the rest, pleasing to the touch. The edges of the book looked singed. Definitely the one he'd rescued.

I gingerly opened it to the middle, to a page with a list:

- *Black Matte, Cone 6*
- *whiting — 17.9*
- *zinc oxide — 8*
- *potash feldspar — 49.2*
- *EPK Kaolin — 19.9*

- *Silica* — 5

Chemicals — for a glaze? It went on with a couple more items. I turned the page.

This one was covered with doodles. No, not doodles — they were patterns and decorative designs. One page was entirely covered with sketches of leaves. The next had drag-onflies. The drawings were precise, balanced, beautiful. I flipped through a few more pages — interlocking geome-tries; flowing waves; swirls like the ones on the vase I'd admired.

The next page stopped me cold.

This was not a pottery pattern. This was a sketch of a young woman, her head down, just one eye visible, a hint of a smile on her lips under the diagonal cut of her bangs . . . I quickly flipped through, and there she was again, and again, scattered among the designs and patterns and lists of chemicals.

She. *Me.*

Something touched my leg, and I almost jumped out of my skin. I slammed the journal shut, looking around for ghosts or Gary.

Instead I saw Pumpkin Spice circling me. She slinked between my legs, jumped up on the nearest comfy chair and regarded me with knowing, yellow-green eyes before lifting and licking a paw.

"Goddamn it, cat," I said. "There goes one of my lives. And I've already used up more than you have."

I slipped the book back into place, feeling overwhelmed with what I'd seen, the pretty drawings from not just the past two weeks, but months, maybe years. They were tender and lovely and strange, and all the more personal because they were secret. I told myself they weren't like the photos. Nothing could ever be like that.

But how could Gary think about me so much? Want me so much? Nobody, I decided, wanted anybody that much without wanting to take a little piece of their soul.

I grabbed my keyboard and stand and purse and snuck down the hallway, ignoring the voices in the kitchen. Before they could find me, I slipped out the front door to my car and left.

My phone buzzed just when I was parking in the little lot behind my apartment building. I glanced at the screen. The text was, as I suspected, from Gary.

"Where'd you go?"

At least he'd given me enough time to get away and think. But I still wasn't sure what I thought.

Warring with my knee-jerk need to run was something else — it had to be a chemical reaction — my pleasure center curling up and purring and stretching and wanting more of the hot sex and slow kisses I'd had with him this afternoon. *Fuck, what is wrong with me?*

"Had to go home," I texted back.

"Scared of my mom? :-)"

I didn't answer, despite the smiley face. *Scared of you. Scared of myself.*

I got up to my apartment, manhandling my keyboard and getting it inside just as he sent another text: "She wanted to tell me she and Jay have set a date."

Reading his message, knowing the subtext — the house would be sold to developers, the gem on the beach would be gone, his family would have to find a another place to live — I forgot about the drawings and just felt sorry for him.

"Glad for her," I responded. "Sad for you."

"Don't be sad for me. I'm happy for her. Wish I could talk to you. Can I talk to you?"

I stared at the phone. Nobody wanted to talk to me. Everybody wanted something from me, but nobody wanted to *talk* to me, except maybe my girlfriends, but that was all on a pretty shallow level. I kept it that way. I never confided in anyone. And I wasn't used to people confiding in me.

My ringtone filled my space with the hammering piano chords that opened Amanda Palmer's "Astronaut." I stared at the phone, willing it to stop.

My index finger acted on its own, touching the screen to pick up the call.

"Ez." Gary's voice was filled with relief. "Thank you for answering."

And he said he wasn't nice? He even thanked me for answering the fucking phone.

"I'm sorry about the house," I said. "Maybe there's something you can do."

"I don't know what. Mom's going to wait until the last minute to announce anything, and then they'll get married at the end of April. She doesn't want to give my dad the satisfaction, I think, but she's going to have to eventually. What really sucks is it could easily be him who buys the old place."

"Maybe he'd keep it in its original state," I said, resigning myself to the conversation and flopping on my couch.

"No way. He wanted to sell off chunks of it when they were married."

"Sometimes life just screws you over, and you have to move on."

He was silent for a moment. "Is that why you moved to Bohemia?"

"What? Gary, I don't want to talk about why I moved to Bohemia."

"I remember you, your first day of school, freshman year. You were so pretty and mysterious. The teachers calling you Esmerelda and you telling them right away you were Esme. But Esmerelda seemed to suit you. You were like an exotic princess from a faraway land."

"A faraway land called Miami," I said drily. "Exotic because Bohemia High was so damn white that a Cuban half-blood looked foreign."

He laughed softly. "I always wondered why you came here, but I was glad you did."

"We had to go somewhere. I suppose Bohemia was big enough for us to blend in and small enough that we wouldn't get lost, or something like that. Also, my dad got a job at the space center."

"Rocket scientist?"

"Information technology. He ran a small company that got a contract to do what I think was essentially data entry. My mom did the books before he sold it. He never talked about it much." *He never talked to me.*

"Huh," Gary said. "I miss you. I mean, I missed you when you left just now. Why did you leave again?"

"I leave, Gary. That's what I do. You'd be better off forgetting about me."

"Because we are not an 'us'? Ez, I'm not going to have this argument again, especially not over the phone. But before you say something like that again, I want you to think about how you felt when you were in my arms this afternoon. Do you want to forget? Or do you want to remember? Because when I held you, I wanted to feel and remember every moment. Ez," he was whispering now, "remember that connection between us. It's powerful. It's real. Remember what it feels like to have my arms around you, to have me inside you. And then we can talk."

The call ended in my ear, and I looked at the phone in disbelief. And then I felt those weird hot springs of emotion bubbling up, boiling through my veins, as I flashed back on Gary hard inside me and the way he held me up, strong and close and so entirely emotionally present it almost hurt.

It was a cliche to hate Mondays, and I usually didn't. Then again, I didn't usually lose my virginity and have a fight and blow my emotional gasket over the weekend before I went to work.

I called in and told them I'd be late. Then I made a quick stop at the clinic and got hooked up with birth control. In a week, especially since good old Aunt Flo had come to call, I could be reasonably confident there would be no baby Esmereldas spawned the next time I had sex, for which, I was sure, the world would be grateful.

My boss greeted me with coffee and his usual cheer, and Irene tweaked me with a snide remark about being late. Today, I paid more attention to her whenever I walked by her desk, wondering if she really could be one of Greer Allighant's daughters. She'd made that remark about growing up with "crappy art." It would serve her right if Greer gave the whole collection to the museum.

I got my answer at lunchtime when I was microwaving a frozen burrito in the break room. Outside in the hall, Irene strolled by, talking on her cell phone. Or, I should say, ranting.

"Mother, you can't let this sale go through," Irene said. "They're ripping you off. Wouldn't you rather see a nice condo building on that property? It's worth a fortune. Don't throw it away!" She paused outside the doorway, just out of sight. "What do you mean, you have enough? You can have so much more to live on if you sell it on the open market. Plenty to take your cruises and lots more besides. We kids could go with you. It would be fun."

Especially if you push her overboard, came my mordant thought.

"You can never have enough money," said Irene, sounding even more frustrated. "Mother. Mother! Don't hang up on me! Mother!"

I hid behind the door and nibbled on my burrito as she stomped by, back to her desk. Her desperation was . . . interesting. And it gave me ideas.

I found myself idly checking my phone that Monday, then not so idly on Tuesday, wondering why I hadn't heard from Gary. I'd come to expect a certain level of pursuit from him, of presence, even when we were at odds. But there was radio silence, and damned if I was going to call him. Not the way we'd left it. If I made an overture, I was admitting there was an "us." And that his sketches of me were perfectly normal. And that he made my cheeks flush when I thought about what we'd done together.

All in all, I wasn't getting a lot of work done. And then my mom reminded me that Sunday was Easter, and I was invited — no, expected at lunch. I wasn't looking forward to the inevitable discussions of Izzy in rehab and how brilliant Reya's two children were and how Mom wondered if she'd ever get any other grandchildren, a rhetorical question always delivered with a sigh.

I went to Wednesday's rehearsal in hopes of a less dramatic session than last week's. Our new drummer Wilson was on tap to play, so Gary wasn't expected. It would be just me and the guys.

First, though, I had a much calmer visit with my sister at her beachfront rehab; I gave her one of the romance novels she liked and diverted the conversation away from anything anyone might consider important. Still, I liked the color in her cheeks, the new clarity in her eyes. Despite myself, I began to hope again, to hope she might get through it sober this time and stay that way.

I got to rehearsal twenty minutes late, expecting to be scolded by Robby and the others. Instead, when I entered the back room of the music store, he greeted me with glossy eyes, a stiff smile and a nervously loud, "Hey, here she is!" I looked at him strangely, then scanned the room. There everybody was, Ace the Bass, Banjo Brian and Wilson the drummer.

And Terry, our would-be record producer.

"Ez, great to see you again," he said in that gravelly voice. He walked over to shake my hand, clasping it a little too warmly as he flashed those white teeth. "I thought I'd check out your new lineup."

I shot a glare at Robby, then turned back to Terry. "Of course. We're glad to have you. We're just starting to gel, so you'll probably get a better idea at our gig Friday, but you're welcome to sit in."

"Thanks." His eyes said he knew that it didn't matter if he was welcome. He was the one dangling the carrot, and he could do whatever he wanted while we needed him. "Robby mentioned that you rehearse on Wednesday nights, so it seemed like a good time."

I smiled thinly and shot Robby another chilly glance as I

sat at the piano, warming up with a few chords from the song I'd played with Gary. I would definitely not be playing that tonight, but just those few notes sent the memory shooting through me again, sweet and warm, melted caramel in my veins. I shook my head slightly to get in the game.

"How about 'Amber Waves'?" Robby asked, and we murmured agreement. It was one of Robby's, a fairly standard rocker about a girl named Amber who's always waving good-bye. It was a perfect warm-up song, catchy but not too challenging.

I needn't have worried. Wilson got in the groove right away, with a more confident sense of rhythm than Stuart had ever had and more creative fills and accents. By the bridge, we were all looking at each other and smiling at the way we fit. We not only had The Sound; The Sound was *sharp*.

From there, we workshopped one of my new songs — one of the less personal ones — and then went over some of our other original material and a couple of covers we liked. I never got tired of singing "These Boots Are Made for Walkin'."

Terry departed after ninety minutes with oily smiles and promises to be at Friday's show at The Junction Box.

He winked at me as he left.

Robby was over the moon. "That's encouraging, right?" he asked after Terry had hit the road for Orlando.

"He likes the new lineup and wants to hear us perform. I'd say that's promising," I granted. "But I wish you had warned me he was going to be here."

"I didn't know until the last minute. He called me and said he was in Bohemia Beach for something else and wanted to know where our rehearsal was."

"This is great, man," Ace the Bass said. "We're finally going to get the deal we deserve."

"We just have to be careful it's everything we want," I said, thinking of Terry's devious dealing. "We're already doing pretty well for ourselves."

"We can always do better. And I mean *money*." Brian plucked a chord on his banjo to emphasize the word. "I looked over the sample contract he sent us. I like that it takes a lot of the crappy business stuff out of the mix so we can just play music. And Robby says these guys made Hood Ornament huge!"

"Or Hood Ornament made themselves huge," I noted drily, "and Crystal Slice Records enjoyed a large slice of the pie."

"We'll make sure it's the best thing for us," Robby assured me soberly. A moment later, the grin stretched across his face again. "But won't this be *great?*"

BY FRIDAY MORNING, I had almost messaged Gary to see how he was doing. I mean, why wouldn't I? It was the human thing to do. He was going through some stuff. And my body seemed to have more say than my brain right now.

But I stopped myself, more than once, knowing we'd be playing The Junction Box tonight and that Gary would almost certainly be there. If I could hold out till then, he'd know I wasn't an emotional cream puff, and whatever we did from here on out would be much more chill. Much more me.

Yet, something happened when the guys were tuning with me before our first set and I looked up and saw Gary enter the bar. A strange little light bloomed somewhere inside me and expanded like the flowering pattern in a kaleidoscope, all color and sparkle until it felt as if microscopic colored pinwheels were spinning out of my pores. And I wasn't even drinking yet.

Despite myself, that feeling wrested the cool bitch expression from my face, and I smiled at him. No angry glare. No aloof glance. A full-on smile. And the anxiety I saw on his face, the crease in his brow and the tension in his jaw, all melted away in favor of a big, goofy, Gary grin. He walked right up to me at the piano, ignoring the other guys plinking and tweaking their amps and the board.

"Hi, Ez." He was still grinning.

"Hi, Gary." I couldn't quell my smile at his mop of curls, black T-shirt and jeans and cut-glass dimples.

"Hello, Emeralds." We both turned to face the unwelcome interruption. Terry was here, wearing a tan linen jacket over a bright white T-shirt and khakis, dressed for a night out. "Looking forward to the show."

"Terry, great to see you!" Robby said, walking over to shake the producer's hand.

Terry turned to me. "Ez, you're looking fine tonight."

He was right. I wore shiny black capris and a sleeveless top with a low, draping neckline. Its shimmering silver, translucent fabric revealed a black lace bra beneath if you looked closely, and if you looked even more closely, you might see more than that.

Terry was looking *really* closely.

And Gary looked closely at Terry, none too thrilled at the scrutiny.

"Thanks," I answered Terry's compliment, pretending not to notice his stare. "Terry, this is my friend Gary. He filled in on the week we needed a drummer. He's really good."

Gary looked torn between pleasure at the compliment and hostility at Terry.

"Gary," Terry said neutrally. Gary nodded, speechless, and they shook hands.

"Terry is a producer with Crystal Slice Records," I explained. Gary's expression softened slightly, but he still regarded the older man with suspicion. I couldn't say I blamed him, given Terry was once again looking me over as if I were a juicy turkey leg and it was Thanksgiving afternoon. I addressed him directly. "We'll get started in about fifteen minutes."

Terry took the hint. "Can't wait. What do you recommend here?"

"Just ask Neil to make you something amazing with your favorite liquor. As long as it's not vodka, he'll treat you very well."

"Why not vodka?"

"You've never *met* a mixologist, have you?"

Terry chuckled and headed to the bar. Gary looked at me quizzically.

"Where'd he come from?"

"We're talking to his company about a deal, maybe. It's all pretty tenuous. But tonight could make or break it. He wants to hear us perform with Wilson and everybody in front of a crowd."

Gary nodded, while the rest of the band went out back to lubricate nerves with a smoke — except Wilson, I noted, who wandered to a corner with a bottle of water and his phone. Could it be? A sober Emerald?

"I guess that's good he's here," Gary said of Terry. "I mean, it's great. I always thought you guys deserved national atten-tion. Though all that guy's attention was focused on you."

"Men like tits. What can I say?"

I swear Gary turned pink as his eyes skated over my top and the secrets it didn't really conceal. He leaned against the piano, closer to me.

"I've missed you this week," he whispered.

"How are things with the house?" I asked, unwilling to admit the same.

"We've had workers in and out, fixing a few obvious things before it goes on the market, though none of us expect anyone will buy the house as is. It'll get razed in favor of a condo complex or, at best, a McMansion or three."

"It's hard to imagine a world without that 1970s kitchen."

"I know, right?" He held my eyes with his. I licked my lips, and he visibly swallowed, stuffing his hands in his pockets. I resisted looking at his crotch. "Can I see you after the show?"

I wanted suddenly to feel his lips on mine and fought the impulse to reach up and pull him to me. "I'll be around," I said with a smile, mentally slapping myself for my schoolgirl eagerness. Damn, being cool was getting harder and harder. Must be old age or something.

"Good." He nodded, then spun and headed back to the bar to order a beer.

By the time the guys in the band were back, I was more than ready to play, warmed up on the baby grand with bits and pieces of our songs.

Our set was both familiar and new. We were Junction Box regulars, and this place and its crowd were as comfortable as a pair of old socks, but tonight, the atmosphere was electric. Part of it was our new drummer; Wilson simply kicked ass. And the other guys, who were always good despite how much I trash-talked them, seemed fueled by adrenaline. We knew how much was at stake, and our keenness showed. We were crisp when we had to be, then soulful and folky and funky in turn. My voice was in good form, spiked with emotion I didn't know I had, and our friends were here, paying more attention than usual, cheering us on. I didn't know how many of them knew about the chance of a record deal, but it didn't matter — we were just that good tonight. Everyone felt it.

At the break, Terry came over and collared Robby and me. "I'd like to take you two out after the show and talk business," he said with a significant glance. Robby grinned, and I felt a rush of happiness, too. I'd had too many doubts, spawned by too many disappointments. This might actually be *it*. We could be the next platinum record on the wall at Crystal Slice.

"Sounds great," Robby said.

"Glad to," I echoed.

Terry nodded, looking satisfied and maybe a bit in the bag with one of Neil's Manhattans in his hand. He headed back to the bar.

"Oh. My. *God,*" Robby whispered.

"Keep it chill, dude. We might have to negotiate."

"Whatever," he said. "Embrace it, Ez. Don't you know a dream come true when you see it?"

Honestly? No. "One step at a time. And one more set. Let's not fuck it up."

"Right," Robby said. "I think I'll tell the guys to take it easy on the break." *As in, don't get so high you can't play,* I thought as Robby headed out back.

Could it really be? Could it be that we were about to sign a contract? With a label, the old-fashioned way? Go on tour? Maybe get big? *Shit.* I felt dizzy. I needed at least one drink to make it through the next set.

I approached the bar, carefully avoiding the side where

Terry was courting an unimpressed Penelope in another one of her delicious pinup-style dresses, and called for Neil.

"Hey, Ez," the bartender said, his mustache slick and his suspenders red this evening. "Manhattans OK?"

"Just one, Neil. I'm working extra hard tonight," I joked.

He laughed. "I noticed. You sound awesome. You have some special attention, yeah?" He nodded across the bar at Terry.

"Yeah. Keep him lubricated."

"No problem." He stirred the rye-and-vermouth concoction and strained it over a martini glass. "He's pretty much handling that on his own." Neil spooned a brandied cherry into my cocktail, and I lifted it, closed my eyes and took a long sip. *Ah, sweet, sweet whiskey.*

When I opened my eyes, Gary was next to me. "You guys are *smoking* tonight."

"Some of us literally."

He grinned. "Seriously. You are going to blow the head off that record guy."

"Yeah, he's taking Robby and I out after the show," I said with not a little self-indulgence. Just saying it made me feel giddy again. "This could be it. So, uh, maybe I'll see you later."

Gary tried to hide his disappointment. "Sure, no problem. You'll have to let me know how it goes."

"Oh, we'll be Tweeting and Instagramming and Facebooking the shit out of this when it's a reality," I said blithely, finally feeling the first ripple of whiskey bliss in my bloodstream.

When it's a reality. Yeah, no reality show, no bullshit, just reality. Just the band — the whole band — making records and making money. This was starting to sound really good, especially as I dove deeper into the Manhattan.

"I hope I don't hear it from Twitter," Gary said as I gulped the rest of my drink. He studied me for a second. "Good luck on your second set."

"We got this." I winked at him, feeling the buzz of alcohol and success. His face was unreadable. "Later."

"I hope so," he said, but his voice wasn't so positive.

I touched him briefly on the cheek, feeling a quick rush of heat, then shook my head and sauntered over to the piano. The rest of the band was rolling in, only mildly awash in smoke, and the air practically crackled. *We are going to do this.*

We totally kicked the second set. We had decided to wrap with "Amber Waves," Robby's song that we'd played for Terry at rehearsal, because we'd juiced it up a little with an extended guitar solo — Robby's idea, of course. Plus, it was the kind of rocker that got the crowd on its feet, and it lured much more than our usual quota of dancers to the floor.

"There goes Amber," Robby sang the chorus, with me on harmony, "Amber waves — always saying goodbye." He launched into his solo, bouncing around more than usual, and Wilson and Ace and I kept a tight leash on the beat while letting Robby reel out his line. Brian played the tambourine and harmonica as if they were tympani and trumpet in a symphony, with a hundred percent commitment.

Robby stair-stepped up the speakers to a tall one at the front, his long hair flying, sweat beading on his forehead as he cranked on his solo. The crowd roared.

And then, in slow motion, our guitarist jumped up, doing a scissor kick in midair — and his feet totally missed the speaker on the way down.

The speakers tumbled with Robby and his guitar, making

a tremendous racket as the band stumbled in mid-note. *Not another disaster,* was my first thought. My second was for Robby as I leapt up and ran over to him.

"I'm fine. I'm fine," he said, trying to get to his feet with the help of me and Brian. "Ouch!"

"What is it?"

"My leg hurts like a son of a bitch."

"Which one?" I touched the left one.

"That one!" he screamed. I dimly heard the bar's canned rock music come on. I guessed our set was over.

"Can you stand?" Brian asked.

"Let's try it," Robby grunted, lifting the guitar off his neck and setting it on the floor. Wilson was there, now, and he and Brian lifted Robby, who rested on his right leg and tenuously touched his left foot to the ground. "Shit!" he yelled.

"OK, OK, let's sit you down," I said, grabbing a chair and bringing it over. We got him in the chair, and Ace got him a glass of water. Sweat now poured off Robby's face. "You're going to have to get that checked out."

"I can't," he said hoarsely, glancing over to the bar, where Terry was looking at us with — could it be amusement? "We have to meet with him. I don't want to kill this deal."

"You probably broke your leg," I said. "We'll meet another time. Or I can bring another one of the guys with me."

"No," said Brian and Ace, both looking bleary-eyed. "I mean," Ace added, "I'm not feeling that sharp right now."

"I'm content to let someone else do the talking," said Wilson. "I haven't been with you long enough."

OK. No potheads or newbies at the business meeting. "We'll reschedule," I said, just as Terry wandered over.

"You guys OK?" he asked. "Should we do this another time?"

"Good idea," I said. "Robby has to go to the hospital."

"I do not!" Robby said through clenched teeth.

"We'll take him," Brian said. "You go, Ez. Fill us in later."

"Yeah," Robby said. "You can still do the meeting. You don't need me there. You can speak for all of us, Ez."

"Yeah," the other guys chimed in.

I was torn. Terry still wanted to meet with us. Maybe it was best to strike while the iron was hot. But I knew from our last meeting that the conversation was likely to go better for all of us if Robby was in the mix.

"I don't know."

"Well, I have other bands to check out if you guys can't do it now," Terry said, his response containing just a hint of a threat. It got my hackles up, but before I could tell him to fuck off, the other guys were talking.

"Go, Ez, you've got this . . . " Their eyes and voices said it all. They needed this. They wanted this. I would have to do it for them.

So, feeling a lot less indefatigable than earlier, I walked out of The Junction Box with Terry, with one last look around for Gary, who was nowhere in sight.

I GAVE TERRY THE CHOICE: diner or bar. Already just a bit more fluid of tongue and loose in his walk than usual, thanks to Neil's cocktails, he chose bar. Making small talk as he smoked a cigarette, I guided him a couple of blocks away to Plumeria Bar, a cozy place on Bohemia's small harbor. We sat outside, on the busy waterfront deck. The plumeria surrounding it were leafing out, a harbinger of tropical weather to come. The warm day had cooled enough to bring temperatures to perfection, accented by a breeze that carried the salty scent of the lagoon. Lights glimmered on the water and illuminated the creaking sailboats and other vessels. The nearly full moon cast the whole scene in a magical light. This was one of those nights when it was great to live in Bohemia.

Terry ordered a vodka tonic (ah, *now* he got his vodka), and I ordered an Old-Fashioned, a Calista favorite, as I recalled.

"I like a woman who knows how to drink," Terry said after the cocktails were delivered and I'd taken a healthy sip.

"More to the point, did you like our performance this evening?" I wanted to keep this conversation on track, and that meant talking about business, not what I drank or what I was wearing.

"You were fantastic. *You,* especially. And at least you didn't fall off a speaker," he quipped.

"Robby was fantastic, too, and he doesn't usually fall off speakers," I said, defending our hapless guitarist. "The injury shouldn't affect his performing, unless he's learned how to play with his toes without my knowledge."

"Unlikely," said Terry, already well into his drink. "Have you thought about what we discussed?"

"Signing the band and taking us to the next level? Of course. And I speak for all of us when I say we're ready to do it, after we look at the final contract, of course."

"That's nice to hear," Terry said, scooting closer, "but I'm talking about what I told you personally. About promoting you as a solo artist, getting you on a reality show. You could go to the moon."

I looked up. "It's about time a woman got up there," I joked, trying to keep it light.

"I'd like to see a high-heeled footprint on the moon."

"Please. Do you see me wearing high heels?"

He made a big deal of scanning my legs, ankles and flat sandals. "No, but I can imagine you in them." He looked at me again, his silver gaze more bold this time, making me more uncomfortable.

"Terry, I'm interested in working with the band on this. We all want to work together and make great music. We can do it for Crystal Slice and, I'm confident, make all of us the money you want. Me, I'm not into the idea of a solo career, and I'm definitely not cut out for reality television. There's been way too much reality in my life already."

He leaned over and pushed my bangs away from my eyes, an intimate gesture that made me want to scream and run. Instead, I sat very, very still, not wanting to blow the deal. This could still happen for the Emeralds, and they were counting on me.

"It's the reality that makes your songs so powerful," he said in his deep, rough voice. "I can sense it in you. You've lived. You've been exposed, vulnerable."

I felt as if he were stripping away my skin with everything he said — making me even more exposed and vulnerable. I deflected him with my standard response. "I just channel personas. It's not really me."

"I don't think that's true. It is really you, only you don't want to open that part of you for judgment. That's the material that will grab listeners by the throats. That's the stuff that will make you insanely famous — and maybe even insanely rich. Without the Emeralds."

I knocked back my drink and straightened my shoulders. "Look, Terry, we're impressed by your company, but I want to make things clear. I'm here as the voice of the Emeralds. I *am* an Emerald. And if you can't deal with us as a band, there is no deal." I picked up my purse, implying I meant to walk, as a wave of whiskey wooziness rippled through me.

"Now, wait a minute, Ez. We can absolutely work with the band. I just wanted to test the waters, you know? You're very talented on your own, but if you don't want to go to the exalted level I'm talking about, we can still all be very successful together. Let's take a walk and see if we can come to terms, OK?"

I nodded, relieved. He put down some money, and we took the stairs that led off the deck to the long wooden walkway that ran around the perimeter of the harbor. He placed a hand lightly on my back, the way he had at the studio, and I tried to ignore it as we walked past the rows of boats.

"What is your idea of a dream contract?" Terry asked.

"A fair percentage of the gross," I said. "Well, more than fair, since it's a dream contract."

He laughed.

"And generous studio time," I added. I would love some serious studio time. We'd cut a couple of tracks, but on less than ideal equipment. "Also, someone to deal with all the business stuff and bureaucracy. The horrible scheduling with nightclub owners. A cushy, comfortable tour." It all sounded so good, a fantasy built on clouds. "And a personal assistant?"

He laughed again. We had passed the condos and other businesses and were well into the darker, quieter part of the harbor, not far from where Gary's home used to stand. There were a few boathouses here and even bigger boats. "Anything is possible," Terry said more quietly. "Look at that." He pointed to a yacht. "I'm going to have one of those someday. You could, too."

"You have a boat now?" The alcohol was making me

fuzzy, and I felt like we hadn't made our deal yet. I had to get this back on track.

"Yeah, but that's the thing. I always want a bigger one."

"I don't want a boat," I said. "I want to make a living making music. If perks come with it, all the better."

"The thing is," he said, slowing down in the shadow of a boathouse and pausing to face me, "you can get all the perks you want as a solo artist with me. With us. But if you want to do this with the band, you'll need to make some compromises."

I eyed him with caution. "I'm open to reasonable compromises."

"You have all the power here, Ez," he said, so quietly I had to step forward to hear him. Next to this boathouse, in this tranquil part of the harbor, I couldn't see anything around us except boats and darkness. "You can make this happen, if you're willing."

He was looking me over again, the way he had earlier this evening, checking out my thin top. Now I was self-conscious about the hint of nipple that showed through the layers of sheer fabric. This conversation wasn't going the way I wanted it to.

"I think we should get back," I said. "Maybe schedule another meeting with Robby."

"He can't make this happen," Terry said, moving even closer. He put his hands on my shoulders. "Only you can make this happen. You can write your own ticket if you compromise."

"I told you, I can compromise."

"Can you?" He leaned in and planted his lips on mine, forced his tongue into my mouth. For a moment I was stunned, drunk and shocked and speechless, and I let him do it. Then I turned my head.

"Can we keep this professional, please?" I asked, but my voice felt small. Old feelings came back, ugly, moldering old feelings that weakened me, shattered my facade.

"I thought you wanted this," Terry said, kissing my neck, moving his hands down to my ass. He pulled his hips into mine, and I could feel his hard-on through the khakis. *Oh, shit. I gotta get out of here.* But still I couldn't move. The band depended on me. If we made this deal, all their dreams — all my dreams would come true. At least, the dreams I thought were mine. Terry ground against me, pushing me against the wall of the boathouse.

"This isn't a negotiation," I said, moving slightly, trying to get him off me without pissing him off.

"Like hell it isn't," he said, slipping a hand under my shirt, cupping a breast, kissing my mouth again. I'd let guys do stuff before. Was this any different? Was it? He grasped one of my hands and placed it against his bulge.

He placed his other hand on my mound and squeezed.

"NO!" I screamed, startling him, breaking away. The nightmares rolled through my head like a B-movie, every frame a photograph, a shot of a scared kid who had no power and no choices.

Now I had choices.

Terry was breathing hard. When he spoke, his tone was threatening, the way it had been when he'd suggested canceling the meeting earlier.

"Do you really want to throw this away?" He stepped toward me again.

"That's what you do with garbage," I spat out. "You throw it away."

And I turned and ran like hell.

AT 2:20 A.M., the Uber car dropped me off at Gary's beach house, barely lit in the darkness, and took off before I even reached the gate. I pressed the button once, twice. Finally, a voice — his, thank God.

"Who is it?"

"Gary, it's me. Let me in."

"Ez?" The gate slowly opened, and I trudged up the driveway, emotionally exhausted, still a little inebriated and completely disgusted with myself. Gary came out the front door in loose sweats and a T-shirt, took one look at me and gobbled up the ground between us, running with his long strides. He wrapped his arms around me and hugged so hard he squeezed tears out of me. Or maybe the tears just needed an excuse.

I think he felt them against his chest. He held me by the arms and looked into my face. "What happened to you? Are you OK?"

"As OK as usual, I guess." I sniffed. "Only I'm never really OK, am I?"

"You're always OK with me." He looked around. "Where's your car?"

"Back at home. I Ubered it."

"From The Junction Box?"

"From the harbor. I had to get away from that asshole."

"The record company guy?" Gary asked. "He had asshole written all over him."

"I should have known better," I said as Gary guided me toward the house.

"Sometimes it's not always easy to know until circum-stances make it clear. What did he do to you?"

I glanced up at Gary and saw fury simmering just below the surface. "He tried to 'negotiate' a deal."

Gary picked up my implication. "Are you really OK?"

"Yes. I bolted."

He led me inside and down the hall toward the den. "Good. You don't need him."

"I hope the band feels the same way."

"This is about you, Ez, and only you know what's right for you." He opened the door to the den, flipped on one dim light with a stained-glass shade and closed the door behind us. "Sit on the couch. I'll make you a drink. Tequila?"

"Bourbon."

"Done." He got ice out of the mini-fridge, poured from a bottle in the globe bar and gave me the whiskey in a rocks glass. He sat next to me, careful not to crowd me, I thought. "You want to talk about it?"

"He wanted me to do things."

Gary clenched his hands into fists. "Did he do anything to you?"

"Not — nothing serious." The tears started leaking from my eyes again. I ignored them and took a gulp of whiskey.

"You got away?"

I nodded.

"Is there something else going on, Ez?"

I set down the glass and looked up into Gary's eyes, dark now with anger at what had happened to me, worry for me. No one ever gave a damn about me like this. I had no idea what to do with his concern.

I sucked in a breath and burst into a full-on crying jag.

"Oh, shit," Gary muttered, and I almost laughed through

the tears. Guys never did know what to do with a weeping woman. He wrapped an arm around my shoulders, and I buried my face in his T-shirt and soaked it with great, heaving sobs.

After a while, the cloudburst dried up, and my breath hitched as I leaned against him.

I tilted up my face and kissed him. He let me, but he didn't jump into the pool of desire as I expected him to. I opened my mouth, licked his lips with my tongue, hoping to lead him there, kill the pain.

He pushed me away. "Ez."

"Don't you want me?"

"I want to know why you just used me like a Kleenex, honey." He paused. "What happened to you?"

This time, I knew he wasn't asking about Terry. I sat up and tried to get myself together. I took another sip of my drink and set it down on the coffee table.

"I'm a fuck-up," I said.

"Not from where I sit."

"Trust me, I'm a fuck-up. If I'd been stronger at any point in my life, my sister wouldn't be in rehab and I wouldn't be in Bohemia Beach."

The corner of Gary's mouth quirked up. "I'm glad you're in Bohemia Beach, at least."

"It has its points."

"But Miami was better?"

"For a while. And then it all went to hell." I stood and moved to the curtains covering the sliding glass doors. I peeked out at the black ocean and let them fall shut again.

"Tell me."

I turned to look at Gary. I never talked to anyone about this. But maybe Gary was the only one who'd ever really given a shit, except for my mom. Maybe he was the only one who ever would. But I didn't know if I was ready to lose my one true fan, either.

"I don't know if you're going to like me very much after I tell you," I said.

"So that means you're going to tell me?" He smiled encouragingly.

"I don't want you to look at me and see — what you see won't be what — "

"What?"

I closed my eyes. "I looked at your notebook."

"My notebook?"

"The one you saved from the fire." I glanced at him again.

"Oh," he said, crossing his arms, something like embarrassment crossing his face. "I like to draw." He cleared his throat. "I like to draw you. I hope you don't think that's too weird."

"I hope you don't think it's too awful that I looked at your notebook."

"Is that what you were going to tell me?"

"No," I said. "But since I'm feeling confessional — those drawings are beautiful, Gary. And I don't think you'll ever see me in the same way again."

His eyes caught mine, those swirls of brown and green and something more. "I'll always think you're beautiful, Ez. Talk to me."

I went to the bar, got out another glass and poured a bourbon.

"You already have a drink," he said.

"This one's for you." I handed it to him, smiled at his look of surprise, and sat next to him on the couch, a few feet between us this time.

I took a deep breath. "I was twelve when it started. No, let me go back." I picked up my glass, took a sip, put it down again.

"I had an uncle," I said. "He was the 'fun uncle.' My dad's younger brother. I have an aunt on that side, too, but she lived — lives in Arizona. Anyway, their father came over from Cuba in 1960. My dad was the boring traditional type, except for his one wild hair when he married my Anglo mother. But my Uncle Ernesto was the one all the kids in the neighborhood liked to hang out with. He was single and into rock music and played electric guitar and drove a cool car. Sometimes he would volunteer to babysit and take us shopping, Reya, me and Izzy. Reya outgrew that pretty fast, though. She was four years older than me and always had a pack of friends to run with, and then boyfriends, and she thought we were hopeless geeks. Izzy and I liked to sing, and Uncle Ernesto played guitar. He'd sing with us.

"When I was twelve, he suggested I come over and we write a song together. He knew I liked to jot down poems and play with chords. My parents thought that was great. Izzy wanted to come, too, but they said this was for me. She was never into instruments. I think she really just sang along with me because she loved being with me, and she kind of — admired me." I paused, took another drink, trying to tame the quaver in my voice, the tremor in my hands.

"I always wanted a brother or sister," Gary said.

"Yeah, it seemed good at the time," I said, welcoming the interruption even as I tried to stay on track. "Anyway, Ernesto had me over to his apartment, and he taught me some stuff on the guitar. We had a couple of lessons like that, and we even wrote a song based on one of my stupid middle-school poems. Izzy was never allowed to go. It became kind of a thing on Mondays after school — I'd go over and get a lesson or write a song and come home with some earrings or a new piece of sheet music he bought me — I was taking piano, too. And then, one day, it was different."

I glanced at Gary, then looked away. I couldn't look at him and say what I had to say. My stomach churned. I withdrew to another place, a safe distance, observing that girl in my memories as if she'd never been me.

"One day he said he had other hobbies, too. He was into photography."

I heard a soft noise from Gary, a noise of distress, and I knew *he* knew the story wasn't going to get any better. But I focused on looking at the dregs of my drink in the glass on the coffee table and spoke.

"He started taking photos of me with the guitar, or lying on the couch, all fun stuff. We pretended I was a model. And then one day, he said he'd put together a studio. It was in his guest bedroom. He'd closed the curtains and set up lights and had a black backdrop. He told me all the models had their photos taken in lingerie. He told me we should take a few in my bra and panties. He said I could be a model. That a cool chick would do it. All the stuff I guess you say to an insecure adolescent who trusts you. So I did it. I posed for some photos in my underwear. It didn't seem that bad. I kind of envisioned myself as a grown-up teenager. That day he gave me my own guitar to take home."

"Oh, fuck," Gary said.

"Yeah," I replied. "I look back now and wonder how stupid I could have been. Wonder why I kept going back. The visits became less about music lessons and more about the photography. He talked me into taking more clothes off and wearing lipstick. At first, I thought maybe I was sexy like the models I saw in the magazines. I felt the — sexuality of the situation. Even when I started to feel that something wasn't right, it changed something in me, sexually. And he gave me things. He made a fuss over me. But over time, when I saw the way my uncle looked at me, the way he posed me — I was in denial for a while, trying to tell myself it was OK, but I finally admitted to myself that it was wrong. He never touched me, but I knew. And then once, he masturbated in front of me, and I flipped. I told him I didn't want to come over anymore, and he — " I drained what was left in the glass. "He said he would tell everyone I was a liar and a slut if I told anyone about the photo sessions. And if I didn't keep coming over, he said he'd rape my mother."

Gary gasped. "So you didn't tell anyone?"

"I was too scared to. And I just got used to pretending it wasn't about the fear. Once in a while we'd have a day and just play music and I could pretend it was all normal. All the time, Izzy was jealous. She wanted music lessons, too. She tried to play guitar, but she, well, she was never as good as I was. And she was only ten when it started, then eleven. I didn't want her to go to my uncle's, ever. I told her she wouldn't like it. I told her everything but what I *should* have told her, what I should have told everyone. And then I won a scholarship to a special summer music program at Berklee."

"Berklee College of Music? That's huge."

"Yeah. It was a really big deal, especially for my family, which didn't have much money. I was thirteen by then, almost fourteen. The grant program would pay for everything, transportation, classes, and I'd stay with a local family in Boston. It seemed like the first step to bigger things. My uncle was angry that I was going. I told him that it was just for two months. He warned me before I left that if I didn't keep his secret, he'd do terrible things to my family. I made him promise to leave them alone, but I resolved to myself that when I came back, I'd do something so I'd never have to see him again."

I glanced at Gary. He looked pale, and he was sipping the bourbon. Good.

"So I went to the music camp, and when I came back, all hell had broken loose."

"Your sister?" he asked.

I nodded. "She'd told my uncle she wanted lessons, too, and the sick bastard just couldn't resist. So she started going to his house."

"He took pictures of her?"

"He raped her."

"Oh, God, Ez, I'm so sorry." Gary's eyes were moist, too, and my heart almost broke. Again.

"And she was ten times braver than me. It happened just before I got back — he waited that long — and she ignored his threats and told my parents right away. My dad argued that we just move and never speak of it again, but my mom fought with him and called the police, and Ernesto ended up being arrested. He was charged with the crime right after I got back, that and more. The police found the pictures. A lot of pictures, not just of me. My mom took me aside and asked me if there was anything I wanted to tell her. And I told her no." The tears started rolling down my face again. Gary reached out to touch my shoulder, but I shrugged him off. "The evidence was so overwhelming, he ended up pleading guilty in hopes of a lighter sentence.

"My parents didn't want us to be in an atmosphere where we had to think about it, hear about it, so we moved anyway. A few years later, after we'd been in Bohemia for a while, I told my mom then. She said she already knew; she just didn't know how bad it was. But still, the whole chain of events just about broke her heart. And my dad barely spoke to me at all after that. I figured he blamed me for his brother, for Izzy, for everything. That was — hard. I tried to talk to Izzy about it. She was never angry with me. But it came out in other ways, and she got wilder and wilder. Reya never knew about me. Kept saying how lucky I was that he hadn't touched me. She still doesn't know about the photos, or she's in denial, I'm not sure which."

"Is your uncle still alive?" Gary asked.

"He was killed in prison."

"Good." From the set of Gary's jaw, he looked as if he would have finished the job himself.

"Yeah, good. I wondered sometimes how many other kids in the neighborhood — if I had just spoken up — "

Gary gathered me into his arms, and I let him this time. "You were just a kid, Ez," he whispered. I buried my face against his shoulder, breathing his scent, wishing he'd been there to protect me, that he'd always be there.

Wait. *Always?* I didn't deserve that kind of ally.

"I'm a loser," I said. "And now Izzy's paying the price."

"You're both paying the price," Gary said. "You pay it every day. You paid it with shitty boyfriends like Stuart. You paid it tonight. You deserve better."

I lifted my face to him again, and this time, he kissed me, gently, sweetly. Then he pulled me to him against the cushions of the couch, wrapping his arms around me, keeping me warm and protected, and we fell asleep to the sounds of the ocean.

A THIN GAP in the curtains seems magnified a hundred times when the rising sun shines through it, piercing the darkness.

Dawn over Bohemia Beach aimed a beam of light into the space where we slept. I felt it through my eyelids and stirred against Gary's body, still wrapped around mine, both of us in our clothes. I opened my eyes and studied the fine bone structure of his face, the subtle shadows, and wondered how I came to confide in him, to find myself here, in his arms. This was the last place I expected to be. With my surprise, I felt something else: gratitude. My heart was lying in pieces around me, cracked open in all kinds of ways, and I was glad.

I traced a finger along his cheek, the stubble on his chin, his nose —which twitched — and his lips.

I gasped when he caught my finger in his mouth, opening his eyes, smiling at me.

I pulled it back, embarrassed to be discovered. He shifted, putting himself more squarely under me, pulling me closer, and he kissed me.

There were worlds in his kiss, promises and assurances and lust. He still wanted me, and I found comfort in his need, opening my mouth to his tongue. He moved slowly, silently, slipping his hands up the skin of my back, under my shirt. How strange and wonderful it felt to have someone I *wanted* touching me. I slid my fingers into his curls and tasted his mouth with more urgency, repositioning my hips over his. He moaned softly into the kiss, sliding his hands down to my behind, pressing me gently into him, making no moves to disrobe me — guided, I thought, by tenderness, questioning how far he should go after last night.

I answered for him by moving my hands to his hips, the sweatpants he'd thrown on when he came to me at the gate. I slipped my fingers under the waistline. There was nothing beneath. I caressed the muscles of his belly, his hips, feeling his agitation as I slipped the pants down and over them. I broke the kiss to pull them off and sat up in front of him. His eyes were cloudy, smoke hiding fire. I slipped my shirt over my head, then removed my bra, and he took a deep breath, watching me, tense now with wanting. But still he restrained himself, even as his cock lengthened and hardened before me. I reached out and touched it, running my hand slowly up and down its length. He closed his eyes and stretched to meet me as I did so. But I wanted more. I stopped, leaned in and tugged at his T-shirt. He helped me get it off. In the dim light, his torso was a thing of beauty, every muscle defined by the shadows. I ran my hands over it, down his chest, thumbing his nipples; I slid my caress down to his hips and his thighs. And then I worked off my tight capri pants and the barely-there thong beneath so that I was naked over him, feeling more naked than I'd ever felt. He knew me, knew the worst about me, and still, he wanted me.

I held his shaft again and guided it toward me, rubbing the tip in my wetness.

"Condom?" he asked hoarsely.

I hated to break the spell by speaking. "I've got prevention now," I murmured. "You OK?"

He just nodded, the fire snapping through the smoke in his eyes.

I inched higher on his long body and eased him into my wet slit. I lowered myself until he filled me, more than filled me, and I groaned.

Oh, yes. Now beyond my virgin pain, eager for him, I began to move up and down, slowly, slowly. His breath stuttered and he grasped my hips, helping me, thrusting up and into me as I slid down on him. The sensation was overwhelming, an aching pleasure as he expanded inside me, then ecstasy as he reached up and teased my clit with his thumb, a hot button that shot throbbing heat from the center of my sex through my body. The tendrils of fire licked at my core, my muscles, skated over my skin as my cells reached for a star that Gary was shooting me toward with his movement, his thumb, his intensity. I fell forward and leaned over him, supporting myself with my arms, lifting and lowering myself faster on his cock; my breasts swung above him, and his face strained with his own agony as he watched me, rapt. And then I felt him convulse inside me, his powerful release tripping the detonation in my body, and I bit my lip so I wouldn't cry out. Instead, a long whimper escaped my lips. Gary consumed my cry with a kiss, crushing me to him, his tongue in my mouth, his cock still thrusting in my pussy as our bodies were consumed by the fire.

I spasmed one more time, and then I felt all the strength go out of me as I drowned in his kisses, sweeping my tongue against his, sucking on it, trying to tell him how much I needed him, needed this. We ground to a slow stop, and I lay my head against his chest, breathing in his scent. I licked his salty skin there, once, and he made a primal sound and ran his hands slowly up and down my back, as if to assure himself that I was really there.

"Thank you," I whispered.

"Ez," was all he said, so much emotion in the word that it seemed explosive. I hesitated to touch it, to unleash all it contained.

We dozed off together, him still inside me. When I awoke again, it was to the sounds of people stirring in the house.

I looked down at Gary. He was awake, too, and he grinned. "Stay for breakfast?" he asked softly.

I shook my head. "I'd rather you drive me home. I just need some time."

He nodded, and we slid apart, donned our clothes. We snuck through the house as if we were fornicating teenagers, to his van in the three-car garage.

On the ride across the causeway bridge to Bohemia, we didn't say much. Gary had an air of contentment about him. I was in some other dimension altogether, wondering if I could ever really be normal, or be with a normal guy like him. A nice guy. A nice guy who made me come like a house afire. I looked in his direction, and his gaze caught my wistfulness at that moment, an ember of the fire still in his eyes.

My phone buzzed.

I frowned and slipped it out of my purse.

"Who is it?" Gary asked.

"Robby. He wants to know how it went with the asshole."

"Why wasn't he with you, anyway?"

"Oh, that's right. You left," I said. "He did a spectacular pratfall and broke his leg, I think. He had to go to the hospital."

"Damn," Gary said. "I'm sorry I wasn't there."

"It wasn't your job. It's OK." I focused on the phone and typed a message back, asking Robby about his leg, and he responded quickly. "So apparently he did break it," I told Gary. "A shinbone fracture. They gave him a brace last night, and he's seeing a specialist today. Looks like he'll be in a cast for a while."

"At least he can still play guitar."

"Yeah," I said. "He just can't pretend he's Eddie Van Halen anymore."

My phone buzzed again. "Did you make a deal?" Robby texted.

I thought for a moment, then typed back: "I have news for you guys, but I want to tell you all together. Can you make rehearsal Wednesday?"

"I don't want to wait that long," he messaged back.

"Nothing was signed, but we have a bright future," I typed. "That's all I'll say now."

"Let's meet Monday night."

"You sure?" I typed back. "What about your leg?"

"I'll be OK. Monday night at the music store. I'll let everyone know. See you then." Robby replied.

"Get better, dude." I sighed and put the phone back in my purse.

"Well?" Gary asked.

"I told him we have a bright future. He wants to meet Monday night. I — I have to admit, I'm dreading this. How do I tell them I kicked our rock-star dreams to the curb?"

"There are other ways to achieve your dreams." Gary turned the van onto my street.

"I think so, too. It's just convincing them. They've, well, they've put up with a lot from me. I'm not sure we'll survive this."

"Worst case, you'll be solo, and you know how good you are, don't you?" He parked outside my building and turned to me. "Why don't I come with you Monday?"

There was a time when I would have scoffed at his offer. I could handle myself. But there was something so calm and reassuring and grounded about him that I wanted to say yes, to draw on his strength.

"I think I'd like that," I said. "Maybe we can walk from here."

"Sure." He smiled. "I can't believe it's only Saturday. Want to do something later?" In his voice was more than a casual invitation. *Something* meant more than dinner or a walk on the beach. Heat unfurled between my legs. But I was tired, bone tired, tired in my soul.

"I need to rest today. Don't hate me."

He looked disappointed, but he shook his head with a half-smile. "Not possible. And you need to take care of yourself."

"I have to see my family tomorrow for Easter. How about you come over afterward? We can have dinner at my place. It won't be much, but I'll steal some ham and we can have sandwiches and watch a movie or — something."

Something again. His eyes twinkled.

"Just buzz me," he said, "and I'll be right over."

I WAS the Catholic Church's worst nightmare. I went to Mass twice a year and enjoyed sin too much to confess to it regularly. But my mother's chronic disappointment in my lack of devotion compelled me to show up for the major holidays, and I endured the Easter service with her and my taciturn father and Reya's family by focusing on the chipped paint in the crown of thorns on the wooden Jesus hanging above the altar. You'd think they'd want that blood touched up for the big day. Then again, this day was about resurrection, and the bloody parts were forgotten in favor of visions and angels and rebirth. And chocolate bunnies and plastic eggs.

That's what Reya's two children, a boy and a girl, five and seven, were chasing around my parents' modest backyard in suburban Bohemia after brunch — brightly colored plastic eggs hidden in mostly obvious places: tufts of grass, under the hibiscus, floating in the bird bath, next to a garden gnome, up in the playhouse by the sliding board, nestled in the coiled hose, alongside the fence, and inside the (cold) grill.

My family, minus Izzy, sat at the wooden picnic table out back, watching the kids squeal under the guidance of Reya's handsome, sainted husband, Robert, he of the Big Job and Deep Pockets. None of us seemed inclined to speak, stuffed as we were with ham; mac-and-Manchego cheese with chorizo; plantains; and guava and cream cheese pound cake. My mom, who'd met my dad while working as an accountant in Miami, had embraced Cuban cooking with gusto, seeing as how she came from a white-bread background of cream-of-mushroom-soup casseroles and Jell-O salads. In homage to her upbringing, she always threw in deviled eggs at Easter.

There was another reason none of us were speaking. It was only a matter of time until someone brought up the missing Falcon.

"I talked to Izzy Friday," said Mama, who was petite like me, only softer and more fair, with gray eyes and graying light brown hair. "She says she might get a chance to do a video call with us at 1. They're giving all the guests ten minutes. She said one of you might be able to figure out how to do that. Reya?"

Guests. Such a Mama euphemism.

"Robert's the computer genius," Reya said. "Have a problem with hair, then I'm your gal." She shot me a mean-ingful glance, ever disapproving of my edgy hairstyles. Reya's meticulous makeup and carefully highlighted, long locks were not only the product of a lifetime devotion to beauty; she worked at a high-end salon in downtown Bohemia.

"You don't have to be a computer genius to do a video call," I said drily.

"Then why don't *you* send your number to Izzy, and you can handle it, OK, honey?" Mama asked. "We can all join in."

My father, his gray-streaked dark hair thin on top and combed back, his face jowly, his yellow golf shirt sporting a grease spot where he'd dropped a bite of ham earlier, grunted in response. He couldn't take his sad brown eyes away from the squealing children, the innocent ones. I tried not to notice and shot Izzy a quick message from my phone with the number.

"Do you want another *cortadito*, Phil?" Mama asked my father. His real name was Filiberto, but he'd gone by Phil for years.

"I'll get it." He got up and made his escape.

"Those things make you prematurely old," Reya said of the high-test Cuban coffee I loved.

"There's something to be said for living at high speed," I replied.

"You would know," she scoffed. I scowled at her as my mother made a noise of frustration.

"You girls should get along. You need each other," Mama said.

"Reya doesn't need anybody," I replied.

"I love and need Robert," she retorted from her Happily Married pedestal.

"Yeah. Cha-ching," I quipped.

"Esmerelda, you are so mean," she said. "Why do you have to be so mean? It's not like you're the one who — "

"What?" I looked at her sharply.

My mother cleared her throat and got up. "I'm going to go help Phil with the coffee." She vanished into the house.

"You were saying, Reya?" I stared her down as she looked away, at her kids. I felt raw today after last night's drama, after leaving Gary's calm presence for this family fraught-fest.

She finally turned to me. "Izzy is the victim here. You're lucky our uncle never touched you."

"You're absolutely right. He never touched me," I said. But there was something in my tone that caught her attention, perhaps for the first time, and a tiny furrow appeared in her silky-smooth brow.

"What do you mean?"

"What I said."

"Esme?"

"Is that uncertainty I hear in your voice, Reya? Are you, perhaps, *unsure* of something?" *Shut up. Shut up!* I told myself. *Why am I doing this?* Something had happened to my filters, and now all the bad feelings were bubbling over.

"Did something — happen?" my sister said.

"Something always happens." I looked at Reya. She had — was it *concern* on her face?

"Maybe we shouldn't talk," she said, offended, maybe scared.

"Bitter silence has always worked for us in the past."

"Will you cut it out?" She was angry now. "There's something you're not telling me. You never did talk to me. So tell me now. Tell me, Esme."

I stared at the children, pretty Bella and little chubby-cheeked Edward. *Named for vampires. Really, Reya?* Then again, if I'd been born a bit later, one might say the same of me.

Breathless from the hunt, the kids had sifted through their baskets and counted their bounty, and Robert was trying to figure out where the grown-ups had hidden the last egg before church this morning.

There's always one more secret.

I looked at Reya and spoke carefully. "Be glad that you thought we were geeks for liking music, for wanting to go to him. For thinking he was cool. I'm glad you never went to him, Reya. I am. Because he was an expert at stealing souls."

"Did he touch you?" she whispered.

"He didn't have to. He had a camera."

Reya blanched. Just then, my parents emerged from the back door, Dad with a newspaper, Mama with a tray of fresh *cortaditos* in tiny cups. I took mine, grateful for the interruption, and sipped the sweet, hot shot of caffeine through the silky froth.

My phone, sitting on the picnic table, buzzed with a Face-Time request. I answered.

"Izzy, how you doing?" I responded to her face, pretty and tired and so like the ones around me. My parents and Reya moved to stand behind me so they could see the screen.

"I'm feeling pretty good."

"Isabel, honey, we miss you," Mama said.

"I miss you and your ham, Mama." Izzy's voice was tinny over the speaker. "They had turkey. Who has turkey for Easter?"

"Did you get my package?" Mama said to the phone, smiling at seeing her daughter. "I told them not to give it to you until today."

"Yes! What a beautiful basket. Thank you! They're rationing the chocolate eggs."

"What?" Mama asked. My dad grunted again.

"They don't want me to have too much caffeine," Izzy said. "I'm making up for it with the Peeps. Apparently a sugar high is OK."

Izzy and Mama and Reya chatted for a few more minutes

about the food and the holiday as my father and I looked on in silence.

"Where are the kids?" Izzy finally asked.

"Bella! Edward!" Reya called.

The kids tumbled over to the table with Robert and crowded between us, eagerly craning toward the phone. I held it higher so everyone could see.

"Aunt Izzy!" Bella said. "You should see what the Easter Bunny left us!"

"What did you get?"

"Pretty eggs!" Edward held a pink one up to the phone. The inset picture showed that all Izzy could see was a big pink blob covering the lens. I couldn't help but smile.

"It's more than eggs, silly," Bella told her brother. "There's stuff inside!"

"There is?" He popped his open, and a bright red Hot Wheels car fell out. "Wow! It's Aunt Esme's car!"

"Mine's not that big," I said as the elated kids took their baskets and eggs over to the swings to open them.

"We're almost at our ten minutes," Izzy said. "I miss you guys."

"I'll visit you this week, honey. You're doing great," Reya declared.

"Yeah, I think I am, actually," my younger sister said. "Papa, how are you?"

"Don't worry about me. I love you. We'll see you soon." Positively effusive for my father.

"OK. Esme?" There was so much unspoken in Izzy's simple query that I almost broke down.

"I'll visit you this week, too," I said. "I'm OK."

She smiled. "Love you, everybody. Happy Easter."

She rang off to a chorus of goodbyes, and then all was

silent again, except for the bubbling chatter of the children. Mama sat and sipped her coffee, her expression far away. Papa picked up a newspaper and buried himself in important things. Reya made an eye movement at her husband, the "let's get out of here" signal.

I got up and wandered over to the kids to get a little aunt time in before they left.

"So what you got?" I asked, pointing to the baskets, which were now full of plastic egg halves and colorful toys.

"We both got candy. And I got a whistle and a bouncy ball and a rubber stamp and an eraser and a finger puppet." Bella waved a piece of paper at me. "And this will get me a doughnut at the Sugar Shack."

"Nice," I said.

"She traded me for another Hot Wheel," Edward said, holding up two little cars. "And I got a wind-up bunny and a spyglass and a glow-in-the-dark lizard and a ring."

"I want that. Let me trade you one of the chocolates," Bella said.

While they negotiated, I fingered the plastic egg halves, smooth and bright and unnaturally happy. They could hold more secrets. Or presents.

"How about I make a deal with you both," I said. "If you give me a few of these empty eggs, I'll give you each ten dollars."

"Ten dollars!" Bella exclaimed.

Edward looked more cagey. "Ten dollars and a ride in your car. With the top down."

"I don't have a back seat for your car seat," I said. "We'll have to see what your mother says."

So, with Reya's reluctant approval, I drove each kid separately around the block with the roof off, crawling about fifteen miles per hour. They loved it anyway. And I left with a container of leftovers and a purse full of plastic eggs.

GARY KNOCKED on my door about thirty minutes after I texted him, an Easter lily and a six-pack of cold Bohemia Brewing Red Ale in hand.

"Mmm," I said. "The last time I drank that with you, your house burned down."

"We'll have to be careful about setting fires, then," he teased, no mistaking his double meaning. He handed me the potted flower. "Here."

"Beautiful." I touched the firm, white petals and placed the plant on the pass-through counter that opened from the kitchen to the living room.

"I confess, I didn't buy them. Grandma did, and they're toxic to cats, so I talked her into letting me take them."

"So Punky and I both benefited from your thoughtfulness." We exchanged a brief smile.

He'd dressed well, in khaki pants and a moss green button-up shirt, cuffs rolled up. The color brought out the emerald glints in his eyes.

I'd changed after my family experience, from a conservative blouse and pants to a short, soft, black knit dress — casual, but I knew I looked good in it. Especially after Gary seemed to get lost for a minute in scanning me.

"Are you hungry?" I asked. "I've got deviled eggs, slices of my mom's ham, and I stocked up on Swiss cheese and hard rolls. I even bought mustard."

"Brown or yellow?" Gary asked, following me into the tiny kitchen.

"Both." I pulled the bottle opener out of a drawer and handed it to him so he could pop the tops as I set out the food.

"Here," he said, and I turned to take the bottle from him. He handed it to me, then pulled me to him for a kiss. For a second, I got lost in his scent, his strength, remembering how he'd held me Friday night.

"Mmm." I pushed him gently away. "Not yet. I have a surprise for you."

"Other than ham sandwiches?"

"Eat first. You'll need your strength," I joked.

"Hmmm," he mused, eyes flashing with interest.

We each made up a plate with a sandwich, eggs and potato chips. I plugged my tablet computer into the stereo and tuned it to an Internet radio station that specialized in funky tunes with a slinky dance beat, and we sat on the couch to eat.

"That ham is freaking incredible," Gary said after he polished off the sandwich.

"My mom is an incredible cook. It's too bad I didn't inherit those genes."

"You probably did. You're just too busy making music to bother," he said. "I think you'd be good at anything you do."

"Yeah, well, you've never seen me snow-ski."

He laughed. "When did the Florida girl snow-ski?"

"One ill-advised weekend in North Carolina with some friends when I was at Full Sail. It was like unleashing a bone-less scarecrow on the slopes. I ended up spending most of the time by the fire drinking, which suited me fine."

"I wish I'd been there. I could've kept you warm."

"Nobody could have kept me warm. It wasn't in my nature."

"And now?"

I ate my last chip. "Remains to be seen."

Gary took a sip of beer and shifted so he faced me on the couch. The light was fading to purple outside, and he seemed mysterious in the deepening shadows. "I've been thinking about you all day," he said softly.

I didn't answer him directly. "Did you do anything for Easter?"

"I went with my mom and aunt and grandma to the sunrise service on the beach. It's one of their traditions, and I never want to go, but it's always pretty when I get there. And then I took a nap."

"So I'm guessing the Easter bunny didn't bring you anything."

"How'd you know? I've been a bad boy," he joked.

"Oh, no," I said suggestively. "You've been a very good boy." I took another sip of beer, set the bottle on the coffee table and smiled at him. "I understand a certain bunny left you something, but you're going to have to hunt for it."

He sat up, his interest piqued. "What am I looking for?"

"It's Easter, silly. Easter eggs."

"You're putting me on."

"I'll give you a hint." I lit a match from the box next to the fat pillar candle on the coffee table. The wick flared as I touched it with the flame, and his eyes danced in the glow. "You might want to start with the hottest place in the house."

"Your pants?" he joked, reaching out to touch my knee.

"I'm wearing a dress, doofus. Go on."

Amused, he thought for a moment, then stood and wandered to the kitchen. I heard the oven open. He came out holding a blue egg.

"Did you hide the chickens, too?" he teased.

"You can be funny. Or you can open it and claim your gift."

Intrigue erased his smile as he considered the possibilities. Gingerly, he popped open the egg and pulled out the slip of paper I'd hidden inside.

He caught my eye. "I claim your kiss, fair bunny."

I stood and walked over to him, wrapped my arms around his neck and slanted my mouth on his, open, teasing his lips with my tongue until they opened, too, and we tasted each other, the beer, the increasing heat. I broke off the kiss before I completely lost control. That could come later.

"Is that satisfactory, sir?" I asked, in vixen mode.

"Sir?" He grinned. "Hmm. Very nice." He looked around. "Any more hints?"

"I think you should work for it, but I will tell you there are two in each room." I crossed my arms and unhurriedly licked my lips.

His expression darkened, and he looked around, figuring out where else I might have hidden an egg. He went back to the kitchen. I heard him opening canisters and the microwave and cabinets. Finally, he opened the fridge, and he came back with a pink egg.

"I should have figured you'd have one in an egg carton." Gary opened it and pulled out the paper. He let out a slow breath. "It says here that you will — touch yourself for me." He lifted his eyes to mine, knowing the game was getting a lot more interesting. He watched me for a minute, as if he were struggling with something. Finally, he whispered, "Touch yourself, bunny."

I gave him a slow smile and lifted the hem of my dress, high enough that he could see I had no underwear on underneath. He swallowed and staggered back to sit on the comfy chair as I bunched the dress' skirt in one hand and touched myself with the other. Staring him down, I circled one finger around my nub, letting myself enjoy the pleasure of my touch, of his gaze. As he dropped the egg and gripped the arms of the chair, I slipped the finger inside my slit and stroked myself. Oh, hell, I was wet. I was doing this for him, but I was getting far more aroused than I could have imagined.

I didn't quite bring myself to orgasm, but I sighed and withdrew my finger, letting the dress fall back in place.

"God, Ez," he said hoarsely. "You're killing me."

"Does this mean you want to stop the egg hunt?"

"No," he said immediately. "But you realize we're going to hell for doing this on Easter?"

"I don't see why," I answered. "Easter is basically the Christian adaptation of a spring fertility festival. It's more pagan than anything."

"OK. Then let's call these pagan eggs. Two per room . . . " He looked around. There weren't many places to hide in the living room. He walked over to the bookcase and started moving tchotchkes. And then he saw two books sticking out and put his finger on the spine of one.

"Oh, you're too good," I said in a silky voice.

"*Tropic of Cancer.* Henry Miller fan?"

"Yeah, though I consider he and Anais Nin inseparable."

"Ah, I see. One of her diaries." Gary touched the other book, then pulled out both to find a purple egg behind them. He replaced the books, opened the egg and read the strip of paper, then set the half-shells next to the books. "Bunny, are you sure you feel comfortable doing this? After last night —"

"You're sweet." I walked closer to him. "But don't over-think what I told you. Don't overthink the moment. There is nothing in those eggs that I don't want to do. And, frankly? This is how I get off. Now tell me what to do."

"This is an interesting — shift in power," he said.

"How so?"

"You've always had it all. Always." His eyes darkened as he adjusted to the role I was asking him to play, and his voice lowered, more intense, a hundred times more sensual. "Strip for me."

I felt a satisfying shiver at hearing him say the words. I let my arms fall to my side and began to sway to the music. The swaying became a dance, and I lost myself in the beat, swinging my limbs, gyrating, swirling so my dress spun out just enough. In a trance, I worked the fabric up my body as I danced for him, stretching it here and there, tossing my hair from side to side. I pushed it above my naked breasts and heard him breathe in sharply. I pulled it off my head and tossed it aside. I danced for another minute, dancing for him, feeling every movement of my body as he stared, until I slowed to a halt and stood still before him, breathing hard.

His mouth was slack, his eyes glowing in the candlelight. He took a step toward me.

"I think you're forgetting something," I said softly.

"What?" He couldn't take his eyes off my body.

"You have another egg to find in here."

Gary's voice was hoarse. "What if I wanted to skip the eggs?"

"Then the game will end until next Easter," I said innocently.

He shook his head with a frustrated smile and looked around the room. It only took him a moment to zero in on the pillows on the couch. He lifted a couple and found a yellow egg.

He opened it, and a tuft of fabric stuck out, along with a slip of paper. "Blindfold. You or me. Your choice. Five minutes," he read, then tugged on the fabric. It was a long, silky black scarf that unfurled as he pulled. He set down the egg and beckoned to me, his voice low again. "Come here, bunny rabbit."

Goosebumps skated over my flesh. "Just a second." I grabbed the wind-up timer I'd set on the bookshelves earlier. "Remember, whatever you choose, you have five minutes to take advantage of it." I placed it on the coffee table.

"Turn around," he said, and I looked up at him, breathless at the desire in his face, his new air of command. He was enjoying this.

I turned my back to him. He touched my skin between my shoulder blades and trailed one finger slowly down my spine before cupping my ass, squeezing. I felt so vulnerable, so deliciously bare before him. He reached around me and slipped the scarf over my eyes, tying it in place. I heard the clacking as he turned the dial of the timer.

"Lie on your back on the floor," he said, and the authority in his voice almost slayed me.

I did as he asked, blind beneath the scarf. The cold tile chilled my back. The timer ticked. Nothing happened. My desire flamed higher. "Baby," I murmured into the darkness.

"Mmmm." I heard him move, and then I felt his lips on my thigh. He kissed me there, leisurely, deliberately, and then pressed his lips higher and higher, again and again, burning a trail of wet fire as he moved toward my V. I squirmed, and he grasped my hips firmly with both hands and ran his long tongue up my slit.

I gasped at the sensual invasion in the darkness, wanting more. In a moment, he licked again, and then his nimble tongue went to work on my bud, light and devious and dazzling. I tried to lift my hips to meet him, but he held me down. I began to whimper with the pleasure of it. I was so close — so close —

The timer rang, and he broke contact, leaving me gasping on the floor. "Please, Gary," I whispered. He chuckled and pulled the scarf away. I blinked in the suddenly bright candlelight.

"Your rules," he said, but I could tell he was affected, too. He offered me a hand and pulled me up, pulled me to him, just for a moment. I could feel his cock through his clothes, rock hard. I wanted it inside me.

"The other two are in there," I said, still shaky. I picked up the candle and led the way to the bedroom, where I set it on a dresser. I put my hands on my hips, trying to get ahold of myself.

Gary walked in slowly, looking me over. "You are so fucking gorgeous," he said. "So fucking hot. I think this is the culmination of years of torture."

"You call this torture?" I asked.

"You have no idea." He started looking. He struck out under the pillows. He glanced around the closet. He pointed to the dresser. "Is that off-limits?"

"I have no secrets, but it's not in there."

"Really. Hmm." He spied my jewelry box on top and opened it. The orange egg lay in a tangled nest of necklaces. He opened it, pulled out the paper. "It says 'Undress me.' But you're already undressed."

"No, my dear. You just gave a command. And I will."

I approached him slowly, swaying my hips, and lifted my hands to his shoulders. I ran them down his sleeves, then over his chest, feeling his muscular build through the fabric.

And then, one by one, I undid each button, parting the shirt and kissing his skin each time the gap widened. When I finally reached the last button, I swirled my tongue in his belly button and pushed the shirt off his shoulders.

Now I gave my attention to his khakis. With my mouth.

It took me a few minutes of biting and tonguing to get the button unbuttoned, and he moved against me, making unintelligible sounds. I used my fingers to unzip him, cupping him as I did so. He rocked into my hand, but I was on the move, inching his pants slowly off, kissing my way down his thighs as I went. I pulled off each shoe with reverence, each sock, and finished taking off his pants. Next came his boxer briefs. I kissed his erection through the fabric, and he groaned; I tugged them off at an excruciating pace. Finally, he was naked and gloriously hard before me, his cock jutting forward, inviting more naughty pleasures. I stood, breathing as hard as he was.

Without a word, I pointed to my nightstand.

He reached it in half a second and yanked open the drawer, pulling out the green egg and his fortune. " 'A blow job, any way you want it.' " He looked at me with so much want, I almost melted. "I know you did this for me on the beach, but you can't know how, on my darkest nights, how I envisioned — "

"For fuck's sake, Gary, tell me what you want," I whispered. "Tell me what to do. I want to please you."

He dropped the egg and walked to me, glancing up and over my shoulder. I followed his glance — ah, the mirror. I trembled as he led me by the hand around the bed so we were in front of it, sideways to it, facing each other. He cupped my chin for a moment, and then his eyes blazed.

"Get on your knees."

I almost came at the stern tone of his voice, suffused as it was with desire; my pussy couldn't have been more wet. I dropped to my knees immediately and looked up at him and licked my lips.

His cock seemed to grow even larger before me.

I licked his balls, first, mouthing them gently, then ran my tongue up the length of his shaft, getting it wet and ready. I licked the tip, where a sinful dewdrop of moisture swelled. And then I closed my lips around his cock. I took him deep, sucking him in with loving concentration and sliding back up his length to the tip. I swirled my tongue there, and he groaned. I looked up into his eyes, his shining eyes. He held my gaze, so obviously turned on, turned up high; then he glanced in the mirror as I sucked and licked and moved my mouth up and down, my hand working in tandem with my lips, taking him deeper and deeper.

"Yes, fuck, Ez, yes, suck it," he said, and he started to push into my mouth as I opened to him; he was so long, I couldn't take all of him without the help of my hands, but I felt his tip touch the back of my throat. A surge of satisfaction welled in my core, my psyche as he possessed me. As I sucked extra hard, timed to his thrust, I used a finger to massage the skin at the base of his shaft. He bucked into my mouth, coming with a cry, his load thick against my tongue. He pulled out and shot the rest of it onto my breasts, looking down at me as he did so, rapt, forgetting the mirror, completely lost in the fantasy, the fantasy now a reality. I leaned back, arching so he could see his seed on my skin, dripping off my nipples.

"Oh, my God, Ez," he said, falling to his knees, wrapping his arms around me, opening his mouth over mine, devouring me. He slipped one hand between my legs, and with one touch to my already aching clit, I shattered, moaning into his mouth. I clasped him tight as the waves of pleasure swept through me. I sucked on his tongue, felt on the verge of surrendering everything.

Tonight, I'd given him a gift, the way he'd given me one last night — the gift of listening, of allowing me to speak of the unspeakable. But now I teetered on a ledge as my brain and body ran with emotion, a flood of unfamiliar feelings. I ignored them, denied them, losing myself in his kisses until he paused and gently guided me to the bed. I lay there, exhausted, while he went into the bathroom. He emerged with a towel and tenderly cleaned me, and then he curled up next to me, kissing my lips, my shoulders, my breasts, my lips again.

This intensity — why had I never felt it before? I melted against him, drifted into dreams, lost in the mists of an unknown land.

WORK MONDAY MORNING SEEMED SURREAL, given the tumult in my life outside the office. I wished I could hurry up tonight's meeting, as much as I dreaded giving the band the bad news. My trepidation mounted with each minute.

And each second, it seemed, I thought of Gary — of all the things he did to me. The things I asked him to make me do. My strange desire to do even more — to do something for him that wasn't just playing the slut. Could it be that when I'd opened up and told him about my past, I'd opened something else? Some crack in my armor?

He'd left my bed early this morning, saying little except that he had to get to the art school. I worried that I'd broken something in him, too, and then I remembered his pleasure.

That had been real, no matter what preoccupied him the morning after.

I tried to think of other things, working at double speed processing documents for Sammy. I went to the warehouse to check on a shipment of small percussion instruments that was heading to a local elementary school so I could give the anxious teacher a delivery date. And I studiously avoided the boxes of Peeps that some dieter had exiled from her house and put in the break room.

My cell phone rang just before lunch, and I fished it out of my purse. The caller ID showed it was Gary. I pressed the answer button.

"I've been thinking about you," I said softly, involuntarily.

"That's good, because I've been thinking about you, too."

"Are you working?"

"Some. And making pottery. And planning to walk you to the band meeting. You ready?"

"I will be."

"And — " he paused. "I wanted to make sure you were OK. That we are OK."

There is no "us." I remembered what I'd said to him, what I still believed. But I didn't repeat it.

Sammy had already gone to lunch, so I went into his office and shut the door before replying.

"Gary, if you believe sticking your cock down my throat and making me come like a volcano would bother me, you didn't get it."

He made a choking noise, but I heard a hint of relief in his reply. "You drive me to the edge and right over it. You take me places I've never been. I just wanted to be sure I didn't run you over."

"I like it when you drive," I said, my voice husky as I

slipped into the familiar language of seduction. "I like being overwhelmed. I like it when you *fuck me*. Own it."

There was a moment of silence, then two. I wondered if I'd really turned him off. And then he whispered: "I want to own you right now, every inch of your skin, your smooth breasts, your wet pussy. I want to lick you and push my dick inside you and make you scream."

I moaned. I couldn't help myself. And then I looked around to make sure no one heard me through the doors, the glass walls. No one was paying attention. "I could so go for a lunch date," I whispered.

"Oh, *fuck*." The sound of frustration. "I don't even know where you are. And I've got to work through lunch today so I don't have to work late and can meet you this evening."

"Thank you," I murmured. "Thanks for meeting me later, and thanks for getting me so horny I may not make it through the next hour without going out to my car and masturbating."

"Don't give me any ideas. I'm in my van right now."

"Hey, if you're not driving, go for it. Want me to talk you through it?" I was only half-kidding.

"I'm parked in the school lot with one hand on the phone and one on my shorts, trying to talk my manhood into subsiding before I go help a class of senior women make pots."

"Gary, if they see that tent pole in your shorts, they'll sign up for every pottery class at the Bohemia School of Art and Design."

"Why did I call you again?"

I laughed. "See you at 5:45?"

"Yes. And please, no games before the meeting. My head will explode."

"That's not the only head that'll explode," I joked and

hung up.

Now I was *really* thinking about Gary.

I quietly exited Sammy's office and caught Irene looking at me. I ignored her and headed for the break room, where I pulled one of my burritos from the freezer and nuked it on a paper plate. While I waited for the microwave, I tore off one of the yellow marshmallow Peeps in the pile of Easter candy and stuffed it in my mouth, savoring the granular sugar against my tongue as I chewed and swallowed. I really was orally fixated, wasn't I?

"What were you doing in Sammy's office?"

Irene's query startled me out of my thoughts. The microwave beeped, and I pulled out my lunch and set it on the table before turning to my grumpy office mate, whose spiky bronze 'do looked especially furious today.

"Private phone call," I said.

"You're not supposed to make private calls at work."

Like the one to your mother?

Her mother . . .

Maybe I *could* do something else for Gary.

"We have some stuff going on in the family. My grand-mother — " I deliberately paused, praying that my grandparents in heaven would excuse the boatload of lies I was about to tell.

"What about her?" Irene's eyes flickered at the suggestion of hot gossip that might be to my detriment. She sat at the table, and so did I, playing the worried gal-pal.

"She's talking about signing over her condo in Miami to some charity, so we're looking into alternatives. She's not all there anymore."

"Really?"

"We're hiring a lawyer and getting a temporary

restraining order. Then we go to court. They declare her incompetent, and my mom becomes guardian and can stop her from being bilked out of her fortune."

"And your mom would get her fortune?" Irene was eager now.

"That's not what she wants," I said, still spinning my fictional scenario. "She just wants to make sure my grandma's well taken care of."

"Well, of course," Irene said with an utter lack of sincerity.

"But since you asked, yes, technically, my mom would have control of her mother's assets with the final ruling."

"Outstanding!" Irene said. "I mean, that your grandma will get taken care of. Listen, I have to go make a phone call. I'll talk to you later."

A personal phone call? I thought with a glee that really should have been vocalized with an evil laugh. There was a snowball's chance in hell my scheming would pay off, but, I thought — dismissing a distant alarm in my subconscious — *why not?*

GARY KNOCKED on my door right on time, precluding any foreplay before the band meeting. Not that I was in the mood. Still, his sweet kiss of greeting settled my nerves. I wasn't used to leaning on a guy, to trusting one, and his presence was comforting.

The music store was about six blocks away, across downtown Bohemia, and we had a pleasant walk in the golden light of early evening that almost made me forget what was to come. Gary talked about the pottery class he helped run for the senior women.

"You'll never guess who's in the class," he said.

"That's true."

"Smart-ass. Greer Allighant."

"The lady who's selling her house to the art school?"

"Yeah," he said, sounding a little depressed. "But she's really nice, and if she's giving the school as good of a price as Alex suggests, she deserves to make her money and go live on cruise ships."

"Yeah," I said, thinking of the seed I'd planted with Irene. I never even considered what it might mean to Greer if her family actually tried to stop the sale in court. *Shit.* "So I guess those ladies really like you, huh?"

"I never realized this about older women, but they have absolutely no filter. Do you know how many times my butt was pinched or otherwise fondled today?"

I laughed again. They probably all thought he was cute as a button with or without a bulge in his shorts, because he was. He'd always been cute. It was just that before the past couple of weeks, I'd never thought of him as handsome. As *sexy.* But how could I not, knowing him as I did now, knowing the way his body felt against, *inside* mine? His eyes glowed in the sunlight; his curls were in charming disarray. Colorful spatters on his gray T-shirt, with its worn image of Salvador Dali's crazy face, showed that Gary hadn't changed clothes since he'd left the school, and I liked that evidence of his work on him. It felt real. *He* was real, not like so many of the guys I'd met.

"Penny for your thoughts," he said, looking at me oddly as we hit the block that held the music store.

"Oh, was I thinking?"

"I could practically hear the gears," he said with a smile.

"It's nothing. Just — thank you again for coming

with me."

"No problem. I figure you might need an ally in there."

"I'm going to need something," I said as we made it to the door. He opened it for both of us.

When we got to the back room, Ace the Bass and Banjo Brian gave Gary a funny look. It's clear they never expected to see him in my company again.

"Where's Robby?" I asked.

"Wilson's bringing him," Ace said through his long blond bangs. "He's awkward with the crutches, and he can't drive yet."

"So he didn't work today, then?" I sat on the piano bench, then slid over and cocked my head at Gary. He hesitated, and then he sat next to me. His hip next to mine transmitted warmth and security and a prickle of desire that I tried to quell. I had some serious shit to get through in the next few minutes. This was no time for my body to get frisky.

"No," Ace said, "they let me in before they closed at 5:30, so I could keep the door open for you all."

At that moment, the door between the showroom and our practice room opened. It was Wilson, and right behind him was Robby, gingerly moving on his crutches, his leg in a cast, his hair pulled back in a ponytail. Gary leapt up and found him a chair, which he fell into immediately. I had never seen Robby look so pale through his beard, and he waved off our chorus of inquiries into his health.

"This sucks," he said. "I'm going to be fuzzy for a while. But I have some good painkillers, and I should be able to make practice on Wednesday."

"You sure?" Brian asked.

"I'm sure. This is no time for us to take a break, right, Ez?" Robby grinned. "Let's get to it. Give us the gory details."

Gary had resumed his seat next to me, but now I needed to separate myself, to harden my shell. This was going to be tough, and they didn't need to know how vulnerable I felt. I stood, walked a few steps and faced them all.

"We are not signing a deal with Crystal Slice Records."

For a moment, they all just stared at me. Robby had obviously stoked their hopes.

"*What?*" he finally exclaimed.

"Terry's terms were unacceptable. The good news is, we're going to have complete control over our own fate. We're going to cut our own record. We're going to have a career on our terms."

Ace gave me the side-eye. "And just how do you anticipate doing all that stuff that we aren't doing now?"

"We are doing it now," I said. "We're just doing it at our own pace. I have training as a producer. We have the material. We have The Sound. We can get a manager and get more tour dates — "

"Fuck our own pace," said Ace. "I want to do it at the super-fast, platinum-record, making-money-hand-over-fist, Hood Ornament pace."

"Terry did not have our best interests at heart," I said. "I suspected it before, but I know it now."

Robby cleared his throat, and everyone looked at him, knowing that he was the other leader of the band. "Just how do you know this, Ez? The contract looked good to me. To us."

"Yeah," Ace and Brian murmured. Wilson, to his credit, kept silent, observing.

"There were terms that were not spelled out in the contract." I heard my own voice shrinking as I relived that moment on the docks, Terry's tone, his hands on me.

"What the fuck are you talking about?" Robby said, forgetting he wore a cast as he tried to get up and immediately fell back into the hard chair.

I stared him down for five seconds. Ten. "He wanted things from me I was not willing to give," I finally said.

"Like what? Song rights?" Ace said. Had he been smoking before I got here?

"No." I was tired of dancing around it. "He wanted in my pants."

Robby's eyebrows went up. Brian closed his eyes. Wilson shrugged with an amused smile.

I caught Gary's eye, and he had a determined look on his face, as if he were feeling my angst as much as I was.

"Are you pranking us?" Ace asked. "Because that's never really been an issue for you, has it? Did you fuck up the deal somehow?"

"What did you say?" I asked, knowing perfectly well what he'd said.

Robby, who was shaking his head at no one in particular, aimed his gaze at me. "What Ace is saying is that you're not exactly known for worrying about who's in your pants."

I laughed. I actually laughed, one short, bitter guffaw. "You bastards. You should know that he not only wanted to fuck me, that he tried to *force himself* on me — he wanted to fuck *you* over."

"Come on," Ace said.

"Let her talk," said Brian, but he looked confused and hurt.

I turned to Robby. "Remember that little meeting in Orlando? When you went to the bathroom and left me in the conference room with him? He told me what he really wanted. Me. Not in that way, then — or he didn't say so — he wanted me as a solo act. He wanted to put me on some reality TV show he's developing."

"We could have been on a reality show?" Ace yelled.

"Not you. *Me*. I told him we were a package deal. The contract had to be for all of us. And then he proceeded to lead us on."

"Or maybe you led him on," Ace said. "Maybe you told him you'd like that solo deal, and after you blow us off tonight, you'll go to him and get exactly that."

"Are you not listening?" It was the first time I'd raised my voice. "He wanted to ditch you guys from the beginning. And then Friday — he made it clear there was only one way he'd do the contract the way we wanted. And then he — "

I abruptly felt nauseous, remembering, remembering everything, that night, all of the memories, the terrible memories. I couldn't finish the sentence. I clutched my stomach and swayed. Gary was at my side in an instant, guiding me back to the bench. He helped me sit, and I lowered my head and tried to breathe as he rubbed my back.

"She's not lying." Gary's voice was low, simmering with anger. "She would never screw you guys over. This Terry is an asshole. You should count yourselves lucky you didn't sign anything."

"Gary, you're a good guy," Robby said, "and frankly, I'm shocked to see you here. But this has nothing to do with you. I think you'd better leave."

"I'm not leaving without Ez." He squeezed my shoulder, and I sat up and tried to focus.

"Robby, how can you not believe me?" I squeezed my hands together to stop the tremor. "I don't think he ever intended to sign us. The guy's a — a predator."

Ace rolled his eyes and let loose a dramatic sigh. "Please, Ez. As if you didn't let him know you were available."

"Fuck you," I spat.

"I think this is finally it," Robby said. He clutched his head. "I can't think right now. But I can't see any way forward as Ez and the Emeralds."

"You're breaking up the band?" I couldn't believe it.

"No," he said. He swallowed and tried and failed to meet my eyes. "We're asking you to leave."

My mouth dropped open. "All of you?"

"Go," Ace said. "We'll be just as good without you. And we'll call Terry and straighten this out."

"I'm sorry, Ez," said Brian, still looking torn but bowing to the others.

Wilson didn't say anything, but I saw pity in his eyes. That was worst of all.

I was beyond pissed off. "You'll be doing it without the name and without my songs."

Robby just stared into the distance. The others stared at me.

I stood and swept the room with a skyscraper-melting Godzilla glare.

"Have a great life, motherfuckers." I walked out, with Gary on my heels.

Neither of us spoke until we'd put a block between us and the store.

"That went well," Gary said.

A chuckle escaped my lips and, halfway out, transformed into a sob. I stopped in the middle of the sidewalk and turned to him and hugged him hard. He held me as I cried into his shirt, into Salvador Dali's wacky eyes and curly mustache, into the scent of clay and art and Gary.

After a minute, I recovered myself, let go and started walking again, slower this time, leaning into Gary as he wrapped an arm around my shoulders.

"I knew they wouldn't take it well," I said, "but I didn't think they'd kick me out."

"They'll reconsider."

"I'm not sure I want them to." I sniffed and looked around, seeing the neon sign with the cursive "Diamond" in pink across the outlined blue shapes of two diamonds. "Let's stop at The Diamond. I want a milkshake."

"Not a whiskey?" he quipped.

"I'd add some, but I left my flask at home."

"Just as well," he said with a smile. "I'm buying. I still owe you a meal here."

"You don't owe me anything," I said as we entered the diner. *And I owe you more and more.* "But it so happens I don't have my purse, so I appreciate it."

Millie was our waitress again. That girl must work all the time, I thought. Gary asked for a big blue-cheese-and-mushroom burger, and I ordered a milkshake with pancakes and bacon, because I could. Breakfast was 24/7 comfort food.

I inhaled the milkshake first — vanilla, the good kind, with real ice cream — until I got brain freeze and sucked the last drops through the fat straw. I looked up to see Gary staring at me.

"What?"

"I've never wanted to be a straw so much in my life," he murmured, and I laughed. It felt good to laugh.

"If only you tasted like vanilla. But you are pretty delectable." I licked my lips, knowing I'd get a reaction.

"*You're* feeling better."

"Yeah," I said. "If those guys don't believe me, don't

believe *in* me, I don't need to be with them."

"They are going to regret tonight sooner rather than later," he said between bites of his juicy burger.

"I'm looking forward to that."

"Are you really through with them?"

"Maybe," I said. "They certainly seem to think so. And I wouldn't go back without an abject apology. But I'd like to see them do a gig without me. It would be — educational."

"I almost felt sorry for Robby," Gary said, "with his leg and everything. He seemed like he didn't feel all that well."

"That's the only reason I would excuse what he did tonight." The anger rose again, and I took a breath and calmed myself. "This is all speculation, anyway. For all intents and purposes, they and I are not a thing anymore."

"Breaking up is hard to do."

I threw a foiled-wrapped pat of butter at him.

"Hey!" He ducked and grinned.

"You're lucky I used the rest on my pancakes." Which were delicious. I was powering through them, too.

"Those look good."

"Try them." I cut a three-layer bite of pancake, pierced it with the fork, swirled it in the maple syrup and held out the morsel. His eyes got that cloudy look, the swirling river light as he caught my gaze, and he closed his mouth over the bite.

"Mmm." He chewed and swallowed. "Delicious." But his eyes had never left mine, and I wondered if he was talking about the pancakes.

"Do you want to go back to my place?" I asked abruptly.

"Yes," Gary said, whipping out his wallet and laying cash down on the check Millie had already bought to the table.

We left the food half-eaten and hit the pavement, headed for my apartment.

PART 3

$\mathcal{I}$ felt wrung out after the meeting with the band, but Gary had lit a spark in me that demanded to be fanned into flame. I was as puzzled as I was eager. *What am I doing with him?* I thought as I let us into my building.

"Ms. Falcon!" Julio popped out of his apartment door. "Hi! When is my next lesson? It's Monday. Can we do it now?"

"Um, no," I said, shooting Gary a glance. "I have a guest."

"He's not a jerk, is he?"

I coughed to cover a laugh. "No, he's a good guy. Gary, this is Julio. Julio, this is Gary."

"Nice to meet you," they said in tandem, and Gary's dimples showed as he shook the boy's hand.

"So we'll do the lesson soon," I said, taking the first stair.

"Tomorrow? I am free tomorrow!" Julio said, all bouncy, innocent eagerness. My heart twisted just enough that I caved.

"OK, tomorrow evening, like last time, but only if your mom is OK with it. Did you learn your new song?"

"I'm really good!" he said, and I laughed. "My mom will be happy. Can Gary come too?"

"No, Gary will be busy." I shot Gary a look, and he nodded. "We'll see you later."

"OK, Ms. Falcon! I'll be ready!"

Julio bounced back into his apartment as I jogged up the stairs to mine.

"You have a pupil?" Gary asked.

"Sort of."

"Is that part of your mysterious job?"

"No. I teach him a lesson once in a while for free," I said, letting us in my door. "He's a good kid."

"So what do you do, anyway?" he asked as I dropped my keys on the kitchen counter. "I mean, why is it so embarrassing? Are you a stripper? Do you do phone sex?"

"Really, Gary," I said, turning to him and staring him down. "Is that all you think I do? Lure men to their demise?"

"Sorry." He looked embarrassed.

"You'd like that, wouldn't you?" I stepped closer, pressed my hands against his hard chest, thumbed his nipples through the fabric until his breath hitched. "You have a thing for phone-sex operators?"

"I never — well, I mean, I only talked to one once, and it was on a dare, and we ended up discussing poetry."

"You're kidding."

"Poetry and the relative seductive value thereof," he said, slipping his hands around my waist.

"Does it work?" I whispered, lowering my hands to his hips and rocking against him.

"I — I don't know. That's not really where my talent lies."

"Where does your talent lie?"

"I'm more of a hands-on guy," he said, lowering his mouth to mine, his hands to my bottom, pulling me in.

Oh, yes. His need was still there, and now, more confidence, more everything. His kiss said so much I didn't understand, and I didn't mind; my brain was fast succumbing to my body. I moaned into his mouth, and he slipped his tongue against my lips, swirling, tasting. He tugged me into the bedroom.

"Wait a sec," he said, slipping into the bathroom, dangerously close to breaking the mood. He came out with a towel and a jar. "I saw this in your — well, I looked in your medicine cabinet last time I was here. Sorry."

I crossed my arms and raised an eyebrow. "See anything interesting?"

"Yes, I did." Gary set the jar on a nightstand and spread the towel on the bed. He crooked a finger at me. "Come here."

I felt a corner of my mouth turn up as I responded to his finger like metal to a magnet. He slipped his hands under my shirt — a plain black knit, today — and pulled it over my head. His eyes flickered with interest at my tan bra, cotton though it was; he took no time to reach behind me, unclasp it and toss it aside. Rubbing my nipples until they hardened to dark peaks, he lowered his mouth to them, sucking each in turn, until I grabbed his shoulders, asking for more. Not speaking, he unbuttoned my pants — the linen dress pants I'd worn to work — and slipped those off, too, taking my sandals with them. He smiled at my panties, tan cotton, nothing a temptress worth her salt would wear. He kissed my mound through the fabric and I shivered.

He looked up at me. "Are you ready?"

I nodded, not knowing what he had in store. He slipped

off the panties and pointed to the bed. "Get on your stomach," he said.

A thrill passed through me. Just what was he planning? I climbed onto the towel he'd laid out, belly down, and crossed my arms under my head, turning it so I could watch him. He went to the dresser and lit the candle I'd left there; it was a perfect light in the descending darkness. Then he picked up the jar he'd pulled from my cabinet, and I realized what it was: coconut oil. It was an indulgent moisturizer I used only occasionally, and its sweet scent was a balm to my nose as he unscrewed the cap.

"Just relax," he said, scooping out a tablespoon of the white stuff with his fingers and smoothing it into my back. In a moment, he climbed onto the bed and straddled me from behind, still fully clothed, working the oil into my shoulders, my spine; he worked his way down to my buttocks, and I thought I'd pass out from the deep massage.

"Holy fuck," I muttered, wanting to push myself against his hands but feeling too much like a wet noodle to do so.

"I told you I was a hands-on guy."

"Why have I never dated a potter before?" I mumbled, and then I bit my lip. I'd just said we were dating. He chuckled. *Oh, hell.* It was hard to say otherwise, given everything that had happened. But I didn't want Gary to get his hopes up.

He'd moved to my thighs, pushing deep into my muscles with his fingers, working out all my tension, my pain. I stopped thinking, closed my eyes and drifted as he worked his way down my legs to my feet. I made primitive noises as he manipulated the muscles. Now I wasn't just relaxed. I was aroused.

He got off the bed.

"Don't stop," I whimpered, turning my head to look at him again.

"Do I look like I'm stopping?" Gary grinned at me as he stripped off his clothes. Oh, my. In the candlelight, from my haze of ecstasy, he looked like a god. He leaned over me and whispered. "I want to turn you over now."

I made it easy for him and turned with minimal help, lying on my back against the towel, closing my eyes, stretching, feeling utterly relaxed. And even more turned on. Because now, from the side, he rubbed more oil on my chest, caressing my slippery breasts, kneading every inch of skin. My nipples tightened to arrow points; he pinched them as he stroked me, making me grunt with pain, pain and pleasure. He licked them, teasing them further until I squirmed beneath him.

"Mmm, dessert," he murmured, and I giggled. I didn't even know I knew how to giggle.

Every inch of my skin was alive, every muscle slack. Between my legs, I was hot and wet and needy, even as I sank further into the delicious torpor created by his strong, wonderful hands. He worked his way to my belly, then my hips, sliding to my thighs, knees, lower legs, ignoring the part of me that wanted him more than ever.

He paused in his ministrations and climbed onto the bed. I opened my eyes to see him above me. He nudged my legs apart and knelt between them, and I sighed at the sight of him, muscled and, *oh, fuck,* so erect it almost hurt to look.

Gary laid his oiled hands on my upper thighs and slid them to my triangle, pushing, pressing, rubbing. He rolled my clit between his thumb and forefinger, slowly. My breathing increased, and ripples of erotic ecstasy radiated from my nub. Still, I couldn't move, could only yield to his pressure, his pleasure. He slipped one finger into my slit, pressing deeper, finding that spot that made me make unearthly sounds of excitement and surrender. His fingers came out again, and one hand slipped between my legs, underneath, caressing my anus. I gasped at the contact, but he'd already moved on, now pressing two fingers into my pussy, so wet now he smiled, his eyes hooded.

"Please," I moaned. *"Please,* Gary."

"What do you want?" He said it so softly, I barely heard him.

"I — " I'd lost all capacity for thought.

"Do you want my cock in your pussy?"

"Yes."

He shifted closer, dragging the tip through my folds, whispered again. "Do you want me to fuck you until you scream?"

"Yes."

"Tell me what you want, Ez."

"You," I moaned, spreading my legs wider for him.

"Good answer." He slipped in an inch, paused, then rammed his cock deep inside me.

"Oh, God." My muscles were jelly, but his were steel. He suspended himself over me, his corded arms bracketing my body as he pounded my pussy. I spread my legs wider, and I saw the satisfaction on his face as he found a place so deep inside me, it started an earthquake. *An Ez-quake,* came the humorous thought, erased just as quickly by the primal passion in his thrusts. I began to cry out with each one.

"So fucking wet and hot for me," Gary muttered, almost as if he couldn't believe it himself. "Come for me, Ez. Feel me inside you and come for me."

I fell apart with a cry and wrapped my legs around him.

He sank deeply into me and held himself there, then bucked, and I felt his creamy explosion inside me, fueling my delicious disintegration. I shuddered and he collapsed against me, breathing hard. I held him tight, still lost on the sea of my surrender, glad to be drowning in his ocean. The scent of coconut gently wafted from our heated bodies; for a moment, I was naked on a tropical beach, Gary possessing me, fucking me alongside the turquoise waves.

Our high subsided slowly. He eased out of me and held me. I was boneless, drifting. I barely remembered the mess with the band or, more to the point, no longer felt it mattered. For now. There would be a reckoning.

But in the guttering candlelight, the soft, sweet heat, I lost all my cares in the satisfaction of melting in Gary's arms.

TUESDAY CAME AND WENT: the routine of work — where Irene spent a lot of time making personal phone calls — and the lesson with Julio. Gary worked late, then worked a construction gig on Wednesday and an evening shift at the school, helping with a raku class. I spent my Wednesday evening with my headphones on, pounding out a new song on my keyboard, trying not to think about the band rehearsing without me.

Thursday, Gary and I texted the occasional double entendre and how-are-you, but it was almost like we were afraid to come together again. Or maybe I was afraid. I told him I couldn't see him Thursday, though I didn't have any plans, but I asked if he would be at The Junction Box on Friday. I really wanted to show my face to the Emeralds — or whatever they were calling themselves now — and I found myself needing Gary as backup. No, wanting. I didn't need anybody. I called my girlfriends, too, determined to have a support network on hand of all those people I didn't really need.

Despite my studied nonchalance, when I saw Gary at the bar, chatting with Neil over a beer, a buzz built inside me that I couldn't explain. Maybe it was the mind-blowing sex we'd had Monday. Maybe it was something else. All I knew is that when he turned to look at me, it felt like slow-motion lightning.

His smile started with a dimple and slowly lit up his face. He walked toward me and, without hesitation, leaned down and kissed me, not so briefly as to be merely friendly, and just long enough to make my toes curl. It was, I realized, our first kiss as — as an *us*. Or what the world would see as an *us*. He'd claimed me, and it felt strange indeed.

"Let me talk to the girls for a bit," I said, spotting Sloane, Cali, Thea and Penelope at a table. "They're looking at me like I've turned purple."

"Because of me?"

"I think because the band is setting up without me." I looked over to where Robby, sitting on a stool with crutches at his side, was tuning up with the others and studiously avoiding my gaze. No piano player was in sight. And only Wilson gave me a respectful nod. I'd have to think about revising my opinion of drummers.

Maybe the band lineup would elicit curiosity, but I knew the women would grill me about Gary first.

They didn't disappoint.

"I just want to say I approve," said Cali, cute in a sky-blue blouse that echoed her eyes.

I pulled up a chair and squeezed in at the square table

while Gary went back to the bar and said hi to Alex and Damien. My friends all looked at me with varying degrees of mischief.

"Of what do you approve?" I asked innocently. "Manhattan," I told the server whose sleeve I'd grabbed, and he nodded and booked it to the bar.

"You have to promise to be good to him," said Sloane, who was working on a glass of red wine. "He's been crazy about you for as long as I've known him."

"Even though he used to cast glances your way?"

"Only when he wasn't talking about you. He was never really into me," Sloane said, sounding a bit embarrassed, "especially when it was clear that I was all tied up with Alex."

"*Really,*" Penelope said with her trademark dramatic inflection. Her pink and blond coiffure and perfect makeup were complemented by a strapless yellow dress with a retro-style puffy skirt that made me feel underdressed in my capris and silky bronze tank. Though Thea set the standard for casual in a T-shirt and jeans.

Sloane was blushing, and I tried not to visualize why. "Just saying. He's a good guy."

Penelope aimed her pale green eyes at me. "So this means you probably know about my semi-secret project?"

"I know nothing."

She leaned in, and we all followed suit. "I'm making the wedding dress for Gary's mom."

"I didn't know you did that!" Cali said.

"I can't live on costuming and bizarre fiber art projects. Anyway, it's going to be very cool. Perfect for the beach. That's all I'll say for now. Are you and Gary in the wedding?" Penelope asked me.

"No, I'm not. Look, I'm not privy to all of Gary's secrets."

"Whatever you say, Ez." Cali nodded and smiled. "I think you two are meant to be. He really has been into you forever."

"Where's Wyatt?" I asked, trying to change the subject.

"Packing for our trip to Tahiti." Cali grinned. "Anyway, I'm glad you're with Gary."

"I'm not with him."

Thea sipped her beer. "Could've fooled me."

I shrugged. "We've spent some time together. He's been very supportive."

"And why do you need support?" asked Cali, who sipped an Old-Fashioned.

My Manhattan had arrived, thank God. I ignored the question, sniffed the whiskey drink and took a long sip to sustain me during the grilling. I caught Neil's eye at the bar and smiled; he bowed to me, his hand on his heart. Neil, privy to the band's transformation, understood me. Cocktails first, questions later. The mustachioed bartender walked out of the oval-shaped bar and toward the band, which looked just about ready to play.

"Ladies and gentlemen," Neil addressed the bar crowd, and my friends exchanged a look. It was unusual to get an announcement before the entertainment. "We've had a change in our lineup tonight. I'd like to present a new group — The Green Rocks."

I took secret pleasure in the weak applause, reflecting the bafflement among those who knew the Emeralds well, and I couldn't repress a bitter smile at my old band's new name. "The Green Rocks" showed an appalling lack of imagination, but it wasn't anything I'd want to sue them over.

They launched into their first tune — a cover of a Foreigner song. Wow. We'd never started with a cover. And it was a pretty lame cover at that. More to the point — it was definitely not The Sound.

I felt four pairs of eyes on me and looked around. "What?"

"What in the hell happened?" Cali asked. "Why are you not up there?"

"So you haven't heard? They kicked me out."

"But they suck now," Thea said, and everyone laughed.

"It's only halfway through the first song," I said, plowing through my drink. "It has to get better."

"Not necessarily," Penelope said, her tone as dry as her vodka martini.

"At least we don't have to feel obligated to listen," Sloane said. "You wanna talk about it?"

"I really, really don't. At least, not until I'm a lot drunker," I said.

"OK," Sloane said. "Then I'll talk about something else. You know that river house that the art school was going to turn into a retreat? The sale's on hold."

"Oh, no." Thea blew a stray red curl out of her eyes. "What happened?"

I put on my game face, feeling a twinge of worry, and listened to Sloane.

"Greer Allighant's children got a temporary restraining order to stop the sale," she said. "They're trying to get her declared mentally incompetent so they can take over everything."

"How is that even possible? Isn't she in her right mind?" Penelope asked.

"Sane as the day is long," Sloane said. "Really sharp, in fact. She's taking clay and painting classes at the school this session. Says she's working on developing hobbies she can take on the cruise ships."

"So there's no way the kids will succeed, right?" I asked, knowing this was my fault. I'd goaded Irene, thinking I was helping Gary, but I didn't consider the impact on a generous woman who'd never done anything to me.

"Greer has a lawyer, but this is likely to be tied up for a while, and now Bohemia Beach is balking at the zoning, probably because her son has friends on the board." As Sloane finished talking, Alex and Gary walked up to the table.

"I see we're sharing the same conversation," Alex said. "What might be even worse is that, if the kids get control of her finances, the museum won't get her art collection, either."

"Shit," I mumbled. I hadn't even thought about that. "Is the art mentioned in the restraining order?"

"No, that's just for the sale, but I know she saw it as a package deal," Alex said. "The trustees still have to talk about what to do, but it might mean we'll be looking at other properties. Maybe even yours, Gary."

"We'd be thrilled, but not this way," Gary said with a frown. "Greer's a good person. She deserves better."

Oh, crap. I'd really done it now.

The Green Rocks broke into a cover of a K.C. and the Sunshine Band song, and I groaned. Gary laid a hand on my shoulder and squeezed, and I saw all the other girls eyeing me and smiling. It was funny, at least to them. And his hand was warm and distracting. But now I was too keyed up to acknowledge humor or pleasure, worried about what I'd set in motion.

I finished my drink, ordered another, ignored the band and thought about how to make it right.

I SHOWED up on Greer Allighant's front doorstep at 10 a.m., what I deemed a civilized hour for a Saturday. I'd slept alone, telling Gary I needed some time to myself, and on the surface, he seemed understanding. He had a construction job today, anyway, and had to get up early. But I saw the disappointment in his eyes when I kissed him quickly goodnight after he insisted on walking me home.

The truth was, I was too upset to think about anything but the mess I'd caused. Gary's mom might get a great buyer for her house, which wasn't yet on the market, but Greer Allighant's life plans appeared to be fucked. I might have a history of not really giving a shit about anything but my own issues, but I knew when I'd screwed up.

It had been easy enough to find Greer's address through online property records. It was a graceful, sprawling, old white clapboard house in Bohemia Beach, right on the lagoon, surrounded by a jungle of palm trees and tropical flowers. All the plants were bursting out in fresh greens and colors, spurred by the heat of spring. I was already perspiring when I got out of the car at the circle at the end of her winding driveway, especially because I was wearing business casual clothes, including a linen jacket, that were too warm for this muggy April day.

I could hear her doorbell echo beyond the grand front door, with its leaded glass insert and flanking glass panels. After a minute, I rang it again, and I finally saw a shape cast a shadow through the glass.

The door sprang open, revealing a woman even shorter than me, spry and not quite thin, with tight silver curls and sparkling blue eyes. She wore a crisp white tennis outfit.

"I have my own belief system. You go on, now," she said.

"What?"

"There's no point in arguing with me. No Jehovah's Witness has ever convinced me of anything. And you keep coming back here. Don't you have somewhere else to go?"

I laughed. "Ms. Allighant? I'm Ez Falcon. I'm — a musician," I said lamely. "I just wanted to talk to you."

Greer looked confused, then pleased. "I know you, don't I? You played at the regional show opening at the museum. And you were quite good. You have spark. I like that. I want to talk to you, too." She grabbed my arm and pulled me inside.

I got over my shock long enough to take in the decor. A spiral staircase and grand crystal chandelier were at the heart of the two-story foyer, but that's not what I saw first. Every inch of wall space, right up to the ceiling, was covered with art.

I followed Greer into a large sitting room whose walls were similarly adorned with every imaginable style of picture. Among them, some styles looked familiar, even famous, but I wasn't sure about the artists, except for the occasional signature: Picasso. Warhol. Monet? *Holy shit.*

When I dragged my gaze away from the walls, I noticed the medium-size grand piano in the middle of the room. It was surrounded by all kinds of furniture and frippery — large vases filled with peacock feathers and that kind of thing — so it wasn't surprising I'd missed it.

"Play something for me," Greer said, gesturing me to the piano. "You know any opera?"

"I have a secret love of Puccini."

"Good, good. Give me an aria. Need the music?" She flipped open a book that was already on the piano — not just any piano — a Bösendorfer. *Nice.*

I sat on the bench and looked at the song. "This one OK?"

" 'Tosca' is more than OK. Go ahead, now," Greer said, standing behind me as I scanned the music. I was so used to playing by ear, it had been a while since I'd sight-read.

I played the sustained opening notes of "Vissi d'arte," and to my surprise, Greer began to sing along. "Vissi d'arte, vissi d'amore . . . " *I lived for art, I lived for love* . . . The lament seemed even sadder in Greer's fractured soprano, but I recognized in her aged voice a real talent and genuine emotion. I had to blink away a tear as I played the last notes.

"That was beautiful," I said.

"Don't kid an old lady," Greer said. "Despite reports to the contrary, I know exactly how 'good' I am."

"*Really* good. You're a musician, too? I mean, not just an art collector?"

"I'm many things, young lady. Why don't you sit down over here, and I'll make us some tea."

She settled me into an ornate antique couch, in front of a similarly baroque coffee table almost covered with pieces of glass art. I looked around, overwhelmed by the forest of colors and textures and gilt. In a few minutes, Greer emerged with a tea tray, which she barely managed to fit on the table. She sat in a fancy chair and poured us each a dose in delicate porcelain cups adorned with roses.

"Sugar?" she asked, holding tongs over a flowery china bowl filled with sugar cubes.

"One would be great."

"Cream?"

"No, thanks." I took the cup and saucer and held them gingerly, wondering how to get around to what I wanted to talk about.

"You're a very talented young lady," Greer said. "I hope you go far."

"Right now, maybe only as far as Bohemia Beach," I said.

"That's perfectly all right, you know, as long as you're happy." Greer sipped her tea with a satisfied sigh.

"Tell me about your music," I said, putting off the inevitable.

"It's funny you should come asking. I'd just been thinking about my music, how I got started. It really brought me to where I am today, which is in a bit of turmoil, unfortunately." She took another sip of tea. "Back then, I was lucky enough that my parents could afford to give me the lessons I wanted, which always helps. They paid my way to Austria to study."

"Wow."

"Yes, I've always been fortunate, and I've never forgotten it," she said. "I believe in sharing one's fortune. But back then, I was just a self-indulgent girl who thought she could make a career out of playing the piano. I sang, too, but I didn't have the chops for opera, not really. Instead, I worked in a cafe for tips, playing and singing when I wasn't studying."

"When did you go to Austria?"

"In September 1955, at the end of the postwar occupation. I was twenty. I started in Salzburg, but the teacher I'd heard so much about was much too severe with me. I think he saw me as a sweet little strudel, not worth taking seriously. Perhaps I wasn't. And then I met Victor, an Englishman who heard me playing at a cafe."

"What happened?" I drank my tea, imaging Greer as a gallivanting twenty-year-old.

"We fell in love. He had a grand apartment in Vienna, and I went with him after only a month of study. I was terribly capricious at the time, and I was so taken with the country. It was gorgeous, old Europe, you know, even though it'd had the hell bombed out of it during the war. And Vienna — my God, when the Vienna State Opera reopened with 'Fidelio' under Karl Bohm, I thought I would have an orgasm right there in the audience."

I almost dropped my cup.

"It was a glorious night," she continued, "and a torrid affair, not just with Victor, but with Vienna, with the music, with the fantasy. Eventually, I realized I was only playing. Not playing piano — not learning to be great — just playing. At first I tried to talk Victor into coming back to America with me, but I realized he was too set in his ways, too much older than me, too enamored of his life in Vienna. It was a very difficult parting, but I came back home and went to college and studied music. I met Mr. Allighant, and I started to have children, and we started to collect art. I gave piano lessons, but I never recaptured my passion for the instrument in the same way. I think my classical ambitions died with my affair in Vienna."

"Yet you have that beautiful piano, and you still sing."

"The occasional Chopin. Church choir. Music still gives me pleasure. But now, like all those years ago, I know when it's time to move on. My husband's been dead for fifteen years. I'm selling it all. The piano. The art. The house. Well, I'm selling the house, but I'm giving away the art. Unless — "

"I heard about the restraining order," I admitted.

"Oh, you did, did you? That's what you get when you do everything for your children," she said darkly.

"Are you going to fight them in court?"

"Of course!" Greer looked indignant. "My lawyer says we'll eat them alive, and I'll retain control. But the head of trustees at the art school — " She looked at me suspiciously. "What is your interest in all this?"

"I have no personal interest now except to help you if I can. I'm afraid something I said to one of your daughters might have led to this predicament."

"One of my daughters? Are you friends?"

I frowned. "I work with Irene."

"That explains it," Greer said wryly. "I didn't think Irene had any friends as interesting as you."

"Is there any chance the school is going to buy your property?"

She looked at me closely, as if determining my sincerity, then shook her head. "I'm sure it isn't. The trustees haven't decided officially whether to keep pursuing it, but there have been other complications. My son has pull with the zoning board, so it's likely Bohemia Beach will never approve this property for the school's purposes. And this court business will delay the sale and my plan to travel. I'm going to live on cruise ships." She smiled broadly, then frowned. "But who knows when, now? I'm eighty. I don't want to spend the next year tied up in court."

I shifted and put down the teacup. "I understand your paintings are not covered by the temporary restraining order."

"No, they aren't, but I'm set on giving them to the museum, and that won't exactly get me into enough money to do what I want to do."

I looked around at the squares of vibrant color all over her walls. "So what if you didn't give them everything? What if you sold one or two? You have valuable paintings here, don't you?"

Greer looked at me thoughtfully. "You know, I really

wanted to see the Picasso and the Warhols and the Monet hanging in Bohemia. But — there may be something else." She stood up and beckoned me to follow. "Remember I told you about Victor? He gave me a present when I left Vienna. I kept it with me always, but I kept it private. The museum doesn't know about it. I don't think they'd miss it. And maybe it's time to practice what I preach. It's time to move on."

I followed her up a staircase — a different one from the spiraling stairs in the foyer — and up another flight to a narrow third-floor hallway. She opened a door onto a small, clean office. It had creamy walls, sloped on one side with a bright dormer window and a window seat. A rolltop desk and bookshelves were the only furnishings.

There was only one painting in here, about four feet square, centered on an empty wall. Greer flipped a switch, and a spotlight shone on it.

It glowed.

"It's from his golden period, just after the turn of the last century," said Greer, her voice full of love. "A portrait of a young woman in Vienna that her family was too embarrassed to make public. Too sensual, you know." She giggled. "Victor bought it from them after the war when they needed money. He gave it to me. Said it reminded him of me."

The style rang bells — the unconventional lines, the beautiful young woman, colorful robe falling off her shoulders, eyes closed, lips red, black hair tumbling, the background glimmering in gold leaf.

"My God," I said. *Gustav Klimt.* I pulled my phone out of my pocket and started searching as Greer laughed in delight.

"I know," she said.

When I found a page about auctions of his work, I almost passed out. "You do realize what this could be worth?"

"I've kept track. I figure at least a hundred million, not that I ever wanted to sell it before. Ez," Greer said, turning to me, "I think it's lucky you dropped by. You've made me think. I've always prided myself on not hanging on to the past — except for my art. I didn't want to give up this painting. I'd planned on leaving this to my children after giving away the rest of the collection. After what they've done, I simply can't."

"So you'd sell it?" I asked.

She nodded. "I think that's a brilliant option. You know, I've always chosen happiness over ambition, over possessions. And maybe it'll be good for my children to learn to live without. It's time to let go and live for the future."

I nodded. "You should have, like, a guard on this or something."

"This house isn't without security, and I'm sure the auctioneers will keep my golden girl safe once I get the ball rolling. I think I'll call my lawyer, have him come over for dinner so we can talk about it. He'd like that. We go way back."

She winked.

I was still stunned, even as her words sank in. *Live for the future.*

I stared at the painting, dazzled by its romantic, exhilarating vision. I'd lived life in black and white for too long. I wanted color. I wanted passion. I wanted *gold leaf.*

I TEXTED Gary later Saturday afternoon to see if he wanted to go out to dinner. He texted back that he was busy — he'd agreed to go out and play pool with some of the guys — and I wondered if I'd put him off for too long. For the first time, I felt ready to give this "us" thing a chance. I had no idea what was involved, really, though I hoped it included a lot more sex. I had too much time to make up for.

To my relief, he texted me about an hour later and suggested a lazy beach afternoon and sunset picnic on Sunday. Also to my relief, he didn't suggest playing music. As enjoyable as it had been last time, it hadn't exactly ended on a harmonic note. I promised to bring the drinks and dessert, and he said he'd deal with everything else.

The forecast promised record heat, so I wore a strapless black bikini under a gauzy white cover-up. I showed up at the Gorski house at 6 p.m. with a cooler just big enough for a bottle of champagne, plastic glasses and some wickedly good cherry tarts I'd found at a bakery downtown. He buzzed me through the gate and kissed me chastely at the door. I heard voices as we stepped inside.

"Everybody's home," Gary said brightly and, I thought, regretfully. So I couldn't attack him in the foyer, even though he wore only board shorts and a golden tan. Still, I put down my cooler and beach bag, leaned in again, kissed his neck and slipped one hand between his legs. I felt a stirring there before he stepped back, his eyes wild. "Don't make me crazy, Ez. Not after depriving me all week."

"Sorry about that," I whispered.

"I'm never sure where I stand with you," he said simply, then picked up the cooler. I followed him into the kitchen, abashed, not sure where we stood, either.

The bright yellow decor seemed even sunnier with afternoon light filling the windows. They showed a gracious view of the dunes and the beach. The kitchen was redolent with the comforting aroma of fresh baked goods.

"Hi, Esme!" Ginny Gorski greeted me, followed by Gary's

Aunt Johanna. The women, so alike with their reddish hair, were seated at the kitchen table, huddled over a tablet computer, flipping through wedding photos on Pinterest.

"Getting ready for the big day?" I asked, then startled as Pumpkin Spice slinked through my legs.

"We're keeping it kind of free-form, but I'm hoping to pick up a few tips to make it special," Ginny said. "In fact, I was going to ask — could you play something for us?"

"I'd be honored," I said. "Do you have a song in mind?"

"Surprise us," she said.

"OK. I'll give it some thought. I'll need power for the keyboard."

"No problem! We're having a sound system, too. I told Gary I want to have a big beach party before we move out, so it might as well be for the wedding. I want him to invite all his friends."

"You're already planning on moving out?" I asked, not sure where things stood.

"Yes, and I hear we may do it with joy in our hearts, but it's still early to say." Ginny smiled, and I knew she'd heard about the school's changing plans.

"Though it may not work out for Greer Allighant," Gary said darkly.

Oh, boy. I dreaded telling him what I'd done. I didn't want to be the subject of his ire.

"Actually, I heard she's found a way to get what she wants," I said, "even if she doesn't sell her place to the school."

Gary eyed me curiously. "What have you heard?"

"Just — just that," I said lamely. His eyes flickered, his lie detector going off. "Anyway, I'm sure it'll all work out."

"Well, the art school's board is now in possession of a

proposal that Gary helped me with," Ginny said. "And the good news is, I'm hearing that Bohemia Beach would be thrilled to preserve this particular piece of beachfront as mostly wild. They might even be able to pitch in with a conservation grant."

"The wheels turn slowly," Gary said, his tone lighter. "Speaking of which, let's get on with our picnic. I'm starving."

"I packed the biscuits in there with the chicken," Ginny said as Gary grabbed a soft-sided cooler off the counter and slung it over his shoulder. He kissed his mom on the cheek and beckoned me toward the den and its sliding doors.

The sun was getting low in the west, but it still beat on us like a blacksmith's hammer. Gary grabbed an umbrella and a towel off the deck. We took the wooden steps to the sand and traversed the dunes through the sea grass and scattered palms. Hardly anyone was on the beach, but a few walkers and surfers were around.

"Do you ever think nature is conspiring against us?" I asked as we lugged the food and gear toward the waves, sweating seriously now.

"Lightning. Fire. Sandstorm. Hellish heat. Yeah, probably," Gary said cheerfully. "You've basically summed up Florida." We stopped not far from the outgoing tide, and he planted the umbrella. He watched me spread out the towels. "You're not going to let Mother Nature get in your way, are you?"

"No, I'm not." I pulled the cover-up over my head and let it drop to the sand.

Gary's eyes widened. "I never get tired of seeing you naked," he murmured.

"I'm not naked!"

"Close enough." He placed a hand on my waist and

leaned in for a slow, searing kiss. I felt even hotter when he tore himself away.

We sat on the towels and unpacked our coolers. He laid out fried chicken, biscuits, grapes and chips, and I set out the tarts and opened the champagne. I handed him a brimming glass, sparkling in the sun, and he held it up to mine.

"To hot days," he toasted me.

I answered his smile and drank deeply, enjoying the bubbles, the dry flavor. I angled closer to Gary so we were both in the scant shade of the umbrella, and we ate, chatting about the surfers, his night out and other agreeable trivialities. And we sweated to the point where the beach didn't seem like all that great an idea.

"Should we go in the water?" I suggested when I'd finished eating.

Gary polished off his cherry tart with an appreciative nod. "First I want to ask you something. What was going on with you this week?"

"What do you mean?" I leaned back on my elbows, watching the light turn the waves gold.

"Whenever I wanted to see you, I couldn't. You wouldn't."

"You were working."

"There was something else," he said. "You're not avoiding me, are you?"

"I'm here now, aren't I? And I want to be here, Gary." I gave him my most sincere look and reached out to touch his knee.

He still focused on my face. The sunset ignited dazzling sparks in his eyes. "Sometimes I think you're not telling me everything."

I smiled, not wanting to tell him about Greer, about my

own fears. "I'm still cultivating my air of mystery. Should we go in the water? It's fucking hot."

He sighed, looking at me as he might a recalcitrant child.

"OK, let's do it," he finally said.

We stood and walked toward the water. The beach here was almost deserted, now, except for an occasional runner or walker. I grabbed his hand, and he looked at me with surprise, and then with pleasure. We started running toward the waves, until Gary stopped and scooped me up and strode waist-deep into the water. And then he tossed me.

I screamed as my body hit the surf, submerged, flailed, came up splashing and sputtering.

"I'll get you for that," I said with a grin.

"I'd like to see you try."

I chased him through the modest waves, but he always seemed to elude me. The sky shifted from orange into purple, and finally he stopped and let me catch him. My skin might be cooler, now that we'd gone for a swim, but my core ignited as I encircled his waist and stretched up on my toes for a kiss. This time, he had no reservations as he pulled me toward him; he opened his mouth on mine, licking, tonguing, tasting of salt and champagne.

"I should confess right now that I have intense water fantasies," I murmured into his ear when we came up for air, the waves bumping around our hips.

He glanced up, nodding toward his house, visible through the scrubby greenery of the dunes. And despite the dimming sky, there were still people on the beach. "This might not be the best place."

"If only you had a pool." I licked his nipple and ran my tongue across his chest.

He groaned softly. "I might have an alternative. But only a real troublemaker would be interested," he whispered.

"Um, hello," I said, and he laughed.

"Let's get the food and stuff back to the house first."

I joined him in packing up and bringing everything back to Gorski manor, wondering what he had in mind. We returned to the beach in just our swimsuits. The light was almost gone, and a few stars had started to twinkle against the purple velvet of evening.

"So where's your pool?" I asked as he took my hand. We walked, just two lovers — yes, that was a good word, I thought — enjoying an evening at the beach.

"It's not my pool. It's this house at the end of our property that's been for sale and empty for six months."

"And you want to sneak in there?"

"Don't you?" He flashed a grin at me, his teeth glowing in the semi-darkness.

I unclasped my hand and lowered it to his behind, giving it a squeeze. He slipped his arm around my waist and held me tighter as we spotted the dark mansion.

I tried to ignore a moment's worry. "This isn't going to get us arrested, is it?"

"Probably not," he joked. Without hesitation, he took the wooden steps that led from the beach up the dune to the house. I looked around and, seeing no one, followed.

The landscaping here was high-end, a lush jungle studded with swaying coconut palms. A stone pathway wound among them. We ignored the massive house and moved through the foliage to the right, to a large screened enclosure surrounded by plants and palms. It hulked in the darkness, hiding what was within.

"Ready?" he asked when we got to the screened door. I nodded. He opened it, and I followed him inside.

All was quiet. The large, lagoon-shaped pool's built-in hot tub was still, as was its waterfall. But the palms and blooming hibiscus around it rustled in the night. I looked up at the high frame of the arching screened enclosure.

"Gary! Security cameras!"

He laughed. "I guess I should have told you. I have it on good authority that their security cameras are not working right now."

"How would you know that?" I asked, still tense.

"Our construction crew did some work here this week," he said. "A woodpecker got to their fancy foam window surrounds, and I had to carve new ones."

"Sneaky bastard." I slapped him on the shoulder.

"Oh, it's like that, is it?" He slapped me on the behind.

"Baby, if you're going to spank me, you'll need to tie me up first. But not now." I grinned and ran forward, cannonballing into the water.

I heard his splash from beneath the surface. We came up at the same time, wet and eager. He swam over to me, dragged me to the shallow end and wrapped his arms around me, consuming my mouth with his, picking up where we'd left off.

I moaned against his lips. I wasn't kidding about my water fantasies. Of course, as an experienced virgin, I'd had a lot of fantasies, but being slippery and naked in a shadowy pool with a guy was definitely one of the top ten.

Oh, yeah. Naked. We weren't there yet. Gary's mouth traveled down my neck to the curve of my breasts, which were buoyed by the water and the bikini top. He licked my skin at the edge of the fabric and peeled it down with his teeth. Then his mouth was on my nipple, sucking lovingly. I slipped my hands under his waistband in the back, savoring the slope where his hips met his behind. Gary's hands moved to my back, working the clasp of my bikini top. He slipped it off and flung it to the side of the pool, then moved to my other nipple with a tug of his teeth. I arched into him at he laved my tit.

"You're making me so wet," I gasped.

"We're both wet," he quipped, then slipped a hand between my legs and squeezed. "Let me see," he whispered, using both hands to pull down my bikini bottoms. I helped kick them off; they joined the bikini top on the side of the pool, and I was naked as a fish before him. He pushed a finger inside my folds. "Yes, baby," he murmured in my ear, "you are wet and on fire," and he stoked that fire by fingering my clit, by pushing two fingers inside me. I lay back in the water, half floating as he stroked me and supported my back with his other hand. He found the spot that enflamed my aching need, that made me whimper. He pulled me close, kissing me; I slid my hands back to his waist and yanked down the board shorts. They floated I knew not where as I wrapped my legs around him and rubbed against his erection.

"Are you ready for me, mermaid?" He kissed my neck and reached under my ass, holding me against his swollen cock.

"I have never been more aroused, Gorski. You'd better fuck me right now," I hissed into his ear.

He nodded, breathing heavily, and after a moment of torturous repositioning, slid his length inside me.

Fuck, this was hot. I could hear the waves on one side of us, and the traffic on A1A beyond the house and its walled garden. But mostly I heard the water lapping around us and Gary breathing in my ear as he pumped against me, stretching me, allowing me to indulge my most wanton dreams; this was almost like screwing in public, but in a secluded lagoon that, on this night, was meant only for us.

Gary slipped out of me and carried me to the end of the pool, where a shallow slope allowed for a beach-like exit from the water.

He twirled me and pushed me forward.

"Get on your hands and knees," he said in a hushed voice, not so much giving a command as casting a spell, delicate and binding.

Tense with anticipation, I assumed the position in the shallow water, my head just above the surface, the cement prickling my knees and palms. He eased himself behind me, pressing his shaft against my slick folds. He slipped inside my slit, deeper and deeper, so deep I groaned. He pumped into me harder as I looked out into the night, tuned to the rustling trees, the breeze, the wild scent of the ocean. His rhythm drove me into a primal trance, an ecstatic state whose soundtrack was native drums and the rumble of a volcano. I lost myself in primitive cries as he came inside me, clutching my hips, and then I came, too, calling out his name as I fell apart. As he slowed, he cupped my breasts, squeezing my nipples, and I whimpered, feeling completely, deliciously owned by him.

Gary eased out of me and flipped me over in the water. He kissed me with gorgeous intensity, a wet burst of fireflies and roses, and paused and brushed my dripping bangs out of my eyes.

"Not quite 'From Here to Eternity,' " he quipped.

"We could go down to the beach and make out after this. You could give Burt Lancaster a run for his money."

He laughed and lay back next to me in the shallows. "I love that you know that movie."

"I identified with the drunk."

"Frank Sinatra. Probably not a coincidence that he's also a singer."

"Probably not." I turned on my side, slipped one arm over his belly and trailed kisses across his chest.

He *hmmmed* in appreciation. "Let's just live here."

"In the house?" I licked one of his nipples, then suckled as he stroked my back.

"No," he said, his voice soft as gossamer as he stretched against me. "The pool. It's magical."

"OK." I nestled against him as the water lapped around us and looked up. A few of the brightest stars were visible through the dark screen. I wanted to fly up and touch them.

"Ez?" Gary asked after several minutes of perfect peace.

"Yeah?"

"Where are my shorts?"

I chuckled. "I guess this means we're not living in the pool."

"I'm not as handsome when I'm all wrinkled up like a prune."

"I don't believe it," I said, but I sat up with him. We found his shorts and put ourselves back together, sneaking out the way we came. We held hands as we walked down the beach, and I didn't question anything, not until we kissed goodbye at his front door and I drove back to my empty little apartment in Bohemia. There, my keyboard and a half-written song perched on top of it seemed to ask the question for me:

Where am I going now?

∾

WHEN MAMA CALLED Monday morning to invite me to a family dinner on a Wednesday, I knew something was up. But since my Wednesdays were painfully free now, I saw no reason not to accept. I could use the distraction.

And in the interest of trying the new paradigm with Gary, I asked if he wanted to go, too.

"Meet the parents?" he asked in something resembling disbelief when I called him on my lunch hour on Monday.

"That's usually what happens during a family dinner."

"Uh — OK. Sounds great."

I harrumphed. "Why am I not convinced it sounds great?"

"It does," he said. "Really. I'm just surprised, that's all. But happily surprised."

"Right," I said. "You busy tonight?"

"Um, yeah, working late, but I'm available Tuesday evening. Want to grab dinner?"

"Yes, please," I said. "How about Mexican? My blood burrito level has fallen dangerously low."

He chuckled. "OK. I'll come by your place at 6? Or I could pick you up from work?" he asked hopefully.

"My place at 6," I said, ignoring his feint. One step at a time.

I spent Monday evening working on a song and watching *La Dolce Vita*. I always saw something new in it, but this time, its lost souls had never seemed so lost. Then I dreamt that I woke up in a fountain naked, with no memory of how I got there, and no one came to rescue me. When I really woke up, I was crabby and thickheaded, and I had to stop at my favorite bakery for an espresso before I dragged myself in to work.

Irene was hunched over her cell phone, her face a scowl. I

pretended I didn't notice and accepted my boss' coffee with a smile.

"Do you have a minute to talk?" Sammy asked me as I put my purse in my bottom drawer. "Come into my office."

Sammy and I talked a lot, given my job, but there was something in his tone that worried me. Something different.

I followed him in. "Close the door," he said, sitting behind his desk and motioning me to a chair.

Uh-oh.

"Ez, are you happy here?" he asked, clasping his hands in front of him. A dark blue ink stain on the pocket of his light blue Oxford shirt caught my eye, and I forced myself to look at his face, trying to read his routinely bland expression.

"Sure," I said.

"I'd hate to lose you as my admin," he began, and I held my breath. "But I think you might do well in another job here. Maybe a higher management level. Not right now." He grinned at my relieved expression. "But I'd like to give you more to do, see how you like it. I like your work ethic and your instinct for instruments. I want to create a school liaison position, someone who could sell our products to the schools, put together presentations and educational programs, that kind of thing. What do you think?"

"I — " I didn't know what to think. This was my day job — as I jokingly called it, my temp job. This was the job I was going to do until I got my big break. But right now, I didn't want to lose it, and the truth was, I actually liked it. And my big break seemed more and more like an illusion. "Would I have to quit being office manager?"

"No. In fact, this is going to increase your workload, but you're so efficient, I don't think it would be too much of a burden. There'd be a raise in it for you. And down the road, bigger things, I'm sure of it."

Bigger things. Like touring with a famous rock band? Maybe. Maybe it didn't matter.

"Sounds like fun. I'd like to do it," I said.

"Excellent. I'll take you to lunch and fill you in on what I have in mind."

The plan sounded good, and the day went fast. At the same time, I thought a lot about what I wanted out of my life, my career. By the time Gary knocked on my door, I was bursting to talk with someone, but I wasn't ready to admit to him how mundane my life really was. He knew my darkest secret, but he didn't know that I worked a 9 to 5 desk job. And how disappointed would my groupie be when he found out?

He kissed me hello, then looked me over. "Nice outfit. New one?"

"Yeah. Part of the post-ketchup wardrobe overhaul." I'd changed after work into this short, flaring skirt in a colorful pattern trimmed in black. The matching top, with thick black straps and cups that boosted my cleavage, showed just a hint of my midriff. I'd accented it with red hoop earrings. "Finally living up to the hot Latina look, right?"

"Hot, at least," he said with a grin, laying a hand on the exposed skin at my waist and kissing me again, more slowly, with exquisite attention to my lips, my tongue.

I let out a low breath when he released me. "You kind of make me want to skip dinner."

"Because all you have in your fridge is frozen burritos."

"And beer!" I defended myself.

"Exactly. I'm taking you to get some real Mexican food."

"It's my treat," I said as we trotted down the stairs. "I got a promotion today."

"Really?" he asked. When we got outside, he added, "Head phone sex operator?"

"How'd you guess? I get to handle all the senators and congressmen now."

"Please," Gary said. "I don't want to know."

"You do so want to know," I said as we walked toward Beso de Queso. "You want to know exactly how I earn my dirty money."

"Oh, no, Ez. It's not really that bad, is it?"

"Hmm, what could be worse than imagining senators with their pants off?" I teased.

"Being a chicken plucker would suck pretty bad." Gary sounded depressed, and his body language suggested he really did worry about what I did for a living.

Maybe I wasn't sustaining my sense of mystery after all, except in a bad way. As in, *What's in that refrigerator that's been unplugged for two weeks?*

"I don't pluck chickens," I conceded.

"Do you work with animals in any way?"

"Not unless you count humans as animals." My response prompted a new crease in his brow.

"Do they — harm you?"

"Gary Gorski, whatever are you thinking? Nobody harms me in any way."

He looked vaguely embarrassed. Whatever he was thinking, it must have been pretty raw.

"Do you like your job?" he asked.

"You know, I kind of do."

"Then it has something to do with music," he guessed. "Though I'm really hoping you don't have to sing to pants-less senators."

I laughed. "Now that's an image. But I will say you're a pretty good guesser."

"I am?" Gary asked. He held the door for me, and we entered the restaurant in downtown Bohemia whose Mexican music instantly made me crave nacho chips. On orange and turquoise walls, ornate sombreros were interspersed with old sepia-tone photos of what looked like Mexican cowboys.

"I am ready for my Kiss of Cheese," I said after the hostess seated us in a booth, handed us giant laminated menus and took our drink order.

"Is that on the menu?" Gary asked, perusing his.

"Kiss of Cheese. Beso de Queso. It's the name of the restaurant."

"Oh! D'oh," he said. "I could supply you with a cheesy kiss instead."

"Please do."

He smiled at my invitation, perhaps forgetting his concerns over my job, and leaned over the table. I had to stretch to meet him, and the kiss was brief, but there was a sweet familiarity in it. I wasn't used to the feeling.

His Dos Equis and my margarita arrived, along with nacho chips and salsa, and we ordered — fajitas for him, enchiladas for me.

"So you don't work with chickens, but you do work with music, and senators may or may not be involved," he said, sipping his beer.

I took pity on him. "How about this. Twenty questions. I'll answer yes or no."

"Does your job have anything to do with sex?"

"No, and that stings."

"Don't be mad," he said. "It's just because — you're so sexy."

"Yeah, try to dig yourself out of that hole." I took a healthy sip of my tangy drink and licked salt off the rim of the glass as his eyes followed my tongue.

Gary cleared his throat. "Does your job have to do with music?"

"Yes."

"Are you a musician during the daytime, too?"

I puzzled over that one. I was always a musician, wasn't I? "Yes."

He looked thoughtful. "Do you play music during your job?"

"Better question. No."

"Do you work in Bohemia?"

"Yes."

"Do you have to leave the office to do your job?"

"No." That was true, though I'd be on the road more with the promotion.

"Do you sell instruments?"

"Ah. I'll say no, but you need a better question."

"OK." He nibbled at a nacho chip. "Do you work for a company?"

"Yes."

"Does your company sell instruments?"

"Very good! Yes."

"Do you test the instruments?"

"No." I just played with them for fun on occasion. "Ten questions left."

"Do you demonstrate the instruments?"

"No, but I really should."

"Do you work for that shop where your band practices?"

"No, and they're not my band anymore."

"For now," Gary said. "Do you work for a retail store?"

"No." He was pretty good at this.

"Do you work for a company that makes instruments?"

"No."

"How about a company that imports them?"

"Yes." I smiled. "Five more shots."

"I don't need five more. Do you work for Melodeon Music Manufacturing?"

"You know about them? And yes!"

He shrugged and grinned. "I've bought a percussion instrument or three from them. I had no idea you worked there."

"But you still don't know if I operate their phone-sex line."

"Ha, ha. Are you in sales?"

"No."

"Do you work in shipping?"

"No. I'm too short to reach the shelves."

Gary laughed. "I'm sure they have a ladder. Does your job involve a lot of time on the phone?"

"Yes, it does." I sipped my drink and licked my lips, sustaining one last moment of phone-sex illusions.

He narrowed his eyes as our food arrived. "Are you a secretary?"

"Damn it," I said. "Don't you know that term is offensive? I'm an *administrative assistant.* To be more specific, I'm the office manager, and now, the education coordinator."

His eyebrows arched. "Seriously?"

"Don't look so shocked. It's insulting."

"I apologize. I just — I just had no idea. I mean, that

sounds like a real job. And it also sounds a lot more highfa-
lutin than secretary. I guess I lost."

I aimed a playful scowl in his direction before relenting
with a smile. "I'm inclined to concede the point. I guess that
means I have to give you a prize."

Those gold-and-green storm clouds rolled through his
eyes, the light of desire. "I bow to the lady judge. And with
her permission, I'll lay claim to my prize after dinner."

I ate faster after Gary won our little game and drank faster,
too, downing a second potent margarita before we were done.
My buzz was palpable as we left Beso de Queso, and I had
more on my mind than a Kiss of Cheese. Though my belly
was definitely full of cheese.

I wasn't one to question my own motives, but after deciding
to see what being part of a couple was like, I still had no idea
what I was doing. I enjoyed Gary's companionship, especially as
we played a giggly game of "Name That Tune," whistling the
notes as we walked down the street, but I didn't know how to
define my attraction to him. Our history, or lack thereof,
suggested I never should have been drawn to him in the first
place. Yet the heat between us was undeniable. It was a different
kind of heat for me, and not just because we were having actual
intercourse instead of all the minor acts I'd performed with men
before him. I still couldn't explain why I was so charmed by him.

Was desire all that was driving me? Was I just using him
for sex? Though I felt comfortable with him, was actually
able to trust him, I was also unsettled around him, vulnerable. My life seemed out of order. Some key layer of my armor

had been stripped away, and I was doing the emotional equivalent of skipping about in my underwear, not sure how to defend myself.

I tried to push these unwelcome thoughts out of my mind as we strolled down the main drag past bars and restaurants. It wasn't a particularly busy night in downtown Bohemia, but there were still clusters of people out, enjoying the pleasant, balmy evening. They seemed giddy, laughing, smiling, a little tipsy as they drifted by or sat on the patios of the most popular bars. Maybe we all shared the same malady: spring fever.

It was my turn in the game. I whistled a few notes, and Gary stopped walking in front of a watering hole with an elevated, covered porch full of people, complete with an outdoor bar. Loud pop music played. He took on a thoughtful expression.

"I know that one," he said. "It's from a musical — do it again with a few more notes?"

I whistled the three notes and added three more. He leaned in so he could hear them over the noise of the piped-in music.

"I've got it! 'Bali Ha'i' from 'South Pacific,' right?"

"Ah, I made it too easy on you." I stepped farther into his space and kissed him lightly on the mouth. "There's your prize."

Gary slipped his arms around my waist. "I have another prize coming, I think," he said softly, and he kissed my forehead, my cheek, my neck, then finally, my lips. I lost myself in the sweet address, in the feel of his sturdy back under my hands as I pulled him closer. Closing my eyes and falling into the kiss, I flicked my tongue at his, turning my head to take on more of him, sipping and savoring his mouth as if he were another margarita.

"Well, if it isn't Cinderella and her footman," came an unwelcome voice I knew all too well.

My eyes snapped open, and we both broke the embrace to look toward the sound.

It was Stuart, descending the two steps that led from the wide bar porch. His scruffy hair and goatee gave him an unpleasantly devilish appearance.

He paused on the sidewalk, a few feet from us, looking me over from head to toe. His bald gaze made me all too aware of the shortness of my skirt, the skin peeking out from under the top. I felt a chill and grabbed Gary's hand.

"Get lost." Gary's voice was calm, the opposite of my inner surge of fear and rage.

Stuart crossed his arms. People walked around us, our island of three on the sidewalk, a tense triangle. "You still interested in her? Despite her well-deserved rep? And you," he said, looking at me, his voice rising, "have you actually taken up with Groupie Gary? My God, are you actually *fucking* him?"

I became dimly aware of an audience, and not the kind I wanted. People on the porch were starting to watch, as were a few passersby. I worried less about how Stuart was making me look and more about Gary. I squeezed his hand, wondering how he felt about being called Groupie Gary, a nickname I'd once used far too often in private.

"Stuart," I said as coldly as I could, "why do you continue to give a shit? It's not like you gave two craps when we were together."

"That's where you're wrong," he said. "I gave a shit about

having you in my bed, but I never could quite convince you, could I?"

"As I recall, it was my bed, and you could barely get off the couch. Until I kicked you out."

"I left on my own terms, as *you'll* recall." Stuart shook his head, his eyes full of malice. "I just can't believe you opened your legs for *this* one."

In a microsecond, I sensed Gary's calm crumble. I clenched his hand as he fisted and raised the other one; he could have thrown me off and given Stuart the thrashing he deserved, but I tugged at him, and something in my grip held him back. Still, overwhelming tension radiated from his arm to mine.

"Leave *now*." Gary's normally moderated voice rang like steel.

"Or you'll do what?" Stuart said, leaning close enough for me to smell the liquor, the weed on him. There was a volatile undercurrent to his hateful confrontation that made me wonder what else he'd been ingesting. I realized it wasn't the first time I'd had that thought.

"Do we have a problem here?" came another voice, and I turned my head to see the cop who'd taken the report at my apartment. In her crisp, dark uniform and cropped blond hair, she exuded authority as she strolled up to us. She fingered her duty belt, which bristled with baton and gun and all manner of taming tools. With a studied air of nonchalance, her partner hung back, leaning on the patrol car I hadn't even seen pull up.

"This guy was about to hit me," Stuart sneered.

"He didn't. But he was provoked," I said.

She looked at me for a few seconds. I saw the recognition

in her eyes, the calculation as she took in my grip on Gary, Stuart's aggressive posture.

"So," she asked me, "is this ketchup boy?"

I almost smiled. "One and the same."

Stuart's gaze flickered as the cop turned her attention to him. "It seems to me you're making a lot of unnecessary trouble, as well as about to commit another act of aggression that could lead to legal complications for you."

"I haven't done anything," Stuart said, but a quaver in his voice betrayed his hesitation. "What complications?"

The officer regarded him coolly. "Arrest. An injunction to make sure you never bother this young woman again. Ugliness on your record that won't look good to any future employer."

I seriously doubted Stuart would ever worry about gainful employment, but I watched the argument sink in. "You have nothing on me," Stuart protested.

"Are you sure?" she asked. "It looks to me like you're harassing these folks, and there are plenty of witnesses." Her gesture took in the all-too-interested crowd at the bar. "My partner took a statement from you in which you denied your fondness for condiments, but those lies aren't going to help you if you force us to investigate further. Do you understand me?"

"I have no idea what you're talking about," Stuart said, but he backed a step away from us.

"I think you do," she said. "Consider carefully the consequences of ever bothering this woman again. I never forget a face. I'll make it my personal business to make sure the next place you sleep will be behind bars. Do I make myself clear?"

Stuart glanced at me again, his hate tempered now with, if not respect, then fear, basic self-preservation.

"I understand," he bit out. "Can I go now?"

"You *may* go," the officer said, jibing at his grammar. Stuart, his shoulders slumped, turned and shuffled down the sidewalk, melting into the clusters of pedestrians.

"Thank you," I said to the officer and her partner, who'd approached and stood behind her expectantly. I let go of Gary's hand.

"Good thing it was us who showed up. And you," she said to Gary, "watch your temper."

I almost laughed. Gary was the most even-tempered man I'd ever known.

"Yes, ma'am," was all he said.

I thought I saw the twitch of a smile on the officer's lips, and then it was gone, and so was she.

The night seemed to relax all around us. The bar patrons returned to their dinners and drinks, and we resumed our walk back to my place, games forgotten. But without Gary's hand in mine, even walking next to him, I felt alone.

"Thank *you,* too," I said, looking up at Gary, noting a hard set to his jaw.

Gary shook his head. When he answered, his voice was rough. "I've never wanted to kick anybody's ass so badly. Something just triggered when I saw him again, heard his voice. God, I felt like a Neanderthal."

"I'm sorry."

"What are you sorry about?" he asked, glancing down at me.

"For dragging you into my life. For forcing you into confrontations with him."

"Dragging me? Forcing me? Ez, I didn't get dragged into your life. I didn't walk. I ran to you. You gave me an opening, and I took it."

"So," I asked, still worried, "you don't mind?"

"What, being a part of your life?" He paused, then added: "Or you guys calling me Groupie Gary?"

My face heated. "I'm sorry about that, too."

"So many 'sorrys' in one day?" Bitterness gleamed darkly through his sarcasm. *Shit.* He was hurt. "It's a perfect description," he continued. "I mean, hilarious, right? You know I've been your fan forever, from the first moment I saw you in high school."

"And now you know the real me, you poor thing," I said, trying to lighten the moment with a joke.

"It *has* been interesting," he said. "It appears I'm only starting to learn what it's like for a groupie to meet his idol. I suppose I should be grateful. Idols have better things to do than hang out with fanboys like me."

He could have been teasing, but I heard no humor in his words, only a raw cynicism that almost scared me. I didn't know how to make it better. It's not like I was worthy of being anyone's idol. And even though I thought I might like to try a relationship with Gary, I'd never really had one. It was like I was trying him on, treating him like a jacket I might grow into. Maybe he was right. Maybe I was wasting his time.

Neither of us spoke as we neared my apartment, and I wondered if I'd pushed him too far. *It's been interesting?* After everything that had happened in the past couple of weeks, he would never see me in the same way he once did, never adore me again. The flawed part of me that craved admiration felt deflated. But even if he disapproved of me, I couldn't imagine him taking his disappointment and disappearing.

"You coming up?" I asked as I unlocked the front door of my building and watched Gary hesitate in the streetlight-tempered darkness.

"I'll at least make sure you're safe," he said. I didn't want to tell him his concern was unnecessary, but it was welcome all the same.

We entered my place, and I flipped on a light. My apartment was secure, its usual messy self.

"Are you OK?" Gary asked.

"Much better," I said, moving to embrace him. He stiffened, and I pulled back, feeling the sting of rejection.

"I'm going to head home," he said. "I'm exhausted. I think it's the adrenaline dump."

"So you won't claim your prize tonight?"

His half-smile gave me hope. He kissed me on the mouth, brief and sweet. "Raincheck."

"You'll still come with me to my parents' house for dinner tomorrow?"

He paused. "Yes."

No regret, no enthusiasm. But it was a yes.

Gary brushed my bangs back, looked into my eyes for a moment and was gone.

GARY MET me at my place Wednesday after work, but I drove us to my parents' house. He was friendly and open and his usual Gary self, asking me about my day, asking me if I slept well after yesterday evening's debacle. He scanned me subtly, in my form-fitting tan pants and thin, draping, cream knit shirt, under which I wore a bra, if only to pacify my parents. But despite his obvious interest, he didn't kiss me once. He was holding back. I knew it. And though I tried to be cool about it, tried to take his lack of passion in stride, I wondered if something was broken between us. I was so used to him wanting me, so used to getting high on his desire and returning it with enthusiasm, I didn't know what to do without it.

Even if we — "us," not that we'd really achieved that status — were falling apart, there was no way out of this evening now. I was taking him to meet my parents. And Gary was so perfectly cordial, I could mount no objection to his behavior.

My mother greeted him with a mixture of warmth and surprise, and my father grunted almost amiably as he shook Gary's hand. Reya and Robert entered the house right behind us, kids in tow; my sister was literally speechless when I introduced Gary. Robert was the only one who acted normal, shaking his hand and complimenting Gary on his button-up dark blue shirt, which, I had to admit, was a sexy change from his usual T-shirts.

"Come out back," Mama said. "We're grilling."

I let the others go ahead, and Gary turned and cocked his head. "You OK?"

"Maybe." I reached out and snagged his hand. A trace of a spark flared in his eyes and was gone; they were nothing but cool lagoon again. I tugged him along, and we went through the neat, outdated kitchen and out the back door to the patio, where the aroma of cooking burgers filled the air.

And walked right into a giddy reunion. Reya was hugging Izzy, who was less pale than when I'd last seen her; her dark hair was secured in a neat ponytail. The kids were hugging a kitten I'd never seen before, while my parents stood by with something like joy on their faces.

"You're — you're here!" I said to my younger sister, taking my turn to embrace her. I'd almost said "You're out," but that sounded too much like she'd left prison.

"I'm going to stay here a while," she said, then looked expectantly at Gary.

"You remember Gary from high school?" I said by way of introduction.

"Yeah. Nice to see you." Izzy shook his hand, then widened her eyes at me in question.

I offered her the slightest shrug. Was he my boyfriend? I didn't know. Was he my fuck buddy? I didn't know that, either. All I knew was that this was awkward as hell.

"Aunt Esme, did you see Aunt Izzy's kitten?" asked Bella, skipping over to me with the little white furball. "Her name is Mallow." Edward was at his sister's side, holding his hands out, hoping to get his hands on the creature again.

"Let me see her," I said, pulling rank and clasping the kitten in my hands. I let her curl against my chest, where she dug in her nails and, after a moment, purred against my throat as I stroked her long, soft fur. "When did you get her, Izzy?"

"Mama gave her to me. I think she thinks if I have a kitten to take care of, I'll take care of myself, too."

"She's beautiful," Gary said, reaching out to pet Mallow, who nestled in my arms. "You can't help but love her."

He looked up at me with a small, ethereal smile that took my breath away.

"I know. She's irresistible," Izzy said, taking the cat from me and cuddling her.

"How are you doing?" I asked her quietly as the kids, distracted by their father and a Frisbee, dashed into the back yard.

Izzy closed her eyes and spoke into the fur of the kitten she held so tightly. "Don't worry about me," she replied, a tiny quiver in her voice.

Gary left to play with the kids and Robert, and I laid a hand on Izzy's shoulder and squeezed. "Let me know if I can help," I whispered. She didn't reply, just kept her eyes closed and cuddled the kitten, swaying slightly as if to coax Mallow to sleep.

At a loss, I walked over to Reya, who was setting out a stack of paper plates, napkins and utensils on the picnic table. I grabbed the pitcher of iced tea and a plastic cup and poured myself a draught.

"Boyfriend?" Reya asked, never meeting my eyes as she unnecessarily sorted the forks from the spoons.

"Boy. Friend," I responded after a long sip of the tea.

Reya stopped fussing and looked at me. "What are you doing with your life?"

"What are you talking about?"

"Are you just going to coast from guy to guy and gig to gig forever?"

"I'm not coasting," I said, sitting at the table. "In fact, my band has kicked me out, and I managed to hose a record label deal and turn down a spot on a reality TV show."

"You turned down *television?* Oh, Esmerelda, where are your values?"

I laughed at her utter lack of irony and glanced over at Izzy, who now sat in an Adirondack chair with the kitten on her lap, watching the children playing with Gary and Robert. "I would think I'm second on the agenda of Falcons With Problems today."

"Izzy's doing great," Reya declared, albeit softly. "As for you, Esme, I just don't get you."

"You never did." But she had a point. I had my real job, but my music career was running on empty. All I wanted to do right now was retreat to the cave of my imagination and write songs. Maybe there was something true in the impulse, something I could act on.

My musings were interrupted by the call to dinner. Mama produced potato salad and baked beans as my father dished up the burgers, an all-American meal. Izzy put the kitten in the house and joined Reya, Robert, the kids and my parents, filling up the table, while Gary and I grabbed plates and sat in chairs on the other side of the patio.

"So," Gary asked between bites of burger, "how's it going?"

"Which part?" I asked. "My sister just out of rehab, my doomed career, or your visit?"

"I thought maybe my visit, but now I'm not sure," he said, a furrow in his brow. "At least the burgers are good."

I smiled in spite of myself. "Yeah. Papa is good at grilling. Talking, not so much."

"He seemed friendly enough. I mean, other than the not talking part."

"Hopefully my disgrace won't rub off on you."

"Don't say that," he said quietly, setting his empty plate on the ground. "You have nothing to feel sorry for. Surely he understands that."

I shrugged, put my plate down, too. I'd lost my appetite. "It's been a lot of years of evidence to the contrary."

I watched the sky shifting into pinks and oranges as the sun neared the horizon. My mother and Reya cleared the plates while the kids went inside to play with the kitten. Izzy followed them; Robert and my father discussed the finer points of the grill. The warm evening, the drone of insects lulled me into forgetfulness, and I let my head fall back against the chair and closed my eyes.

"Izzy!"

The shriek ripped me from my doze, and I jumped out of the chair, unsteady on my feet. My mother was looking up.

Izzy was scooting slowly across the roof.

"My God, she's going to jump," I heard Reya whisper to her husband.

I shook my head, confirming that I was awake, that this was no nightmare. Gary, also standing, shot a glance my way. By mutual agreement, we dashed into the house.

I led him up the stairs and to the bedroom Izzy and I had shared as kids. The twin beds were still there, and the children, Bella and Edward, sat on one of them, clutching each other and crying. *What the hell?*

We'd often climbed out the dormer window and onto the roof as teens, perching on the nearly flat part that extended over the front porch. From there, we could sunbathe and spy on the neighbors. But we'd just seen Izzy on the other side, the steep side. A chill swept through me, and I climbed out to see if I could catch her.

Gary, bless his heart, followed me as I worked my way gingerly across the shingles and up to the peak. There was Izzy, balancing awkwardly on the steep back side of the roof.

"Izzy, please don't do anything," I called to her, unwilling to articulate what I was really thinking: *Please don't jump.*

Her head snapped around and she lost her balance for a moment, sliding two more feet toward the edge. I gasped. So did she as she found her grip again, and then she looked up at me. "Esme? What are you doing out here?"

"I'm here to get you back inside." I moved to her side of the roof and inched my butt along the peak, toward her.

"Don't be foolish!" she said.

"Well, what are *you* doing, then? Izzy, it's not worth it.

Please." Tears welled in my eyes. "I can't go on if you leave me."

She looked at me quizzically. And then, to my surprise, she laughed, a long peal of laughter that invited an echo of humor. I didn't know what to think at hearing it.

"Ez," she said, finally quelling her laughter, still smiling. "Dear Ez. I'm trying to rescue my stupid kitten."

You couldn't have colored me more dumbfounded. "You are?"

"Let me." It was Gary. He clambered past me and reached Izzy in a moment. "Where is she?"

Izzy pointed beyond her and to the edge of the roof. I shifted so I could see what her body had blocked. Mallow was crouched in the gutter at the corner of the house, trembling. I saw the little pink mouth open, heard a soft meow. Craning, I could just see over the edge of the roof, where my parents, Reya and Robert watched the drama with tense faces.

I held my breath again as Gary eased down across the sloping shingles toward the ball of white fur. "Come here, little one," he called, reaching out a hand. The kitten didn't move. I thought I heard Gary mutter a "damn it," and then he was at the edge of the roof, scooping up Mallow with one hand. He stuffed her in his shirt. "Ouch!" he said as he began the climb back up toward Izzy, and I was too scared to laugh at what the kitten must be doing to his chest. "Go on ahead of me," he said to my sister, acting as spotter as she slowly eased toward the peak and my position. In a few moments, she'd made it and was coming down the other side with me. I watched her go into the window, then waited for Gary.

It was another minute before he came over the top. I let out a long, stale breath and felt the tremors in my hands

ease at the sight of him. He caught my eye and smiled reas-
suringly; together, we went through the window, where Izzy
and the kids, and now Reya, were waiting. Reya clung to
Izzy and the children as Gary slipped open a couple of
buttons and pulled Mallow out. The kids broke into new
wails, Izzy laughed and grabbed the kitten, and I hugged
Gary with the strength of ten deeply fucked-up piano
players.

"Easy," he said. "I think that cat took a layer of my skin
with her."

I let him go and parted his shirt to see the red welts where
the kitten had scratched him.

"What happened?" Reya demanded of Izzy and the kids
as I grabbed Izzy in a hard, fast hug.

Bella responded with gulping sobs. "We wanted to play
with Mallow and took her out of her crate and were playing
on the bed and the window was open and she jumped out!"

Edward burst into new tears, and Izzy and I exchanged
a grin.

"I'm going to patch up Gary," I said, taking his hand and
pulling him down the hall to the bathroom. I closed the door
behind us. We were trapped in a tiny world of retro pink tile
and my mother's frou-frou lace-edged pink towels. "Take off
your shirt."

"You're kidding."

"Gary, as much as I'd like to ravish you," I said, opening
the medicine cabinet, "I'm going to give you first aid instead."

"Oh." He sounded a tad embarrassed as he unbuttoned
and removed his shirt, looping it over a towel rack. I watched
in the mirror, admiring his physique and, even more, feeling
overwhelmingly grateful.

I unscrewed the top of the tube of ointment, set it on the

sink and faced him. Before I did anything, I leaned in and kissed his chest, his red-streaked skin.

I heard his intake of breath, and it made me want him even more. But here, in my parents' house, after he just went out of his way to save a kitten and my sister, too, I restrained myself. I used one of the pink terry cloths to wash his chest with cool water, gently, slowly. He shifted under my touch, watching me as the air heated between us. Then I dabbed the ointment on my finger and eased the antibiotic salve across the scratches, one by one, savoring the feel of his skin.

"She didn't draw blood," I murmured as I finished, closing the tube and setting it on the sink. "That's good."

"I've suffered worse," he said softly. I looked up and into his eyes. So much emotion swirled there, so much I didn't understand. He reached up, held my face with both hands and leaned close, pausing bare inches from me until my heart raced. Then he covered my mouth with his.

I lost myself in the kiss, so deep, so heavy, a drowsy, drugging dream. He stroked his tongue against mine and savored my lips with heated assurance until I whimpered and grasped his hard, naked waist, wanting all of him. But my touch seemed to arrest him, and he withdrew. His eyes fluttered open and caught my gaze again. With a smile, he stepped back and donned his shirt, buttoning it as I watched, my breaths slow to ease in the face of his bravery, his beauty.

"Thank you," I said.

"You know how I love cats," he answered lightly.

I held his gaze for another moment, marveling at his modesty, his ever-present good humor, and then I opened the door so we could go downstairs to say our goodbyes.

I gave everyone a hug, even Reya, until I got to my father. To my surprise, he hugged me.

"I like him," he said gruffly, nodding at Gary, then lowered his voice. "I'm so glad you — I always worried for you. That I — that I let it all happen. That I could never fix it."

My eyes widened in surprise at the concern in his deeply lined face. "Papa?"

"I'm sorry, honey," he said. "I love you."

Tears stung my eyes for the second time today. The world was topsy-turvy. He was apologizing to *me?*

I hugged him, unable to speak.

Filled to the brim with feelings I didn't know how to handle, I left with Gary.

GARY DIDN'T SAY a word as we got to my place, but he followed me up the stairs and into the apartment. Whatever was between us after the kitten incident was loudly unspoken — physical, yes, but something more. I felt a connection that cried out for consummation.

I dropped my purse by the couch and turned to him in the dim light. Outside, dusk had descended, and only the street lights shone through the living room window. The patchy glow set off his cheekbones, his fine features, his turbulent eyes. I studied him, admired him; he looked as if he were about to take flight. But I needed physical reassurance as much as I wanted to show him how grateful I was. Touching him was the only way I knew how.

"I should go," Gary said, still standing near the door, almost as if he'd read my mind and rebuffed me.

"Don't go." I approached him slowly and put my hands on his shoulders, slid them down his muscled arms and clasped his hands. I kissed his neck, enjoying his height, the way he seemed always to stand over me like a watchtower.

"Ez, this isn't what I want."

"Are you sure?" I kissed his neck again and slipped a hand between his legs, feeling the stirring in his jeans.

"Just because you flip my switch doesn't mean I need to run the engine," he said, his voice more strained.

"Why not? It feels like you have fuel to burn." I squeezed lightly, and he groaned.

"What are we doing?"

"Why do you ask?" I unbuttoned and unzipped his jeans in one movement.

"I'm in too deep," he whispered, barely audible.

I slipped to my knees.

He gasped, his protests overcome the moment I pulled down his pants and briefs and set his cock free. I touched it, marveling at its length, its eagerness as he grew harder. I stroked and caressed him, then held his rod with one hand while I licked the tip, tasting the pearl of desire that had already formed there. He slipped a hand into my hair and held on as I opened my mouth and took him in, sucking slowly, tasting his salty, masculine flavor as I worked my lips up and down his shaft. I used one hand to guide and stroke the rest of his length as I savored as much of him as I could take in my mouth. I glanced up as I sucked; his head was back, his eyes closed. He dug into my hair with his fingers, coaxing me almost unconsciously as he moaned and thrust, ever so gently, sliding against my tongue. His pace subtly increased, and I relaxed, opening to him, drawing him deeper. When he came, shaking, I swallowed his eruptions of come and felt a tingle of my own, a heat between my legs that was fanned by my own power. I damn near came with the thrill of it.

In a moment, Gary staggered backward, pulled up his jeans, zipped up. So maybe I wasn't getting what I wanted tonight. I flipped on the living room light and looked at him with puzzlement as I deliberately licked my lips.

"God, Ez, I can't resist you."

"Why would you want to?"

He seemed lost, and his expression both pricked my heart and scared me. He sat on the couch, numbly staring at the coffee table and its pile of magazines and mail.

I went to the kitchen and brought back a couple of beers, handed one to him and sat next to him.

He was distracted, looking at the mail, at a postcard sticking out of the heap. He picked it up.

"From Greer? Greer Allighant?" he asked, looking at me questioningly.

I had a feeling this was not welcome news to Gary, so I just nodded.

He flipped it to the photo, of a port in the Bahamas, then flipped it over again.

"That's private mail, you know," I said with indifference, hoping he wouldn't make a big deal of it.

"She says she's on a cruise."

"I believe her exact words were, 'a short cruise, a preview of my new life.' " I took the card from him and read it. He might as well know now. " 'Thanks for the idea. The golden girl is at the auctioneer and my family is going to lose in court. The museum will get the art, and I've decided to give my land to Bohemia Beach for a park. Suddenly the city officials are much more amenable to my plans. I'm selling everything else, though I'm going to send you a little gift to express my appreciation. Cheers for now.' "

I glanced up at Gary and was surprised to see his mouth set in a hard line.

"What did you have to do with foiling the sale to the school?" he asked in a low, steely tone that completely unnerved me.

"I didn't. I mean, her kids did." I blanched, knowing I had to come clean. "I work with one of her kids, and I may have mentioned something to her about lawsuits and restraining orders."

"How could you? You knew how important that deal was to the school."

"Gary, I did it for you!"

He slammed the beer bottle on the table. "You're playing with people's lives. Good people."

"But it's all going to work out, don't you see?" I was fast losing my cool. "Your mom gets to sell her house to the school, and Greer is going to be all right. I went and talked with her — "

"And now her children are dragging her to court to try to prove she's crazy!"

"But she's not! And her lawyer assures her she'll be OK. We had a conversation. She's still giving the museum the art, well, most of it, and she still gets to live on cruise ships. It's a win for everybody. And, like I said, I wanted to do it for you. To thank you. You've been so good to me."

He stood, his height now intimidating from my position on the couch. "This is not how you thank someone. God, is that was this was, tonight?" Anguish crossed his features.

"What's wrong with doing something nice for you?"

"This is serious shit," Gary said. "You didn't trust me

enough to ask me about something that would affect my family so profoundly, not to mention the school we helped create?"

"I — I hadn't thought of it that way," I said in a small voice. I drank a gulp of the beer, wanting the comfort of the alcohol, hoping it would calm my now-trembling hands.

Gary seemed more hurt than angry, now. "You said you wouldn't lie to me."

"I also said I wouldn't tell you everything. And I didn't want to until I'd sorted it out, and now I have. So I'm telling you."

"How can I ever trust you?"

I flipped from worried to pissed off in an instant. "Why would you want to?" I snapped, standing. "You can't even accept a thank-you from me!"

His eyes flared. "Let me tell you something, Ez. I always wanted you. From the first moment I saw you walk into my homeroom freshman year, I wanted you. More than that, I loved you. Maybe it was naive teenage mutant love, but I would have done anything to be with you. I loved your dry humor, your go-to-hell attitude, your talent, even the darkness I felt you carrying with you; I wanted to bring you light. For the first time in my life, I realized love songs weren't bullshit. Maybe they were odes to chemical attraction more than anything, but I was all in. I loved you, even though you ignored me. But I didn't really know you.

"And then, just in the past few weeks, I've seen what you're really like. And you know what? You are everything I thought you were and more. More complicated, yeah, but more talented, more driven, more intelligent, more beautiful. Funnier. More kinky," he said with a fast, tart smile. "Even kind and thoughtful when you want to be." He paused. "And then I understood the deeper love songs. I understood obsession. You've never written a love song, have you? If you had, you'd understand. In the best love songs, the heart is naked, fragile, offered as a gift, as delicate as the tissue paper it's wrapped in. It's ephemeral as a flame. And if you take someone's heart, you have to be willing to be burned, too. But the fire is worth it, because you understand that love is pain along with joy. You understand that fire burns through to the truth, factual and emotional. Love is never a transaction. Love is never a tit for tat. Love is given freely, with the expectation that it may blow up in your face and singe your heart forever. It's given in complete trust. *Trust.* You give, and you don't expect anything, but you *hope* for the best gift of all — love given in return. At least until you can't hope any more."

Gary stared into my eyes. I felt his passion, but I had no idea how to respond. Love? Was he actually declaring that he was in love with me?

He shook his head, and now his tone was more mild, resigned. "You have no idea what I'm talking about, do you?"

"I'm trying," I said lamely. I at least understood how vulnerable he'd made himself. "I'm sorry you're upset. I don't understand what has happened between us, but I'm trying to tell you I'm grateful for you."

"Sadly, that's not enough." His voice was low, devoid of the passion I'd heard only a moment before. "I think it's best if we don't see each other again, Ez. Not like this. I'll see you around."

He headed toward the door, and before I knew it, I'd sprinted after him and grabbed his arm. "Don't go. I need you, Gary."

"You need a groupie, I think," he said, and his half-smile

killed me with its uncharacteristic melancholy.
"Goodbye, Ez."

Gary shut the door behind him. For a long time, I just
stared at it. I pressed my hands together, willing the tremors
to stop, but they ignored my wishes, and in a moment, I
shook all over. My head felt as if an off-key opera singer had
been screeching inside it. Maybe I was coming down with
something.

I turned out the light and went into my room. I crawled
into bed and tried to process the dark, grinding ache as it
consumed me to my bones.

I DEVOLVED into a poorly functioning robot the next morning,
my emotional circuits overloaded and shorting out. The
family dinner had been a bit too eventful, though I was
happy to see that my sister Izzy seemed to be in a pretty good
place. And the confrontation afterward with Gary — I mean,
what was I supposed to do here? I'd set out to help him with a
pressing problem, and then I'd undone the collateral damage
to the best of my ability.

I was pretty sure Greer was in the clear when I saw how
pissy Irene was. I ran into her in the break room when I was
heating up my frozen burritos, and she practically spat
at me.

"How's that situation with your grandmother?" she asked,
scowling.

"It turns out she's made a miraculous recovery," I said,
again mentally apologizing to my ancestors. "She's perfectly
fine and is marrying her ballroom dance teacher."

"Ha! I knew I never should have listened to you," she said,

leaving the room in a huff with her cup of chemically sweet-ened coffee.

So, Irene's misery was one bright spot in my day.

And the other came when I was halfway through my afternoon, most of it spent talking to schools and setting up appointments, when my phone buzzed. It was a text from Robby.

"Would like to talk. Can I call you now?"

"I'll give you five minutes," I texted back. I walked my phone outside to the parking lot, where the toasty spring sun glared off the cars. The jacaranda tree at the edge of the pave-ment was practically exploding with lavender flowers, and I walked into its shade, amid a carpet of fallen blossoms, as my phone rang.

"Yeah?" I answered.

"We need you," Robby said, words that immediately shot me back to my plea to Gary last night: *I need you.*

"You need a punch in the mouth. Or maybe in the leg. How's that going?"

"I deserved that," the guitarist said. "The leg is coming along. How are you?"

"Cut to the chase. I've got to get back to work."

"We want you back in the band."

"Really?" I let the silence cook for a minute. "All of you?"

"Yes."

"Because all of you pissed me off, but Ace needs a kick in the balls."

"He's working really hard on his grovel," Robby said.

I laughed, still tasting a hint of bitter. "So how'd it go with Terry?"

"He cut us cold. Told me signing us now would be like buying an udderless cow for the milk."

"Typical classy Terry. Of course he'd mention udders."

"Yeah, well, funny thing is, I got a call from a woman he works with, or used to work with, who's become an independent agent. Remember meeting Poppy? She said she'd heard us perform? She's quit Crystal Slice and was looking to get ahold of you."

"What for?"

"She wants to represent your songs. She has a lot of contacts with big artists. Thinks you're a great songwriter."

"Interesting. I haven't heard from her." I tried not to get my hopes up, but I felt a little butterfly of optimism breaking out of its chrysalis.

"You will. While I had her on the phone, I asked if she might want to help us out, too, and she said she only would if you were on board. So what's it going to take?"

"Your unqualified obedience and a dozen Sugar Shack doughnuts."

"Done." He chuckled.

"I don't want to sign with a label. I'm open to touring around Florida, for now. And I want to record an album where we call the shots."

"Given none of us are too thrilled with our record label experience," he said, "I can speak for all of us when I say we heartily concur. Does this mean you'll come back?"

"A dozen Sugar Shack doughnuts a month for a *year*. And Ace grovels."

"Done, if you'll play with us at The Junction Box on Friday."

"Ah," I said. This was it. A chance to reinvent us. Me.

I wondered if Gary would be there.

"I'll do it," I said, "under our old name."

"Thank you so much." The relief in Robby's voice was almost comical. "I never should have let you go."

"Told me to go, you mean."

"Either way. My head wasn't clear. I got wrapped up in dreams of success. I should have trusted you."

"And don't you forget it, pudwacker."

He laughed again. "Yes, ma'am. See you tomorrow."

I ended the call thinking not about the gig, but about seeing Gary there.

I FELT the buzz in The Junction Box as soon as I walked in the front door. The folding chalkboard sign outside had said "TONIGHT: EZ & THE EMERALDS!!!" Three exclamation points. I smiled, attributing at least two of them to Neil.

Inside, it was crowded and warm, with the giggle and fizz of happy drinkers with spring fever. I saw several of my friends gathered around the bar, but not Gary. *Not yet,* I told myself, tamping down a disconcerting surge of emotion.

The band was already setting up. Robby, who was fiddling with an amp, his pony tail hanging down over his shoulder, caught my eye first. He stood and grinned sheepishly through his beard, then hobbled over in his clunky, black orthopedic boot (almost matching his combat boot) and gave me a big hug.

"It's great to see you," he said in my ear. "The doughnuts are on the piano."

I laughed and released him. "As long as there are a couple of glazed in there, we're good."

"Of course."

"I heard from the agent today. I'm getting songs together to send to her."

"Excellent," he said. "You deserve it."

"So you've graduated from the cast." I gestured to his leg.

"Yeah, this is a lot better," he said as he clumped back toward the band. I followed. "But I can't jump off speakers yet."

"Or ever, I hope," I said drily.

Brian looked up from tuning his banjo. "Ez." He turned a bit pink. "I'm sorry about everything. And I'm really glad you're back."

"Thanks, Brian. You pickin' and grinnin'?"

"Yee-haw," he said with a smile.

Wilson walked in the back door with the last of his cymbals, set them down and approached. He shook my hand with an approving nod. Ace entered right behind him with an armload of cables and the stink of patchouli. When he saw me, he threw the cables on the floor and dropped to his knees. The others cracked up.

"Forgive me, Ms. Falcon," he intoned, half-hidden by his bright blond bangs. "The next time you tell me someone is an asshole, I'll believe you, even if you're talking about me."

"Especially if she's talking about you," Robby said.

"Get up, fool," I said, but I allowed him a small smile. "So what's the playlist?"

We quickly went over the song list, and then I wandered to the piano, sat down and played a warm-up song, quietly so as not to compete with the canned music booming over the speakers. Still, when I finished, there was a rumble and a smattering of applause. I looked up to see several people grinning at me, especially Sloane, Penelope and Thea. I grabbed the Sugar Shack box from atop the piano and walked over to greet them by the bar.

"Aren't you the hot tamale tonight," said Penelope, who was retro-chic as usual, this time in a flaring apple-green dress with a boatneck collar and a pink crinoline peeking from beneath.

"Had to look good for my comeback." I glanced down at my new, silky purple pants, which clung suggestively to my tight curves, and my favorite draping, translucent, black sparkling top, sleeveless and showing just enough breast above the black bra, which was visible beneath the shirt. Long rhinestone earrings dripped like sparkling rain at my ears, and dark lipstick tinged with purple complemented darker eye makeup. Sandals with low heels looked good but would let me work the pedals.

"Where's Cali?" I asked after hugging the others and offering them doughnuts. Bless them, they all took one. No diet was worth denying the Sugar Shack.

"Tahiti," Sloane said around a salted caramel confection.

"Ah, hot tropical love with her surfer boy?" I asked.

"God, I hope so," Thea said wistfully. "Speaking of which — where's Gary?"

They all looked at me expectantly.

"I don't know," I said. I'd wanted to ask them the same thing but couldn't bring myself to do it.

Sloane frowned. "You don't — you aren't —?"

"I don't know anything." My tone invited no further discussion.

"But you're back with the Emeralds, and that's exactly where you should be," Penelope cooed, patting my arm just as Neil set a pretty amber cocktail garnished with mint on the bar in front of me.

"Great to see you back," he beamed. "And not just because my tips double when you play."

We all laughed. "What's the potion du jour?" I asked him.

"Mai Tai. I suggest limiting yourself to one at a time." He raised his eyebrows significantly, and his mustache rose with them.

"Is that right?" I took a sip. "Holy shit."

"Strong?" Thea asked. She had a beer in one hand and a peanut-covered doughnut in the other.

I nodded, savoring the rum concoction. "And fucking delicious."

Neil bowed with a smile, and I leaned back against the bar, sipping, munching a glazed doughnut and listening to the other girls talk.

"How's the wedding dress coming along?" Sloane asked Penelope.

"Final fitting this week," she said, fluffing her blond-and-pink hair. "I love it. I hope Gary's mom does. So you're all going to be there next Saturday?"

I nodded. "I'm supposed to perform a song for them, so yeah, I'll be there."

Now they looked at me with pity in Gary's absence. I scowled and took another sip.

"We'll all be there," Sloane said, glancing over to where Alex was talking to a couple of guys on the other side of the bar. "It's going to be one crazy beach party."

"I'm told there are unusual elements in the ceremony," Penelope said with a wink.

"Besides me?" I asked.

She laughed. "Yes. Besides you. Including some hot Broadway actor doing something dramatic, I hear. It's going to be a blast, and not just because of the wedding. They're celebrating the deal. The art school is buying the property as a retreat."

"It is?" I couldn't keep the relief out of my voice. At least that was settled, and it was good for the Gorskis, even if Gary was pissed about it. Pissed at me.

"And Greer is giving her art to the museum anyway," Sloane said. "Though she apparently sent one to auction, one Alex didn't even know she had. A Klimt."

"I saw the picture in the online catalog," Thea said dreamily. "She's gorgeous. And Greer is going to make a fortune."

We were all quiet for a minute, enjoying drinks and doughnuts and the idea of having a fortune. Or other things. Like making music. Like being with . . .

"I've got to get ready," I told them, chasing the last of my doughnut with the rest of the tiki drink. "Whew, that's a rush."

"I think I'll order one of those," Penelope said with a frown. "I could use a rush. I'm between boyfriends."

"I thought you always had a few on deck," Thea said. "I was waiting for your extras."

Penelope shot her a look. "You can do a lot better, believe me, darling."

I waved at them and walked toward the piano, feeling the buzz of the Mai Tai. This was going to be fun, goddamnit, even if it killed me. I swayed a bit as I settled onto the stool and pressed the pedals, ran a couple of arpeggios. I felt the band coalesce around me, getting into position, into tune. Everything felt right.

Almost everything.

Neil announced us — "Ladies and gentlemen, please welcome the return of *Ez* and the Emeralds," with the emphasis on my name — and I scanned the room full of clapping friends and fans and didn't find the face I was looking for. A strange feeling of loss overtook me, accompanied by anger — anger at myself. I'd dealt with my own shit for a long time before Gary came along. I didn't depend on anybody. I didn't need to.

But did I want to?

Robby counted off, and I automatically switched gears, focusing on the music, digging into the rocker we'd chosen for our first song — one of my older compositions, a paean to badassery, mythical bad boys and, of course, bad relationships, all delivered with dark humor.

We followed that with an edgy ballad, then one of Robby's, and then a cover I could appreciate: "Great Balls of Fire." I tweaked the gender but gave it the gusto, Jerry Lee Lewis-style. I was hammering the piano during a solo when I felt the air change in the room, a subtle shift, a presence. I looked up to see Gary walking toward the bar. He wasn't looking at me at all.

I tore my gaze away and launched into the final verse and chorus, glancing at Robby as I did so. He was into his own jam, but I could see it in his face: He'd seen Gary, too, and his eyes held a trace of sympathy. Maybe the word was out. What had been was no more.

The crowd, at least, was eating it up. The Emeralds' old chemistry strengthened with each song. They may have been losers, but now they sounded great, and they were *my* losers. And I felt different, too. I could hear myself performing with more emotion, more depth.

When I played to the crowd, I didn't let my eyes rest too long in one place. I skimmed over the patrons, barely seeing my friends, but noted Gary by the bar, watching me. I refused to catch his eye. Instead, I put my heart into my songs, all my old songs about loneliness and isolation, even the one that had made Stuart flip out at Cali's gallery.

By break time, my face was moist from perspiration, and I was only too glad to walk away from the piano for a bit. Wilson retreated to a corner with a water and his phone, but instead of going to the bar, as was my wont, I followed the guys out the back door. They went out to the parking lot, to Robby's truck. I sat at one of the picnic tables, next to a couple of small parties of drinkers laughing among themselves, and tried to breathe in the stifling air. The heat had come — not the summer heat, not yet, but a heat that signaled that cool evenings would be rare indeed for several months. The short spring had broken.

Fuck. Why hadn't I gone to the bar to get my drink from Neil?

I knew why. I was too chicken-shit to face Gary. I closed my eyes and steeled myself for the trip inside. I didn't know what to do with this anxiety. No guy had ever made me anxious. Then again, no guy had ever made me talk. Or feel. Or screw. Not until Gary.

I walked in the back door and almost ran into him.

"Ez." Gary looked the way I'd always remembered him, casual, quirky, in a Dr. Teeth T-shirt and long shorts. But there was something more, now, an energy I felt burning beneath the surface. He held a Mai Tai in his hand. "Neil said to send this out to you."

"Oh." I took the drink from him, trying to detect any emotion on his face. I didn't know he was such a poker player. Everything was back to status quo, only it wasn't. That current flowed between us, an electricity that crackled as soon as he came into my space, a feeling that hadn't been there before the fire and everything that followed.

"Thanks," I managed, trying to ignore the sizzle. "How are you?"

"Fine." There — was that a whisper of a hitch in his voice? We moved aside and pressed against the office door as patrons shouldered past us, heading outside for a smoke. Some nodded and smiled at me. "You sound good," Gary continued. "I'm glad you're back with the band, as long as they're treating you right."

"Right down to a monthly tribute in doughnuts," I said.

"What kind?"

"Sugar Shack."

"You deserve nothing but the best," he said, a tiny smile tugging at the corner of his mouth.

"Gary?"

"Yeah?"

I opened the office door, grabbed his hand and pulled him inside. The tiny, cluttered room was nearly dark, with a small window — mirrored, I knew, on the other side — looking out into the crowded bar.

"What are you doing?" he asked as I set my drink on the desk and closed the door.

"I miss you."

"You do?" He swallowed and, in spite of his attempt at reserve, let his gaze rove over my clingy, revealing outfit. A smoldering light kindled in his eyes.

"Don't you miss this? Us?" I stepped closer, looked up at him and put my hands on his chest.

"Ez . . ." His voice wavered. "I told you, I can't do this anymore."

"What?" I leaned in to kiss his neck, to tongue his salty

skin. I didn't know what I wanted, except that I wanted him. The electricity shot through my veins to my center, sparking a growing heat.

"This dysfunctional seduction. Whatever it is you're doing," he said hoarsely.

I pressed my body against his, my breasts against his hard torso. That wasn't the only thing that was hard.

I slid my arms around his waist and trailed kisses along his jawline. My lips touched his, coaxing, tasting, and after a few moments, his mouth engaged mine. He gripped my shoulders as he opened to me. I sucked on his bottom lip, tangled my tongue with his, and he moaned. I clasped his behind and pressed myself harder into him.

"We're good together," I whispered as I rubbed against him.

"You mean — this?"

"What else?" I slipped my hands under his T-shirt, caressing his hot skin, trying to take another kiss.

He shook his head, grabbed my arms and pushed me gently away. "Why?"

"Why does there have to be a 'why'?" I asked, frustrated and flustered, unwilling to admit that something more complex than attraction was at work here.

"What do you want?" he asked, his voice harder.

"I thought that was obvious. You."

"But what do you feel?"

"Gary, Jesus." I picked up the drink and drained half of it, then leaned against the desk. "Why are you asking about feelings? Seriously, who's the fucking girl here?"

"I can't believe you, can't believe you would say something like that after everything I told you the last time I saw you. Or maybe I do believe it. Maybe it shouldn't surprise me." He took a step closer. "Maybe you should be asking another question: Who's the human being here? Who's the one with a fucking heart?"

Ouch. I froze, feeling my glare break down into something much more vulnerable. Beyond the window, the muffled sounds of the bar, the rock music on the speakers, the colorful throng of revelers made our little pocket of quiet gloom seem all the more intense.

"Then let's talk." I tried to sound cooler than I felt.

"How about I just listen to you from the other side of the room like all the other people you aren't in love with," he said bitterly.

He walked out of the room, leaving the door open. Through the window, I saw him stride through the bar and right out the front door.

I knocked back the rest of the Mai Tai and hurled the glass hard against the wall, where it shattered in an explosion that wasn't nearly satisfying enough.

I performed the second set with a soft buzz that couldn't drown out a new kind of pain. As I sang, the persona who wasn't me, the one I always said wasn't me, talked back. She became me. She *was* me. The music soared, agonizing, raw, seductive, and I could feel the crowd drawn to its purity, resonating with each refrain, rapt.

She sang of loss and love, and she knew what it meant.

I knew what it meant. Finally.

Gary.

I HAD a week until Gary's mom's wedding, and I'd agreed to perform a song. I wouldn't back out now, though I was mortified at the idea of facing Gary again. The question was, which song?

I was still contemplating the question when Julio button-holed me in the foyer of my building Tuesday evening and talked me into a piano lesson. It was hard to resist the boy's plea, and besides, the distraction seemed like a good idea.

"Are you upset, Ms. Falcon?" Julio asked me after we'd gone through a song as his mother bustled in the kitchen. "Wasn't it any good?"

"It was *really* good. You must have practiced a lot."

"Then why are you sad?"

"Because — because of a guy."

"He was a jerk, huh?"

I laughed. Julio had a good memory. "No, not this time. I was kind of a jerk."

"But you're nice."

"Not always."

"Then why don't you tell him and say you're sorry?" he asked. "Miss Connor says we should always say we're sorry and talk about it when we did something wrong."

"Who's Miss Connor?"

"My teacher." He grinned. "She gives me lots of gold stars on all my papers."

Ah, yes, I remembered when life was defined by gold stars.

I sighed. "I think it's too late to say I'm sorry. What song should we do next?"

"It's never too late as long you mean it," Julio said. "But mom says if you don't mean it, you're going to hell."

I turned my laugh into a cough. No doubt his mother was thinking of her ex when she told him that. Anyway, I had too many other reasons to worry about hell.

"I would mean it," I said. "I mean, if I thought it would do any good."

"He just doesn't know how nice you are," Julio said with confidence. "Can we play the Superman theme now?"

Later that night, over Chinese takeout, I sat on my couch and watched *La Dolce Vita* again, pondering the weary reporter's journey through meaningless nights and days, wondering if Julio was right. I'd never thought of myself as nice. Never thought of myself as worthy of anything great, especially love. I'd never believed anyone could love me; one, I wasn't lovable. Two, men were easily manipulated at best, treacherous at worst and, in my experience, never really desirous of love. Since a man had never truly loved me, how could I ever love one of them?

The gossip reporter stands with the glamorous movie star in the gushing fountain. The film is gorgeous, black and white, a dream world, and she is spellbound, her eyes closed. Poised at the edge of a kiss that never comes, on the trembling cusp of dawn, he tells her she is everything — mother, sister, lover, friend. She doesn't really hear him. And, I thought, he doesn't see her, either. Not the real her. They act a play within a play, somewhere in their heads, seeing around each other, skimming the surface, fanning a fantasy, until the water turns off and they stand exposed in the stark light of day.

I'd been living in a fantasy, too, one in which I could stay at a distance and still have everything I wanted. Even if, I realized now, I didn't know what the hell I wanted. Love?

Love was a seriously scary word. And thrilling and dangerous and gorgeous, a sword to the heart, a cloud to catch me when I fell. It was passion, and it was safety. It was challenging, and it was comforting. I kept thinking that Gary was giving me a gift by listening to me, or backing me up, but I didn't see just how big the gift was. He'd given me all of himself, had offered his soul to me, and I'd whacked it back at him like a tennis ball.

He'd accepted me, the real me, every dark moment, every foolish impulse, every sharp shard of my heart.

Gary loved me. Or, at least, he *had* loved me.

Had I completely blown it? I'd repeatedly deflected his feelings, even mocked them. He was beyond pissed off the last time he walked out on me. I didn't think he'd listen to me again. I'd never had the right thing to say. Never had faith in the words, even if I'd wanted to say them.

Now I did want to say them, but I didn't think I could take the rejection I'd made almost inevitable. How would he ever believe me? Even if he did, how could he possibly feel the same way, after I'd run his heart through a blender?

And how would I get him to listen to me anyway?

I stared at the TV screen. The movie blurred. I wiped my eyes and grabbed my notebook and pen off the coffee table.

There was one way he couldn't get out of listening to me.

I began to write.

THERE WAS a guard at the gate of Gary's mom's house on the glaringly sunny afternoon of the wedding, which didn't help my nerves. I had a sudden fear that he'd been hired just to keep me out.

But upon closer inspection, he didn't seem all that scary. He was more like an usher than a security guy. He was a flustered young man with a buzz cut, wearing khakis and a golf shirt with some sort of event company logo on it, and he had a clipboard.

"There's a shuttle bus if you park down the street at the shopping center," he said when I rolled my window down.

"I'm performing, and I have a keyboard to unload. It would be a lot easier to park here," I told him.

"Maybe you're on the list. Name?"

"Ez Falcon."

"Let me see — Esme Falcon? Is that you?"

"That would be me," I said.

"OK, just pull up by the garage, but don't block anybody. There are a lot of comings and goings."

"No problem." That was one advantage to having a roller skate of a car. I could park almost anywhere.

The ceremony was scheduled for 4 p.m. I'd arrived an hour early to make sure I could connect with the event people and plug in to their sound system.

I took a sip from my water bottle and braced myself for the hot afternoon. I loved my strapless dress: a chocolate-brown satin corset top laced with gold cord and a light gold and brown skirt — layers of chiffon over a short opaque underskirt, cut higher in front than in back. Still, with temperatures flirting with eighty, it might be a sweaty wedding.

Then again, I didn't count on the ocean breeze that we so often lacked just over the river in Bohemia. Here, in Bohemia Beach, the fresh wind lofted my skirts, lifted my hair and fluttered my bangs around my face as soon as I climbed out of my car. It cooled me instantly. The scent of the air and the sound of the ocean filled my senses and reminded me of Gary.

Hell, everything at this point reminded me of Gary, especially given what I planned to do. I looked around, wondering how to approach. I wasn't ready to see him yet. Should I go into the house?

Then I noticed the people in telltale service uniforms popping in and out of a wooden gate adjoining the garage. The caterers and techs were using it as their path to the beach. I decided to get the lay of the land before unloading my keyboard. I hid my keys under the visor, shut my car door and followed a guy carrying an armful of unlit tiki torches through the gate and down the path over the dunes.

And was greeted by something akin to a wedding circus.

The beach that had been nearly empty when Gary and I went swimming (again, I looked around for him but saw only worker bees) had been elaborately staged beyond the house, well above the high-tide line.

The long tent to my left drew my eye first. It had a clear vinyl top accented with intermittent swaths of white fabric that draped from the peak and down the open sides, giving the illusion of open sky above, between the swags. There were chandeliers, too, dripping with flowers, hung along the center ridge of the tent. Beneath were two long tables draped in white tablecloths and bedecked with blooms, with chairs to accommodate perhaps a hundred guests. Nearby, a white tent served as the base of operations for the caterers.

Directly ahead of me were dozens of flowery beach towels laid out on the sand in front of an arch decorated with ivy, white tulle and fluttering ribbons of sea-foam green. It seemed the guests would be lounging on the towels for the ceremony, on either side of a makeshift aisle sprinkled with white rose petals.

To the left of the arch was a platform, probably for performers like me, I thought. Or maybe for a band after the ceremony. An easel sat on one side of the stage, a blank canvas on it. A couple of guys were setting up and testing a microphone, and their *one-two-three* reverberated across the sand.

But to the right of the arch was — a grand piano?

What the hell?

The piano was set up on a temporary floor, and it was also miked. So these guys understood the main challenge of music at a beach wedding: With the roar of the waves, generally, no one could hear a goddamned thing.

I wandered toward the instrument in a daze. It looked familiar. Sure, all pianos looked kind of the same, but there was something about this one that struck me. I'd seen it before.

I stepped onto the square wooden floor set on the beach, took the few steps to the closed piano and sat on the bench. I lifted the fallboard to reveal the keys and caressed the logo on the dark wood. A Bösendorfer.

A creamy square envelope rested on the instrument's music rack. *Ez,* my name was scrawled across it.

For just a second, I hoped it was a grand romantic gesture, but I realized quickly that it was something else entirely.

The letter inside was written in a large, looping hand on thick paper that matched the envelope.

Dear Ez,

I told you I wanted to give you a little something. Here it is. I've always been friendly with Ginny, and when she told me you were playing at her wedding, it seemed like the perfect time to give it to you. Afterward, the gentlemen I've

hired will deliver it wherever you'd like it to go. Thank you!
And never lose your spark!

Sincerely,

Greer Allighant

SHE'D GIVEN me a freaking *piano*? And not just any piano: her
beautiful Bösendorfer. Where the hell was I going to put it?
Actually, that was the wrong question. How was I going to
give it back to her? Because there was no way I could keep it.

"Ms. Falcon?"

I looked up into the face of a blocky blond guy with a
high and tight haircut and a barrel chest who should have
been dominating a football field somewhere. "Yes?"

"Mrs. Allighant sent us." He gestured toward the dune
line, where three more beefy guys waited, all in the same
khakis and white shirts, gripping bottles of water. "When you
get a moment, let us know where you want the piano, and
we'll make sure it gets there tomorrow. We'll clean and tune
it, too."

"OK," I said, still a little stunned, not yet ready to let go of
this marvelous gift, despite the utter impracticality of keeping
it. He smiled and nodded and went back to his buddies, and I
blinked into the sun and took in the rest of the scene.

Between the tent and the water, a circle had been dug. In
the center, logs were piled high, a bonfire ready to be set
alight. Adjoining the tent, bartenders were setting up under
an awning. I narrowed my eyes at them, wondering if I could
finagle a drink. Could that be — ?

I hastened to the tent. "Neil!"

"Ez! I heard you were performing," my favorite bartender
said, coming out from behind the counter to give me a hug.
He and his two colleagues, a man and a woman, all wore

white shirts, red suspenders and black bow ties. But only Neil had the grand mustache.

"You got anything to take the edge off?" I asked him quietly.

"We're not open till after the ceremony, but for you . . . bourbon OK?"

"Remind me to tip you heavily next time I have money with me," I said as he handed me the glass, actually a plastic cup with ice and two fingers of sweet, burning, beautiful whiskey.

"You can't be nervous," he said as he worked to arrange his garnishes.

"This is different."

Neil glanced up at me knowingly after fluffing a bunch of mint in a silver cup nestled in ice. "Because of him?"

I held Neil's gaze for a moment — Neil, who'd always been sweet on me, who smiled at me kindly now and nodded toward the beach.

I turned slowly. Gary was walking down a path from the house that had been delineated with stakes looped with the same kind of tulle and ribbon that decorated the arch. He headed for the techs who were putting the finishing touches on the sound system. He hadn't seen me, but I took him in like a parched girl confronted with a waterfall. When did he become so devastating? His dark curls were long and loose and flopping in the wind. His eyes seemed to glow in the late afternoon light. He wore tan linen pants, so light they were almost white, and a white shirt buttoned all the way to his neck. No tie. But his linen jacket matched the pants, and he looked as if he'd just stepped off a yacht. A millionaire — rich in confidence if not in dollars — who maybe, charmingly, needed a haircut.

I caught myself sighing.

Neil chuckled. "Don't be nervous. He's a fool if he turns down what you're offering."

I turned back to him and set down the empty cup. "Thanks." I leaned in and kissed him on the cheek. "You're still my favorite bartender."

He touched his cheek where I'd kissed him and turned ever so slightly pink. I smiled and walked away from him — this time, toward the house and away from Gary, eager to put off a confrontation. This wasn't how I wanted to talk to him. Not yet.

INSIDE, people I didn't know bustled around the corridors. I headed to the kitchen and found Gary's cousin Kayla and their Grandma Helen tying ribbons on a big white basket full of bubble-blowing stuff and sunglasses with heart-shaped lenses.

"Ez!" Kayla said. "Here, have a pair."

I took a pair of the white-plastic-rimmed glasses and put them on. "With the piano and these, I'll really feel like Elton John."

Kayla laughed as I perched them on my head. "Isn't that piano something? That Greer is a pistol. Too bad she can't be here today."

"On another cruise," Grandma Helen said.

Kayla nodded. "Do you want to talk to mom and Aunt Ginny?"

Kayla brought me down a hallway to a big master bedroom overflowing with packages and clothes and all the accoutrements of wedding preparation. A hair-and-makeup gal curled Johanna's red locks, and my friend Penelope fussed with Ginny's dress. Cali was there, back from Tahiti, apparently, shooting photos. They were too busy to notice me enter. Kayla waved, closing the door quietly behind me, and I got a good look at Ginny Gorski in her wedding finery. She was gazing dreamily into a full-length mirror as Penelope finished looping the last of the pearl buttons on the back.

The dress' color was a delicate sea-foam green like the ribbons in the décor outside. The sleeveless, form-fitting bodice was trimmed with white seed pearls arranged in swirls. The fabric was shot through with spiraling silver threads. The tea-length skirt was layered in what looked like long leaves of satin, chiffon and iridescent fabric in white, silver and shades of pale green, the perfect palette for Ginny, with her reddish hair and fair skin.

"You look like a fairy of the sea," I said in wonder.

"Ez!" Ginny said, spinning away from the mirror to face me. She was beaming. "Thank you!"

"Yes, thank you!" Penelope said, looking pleased and pretty herself in a hot pink pencil dress that matched the pink in her hair and her tie-back wedge heels. "Wait till you see how it flows in the wind."

"She's a genius," said Johanna, wearing a simple satin dress in pale orange, so as not to look too much like the bride.

Cali came over and gave me a hug. "Good to see you."

"You look tan," I said.

"For a blond girl." She grinned.

"So," Ginny said to me, "how do you like the piano?"

"How can I not love it?" I said. "Though I'm not sure what to do with it when this is over."

Ginny smiled. "You'll figure something out. Have you seen Gary?"

I paused, catching Penelope's curious glance. "I haven't talked to him yet, no."

"He's seemed a little withdrawn leading up to the ceremony. I think he's worried about me, and I wish he wouldn't. Maybe you can talk to him."

Or maybe I'm the one making him miserable.

"Would you mind sitting, Ginny, so I can touch up your face?" the makeup lady interrupted.

Gary's mom sat on the edge of the bed for final primping as Penelope packed up her sewing kit and Cali snapped more photos of the process.

"Do you have your song ready?" Ginny asked. "I can't wait to hear what you came up with."

"It's all brand new," I said. "A lot mushier than I'm used to writing, but I hope you like it."

She and Johanna both laughed as Penelope shot me a quizzical look.

"It's amazing how mushy I can feel at my age," Ginny said. "Jay has been a doll all week. And now with the house and the land going to the school, I'm so happy. Happier than I've been in years."

I felt the tiniest twinge of jealousy. I wanted a taste of that happiness. "So you still want me to play a few songs beforehand and the processional, right?" I asked.

"Yes. The ones we talked about and 'Moon River.' You're ready?"

"Of course," I said. "I've always liked that one, and I practiced this week, just to be sure. No vocals, just like you wanted."

"Perfect," Ginny said. "Pick up a program from Kayla so you know the order. She'll give you a wave when it's time for us to walk down the aisle."

"See you out there," I said.

Penelope was hot on my heels as I left the room.

"You and Gary are still on the outs?" she whispered to me as we walked down the hall.

"I don't want to talk about it."

"And his mom doesn't know?"

I stopped and turned to her. "Look. I have one shot to fix this. I don't want her to know anything she doesn't need to know. This is her day. She doesn't need any distractions."

"Chill, Ez. I'm on your side," Penelope said. "I'm glad you want him. I'm glad you know it. If you want him, you'll get him."

I got a little choked up at the pep talk. I still wasn't used to confiding in friends.

"Thanks," I managed to say. "We'll know soon enough."

"Oh, really?" she said, sounding more like the dramatic Penelope I knew. "By the way, that dress is a knockout."

"Gotta have honey if you're gonna catch the bee." I slid the heart-shaped sunglasses down to my nose, and she laughed.

I picked up a program, went out the front door, grabbed sheet music from my car and scooted around the side of the house to avoid running into Gary. He was nowhere in sight. I opened the piano and did a quick sound check with the events folks. Then I started playing the songs Ginny had asked for — all from movies — and waited for my cue from Kayla as the guests wandered onto the beach and took their seats. Alex and Sloane, Thea, Penelope, and Cali and Wyatt shooting photos — so many of my artist friends were here, along with a lot of museum patrons and art-school types.

And then came the signal from Kayla, who stood at the

top end of the ribbon-bordered path that led toward the house, and the processional began.

I slipped off the goofy sunglasses and began to play a lush version of "Moon River." The miked piano echoed over the sand, nature's concert hall.

The officiant — a gentleman from the art museum board who was also a notary — took his place under the arch in his dove-gray suit. Jay walked down the aisle first, dressed in a natty white linen suit with a tie that matched Ginny's dress, accompanied by one of his friends, a ruddy, fun-looking guy in white pants and a tasteful aloha shirt. Golfing buddy, I figured.

Next came Johanna, happy and lovely, her reddish hair curled and now festooned with small yellow roses. And then came Ginny, her hair adorned with white roses, woven into her loose up-do. She carried a bouquet of white roses and seashells, and her dress flowed like water in the breeze; its silver threads flashed in the sunlight.

Escorting her was Gary, tall and strong next to her.

It's a good thing I wasn't singing the song, because my voice would have cracked at the sight, a handsome son with his happy mother, the love and respect between them palpable. He escorted her to the arch and kissed her on the cheek. She smiled, nodded and turned to Jay.

Gary turned to take his seat in the front row, but not before he stole a glance at me. It gave me hope, that look, that glimmer of light in his eyes tempered by restraint, torment. It meant he still felt something. I tried to hold his glance, to convey my feelings, but he turned away, and the ceremony began.

As Penelope had hinted at The Junction Box, there were unusual elements. Besides the guests sitting on their beach towels, most wearing the comical heart-shaped sunglasses, there was a woman in a smock, beret and high heels painting the wedding as it happened, making big, colorful swaths on the canvas set up on the stage.

A handsome young actor who looked vaguely familiar — must be the Broadway guy Penelope had mentioned — got up and, a bit nervously, I thought, recited a Shakespeare sonnet. Still, the women in the audience got a bit swoony at his silky delivery of "Let me not to the marriage of true minds admit impediments ... "

And a juggling magician pulled the rings from behind the couples' ears when the time came.

At last, it was my turn to perform. There was already a lot of pressure to do well, given it was the last item on the agenda before Ginny and Jay were declared man and wife, but I was nervous for other reasons. And though I looked at the couple while I played the opening chords of my simple new ballad, as soon as I started singing, I shifted my eyes to Gary.

He wasn't looking at me. His gaze was focused out over the couple, over the ocean, fixed on the blue horizon. But still, I sang to him. I didn't think his mom would mind. After all, a love song was a love song, wasn't it?

> *I see the ocean in your eyes,*
> *the depth, the strength, the light.*
> *I see eternity shine there,*
> *sweet days and sweeter nights.*
> *Please say forever can be real.*
> *I never want to part.*
> *You finally made me understand,*
> *and now you have my heart.*

Gary's eyes lost their focus on the horizon and turned to me.

> *I thought my soul had closed up shop*
> *and then I let you in.*
> *Your power took me by surprise.*
> *I should have known you'd win.*
> *I may have fought you on the way.*
> *My song went out of tune.*
> *You played the pulse that brought me back;*
> *my heart beat none too soon.*

His mouth parted ever so slightly, and his sparking eyes narrowed. They may not have been hidden by stupid sunglasses, but I still had trouble reading them. Was he angry? Interested? I didn't know. I couldn't stop. I kept singing, watching him, willing him to understand, pouring my emotions into the song for him. And for me. The love, the tenderness, the fear, the joy filled me, all I'd learned to feel for him, and the bright afternoon blurred as tears sprang to my eyes.

> *You fanned the flames and caught the rain*
> *and scaled the heights above.*
> *You saved me like a kitten lost*
> *and turned my life to love.*
> *A few rough spins around the wheel*
> *have made a work of art.*
> *And finally, yes, I understand.*
> *You'll always have my heart.*
>
> *You're all I need for all of time.*

You'll always have my heart.

A murmur of sentimental appreciation followed the song, and a quick glance confirmed the couple were pleased, too. I knew it wasn't my best work, but it was a wedding, and people expected songs about love and eternity. Even if I was really singing a song to Gary about fire and rain and kittens and music and pottery — and love and eternity. Did he know it? Did he understand? Did he care?

I looked back at him. His eyes were closed, his head slightly bowed, the striking planes of his face shadowed. *Oh, hell.* Had I blown it again?

It's not as if I could confront him. The ceremony was finally tumbling to its close, and in moments, Ginny and Jay were married, and the crowd stood and cheered and blew bubbles as the couple made their way to the water's edge for photographs. I banged out Mendelssohn's "Wedding March," the only traditional piece I'd played all afternoon.

When I was done, I looked up to see the guests hanging around the couple, dipping toes in the waves or going to get their first drink. No one was in the audience. No one.

I carefully folded my sheet music, put it back in its folder and wrangled the piano's top board shut to protect the delicate strings and hammers from the salt air. I didn't feel up to dealing with the question of what to do with it. Besides, the piano movers had graduated to quaffing beers by the water's edge.

I just needed to find someplace quiet. Maybe escape altogether. I wasn't sure I could be around a happy couple, especially when my only hope of happiness, the man I now knew I wanted, had ignored the open-heart surgery I'd offered with that stupid song.

I stood and saw Penelope threading her way among the beach towels toward me. I waited for a moment, thinking maybe I could make my excuses to her, and she could pass them on.

"Loved the song," Penelope said, and she hugged me. Her pale green eyes were bright.

"Lot of good it did me."

She raised her eyebrows. "Maybe. Maybe not. I have a message for you. It's a little strange."

"OK," I said, trying not to look interested.

"Gary asked me to ask you to meet him on the moon."

"On the *moon*."

"That's what he said." She shrugged. "I figured you'd know what it meant."

I looked off toward the blue ocean, the crowd, the tents, a band that had begun to set up on the stage. Then back toward the house.

"Yeah," I said. "I think I do."

I knew where. But I dared not hope what it meant.

THE HOUSE WAS quiet and empty.

I set my music down in the foyer and climbed the stairs. I wasn't sure if I remembered which room it was, but I recognized the door when I got to it. I knocked.

Gary, still in his wedding suit, opened the door.

I stepped inside. "The lunar bedroom," I said, much as I had when I'd first seen it.

Gary didn't say anything. He closed the door behind me and locked it. And pushed me against it, his hands tight on my arms, his face close to mine.

"Did you mean it?" he asked, his voice low and penetrating, his eyes almost wild. "Or was it just your persona talking? Was I just a handy metaphor for a song?"

"I mean it, Gary," I whispered. Heat coursed through my body at his touch, at his intensity.

"You're not playing games with me?" He moved even closer. I could sense his barely controlled fervor, feel his hot breath on my lips, and I longed to taste him again.

"No games." I strained toward him. "I love you, Gary."

"How can I believe you?" he asked, his voice softer, his eyes roving my face, the want in his expression almost painful.

"Because I'm smarter now. You've made me smarter. I love that you're strong. That you're clever. That you love music and art and me." I shifted, wanting to press my body against his, but still he pinned me against the door. "I love that you always do the right thing and that you are on my side, no matter what. I love that you're *nice,* goddamnit."

For a microsecond, a smile crossed his lips. And then they were on mine, demanding, devouring. He pinned my arms higher and pressed against me. I moaned into his mouth, opening to his kiss. New tears pricked at my eyes as he released my arms, and I clutched him to me, burying my face in his chest, lost and found in this wonderful man, my friend, my lover, and — I hoped — my forever.

He pulled me away from the door and pushed me onto the bed.

I smirked. "So we're finally going to do this on the moon?"

"We're going to do this every way and everywhere possible," he growled.

He shrugged off his jacket and started unbuttoning his shirt. Lying back on my elbows, I watched, transfixed, as he slipped it off and tossed it aside, revealing his lean physique.

"Have I mentioned that you're gorgeous?" I asked him.

"Now you tell me." He advanced slowly toward me, then dropped to his knees and slipped off my sandals. He slid his big hands up my legs, leaving trails of fire. "This dress on you — you're such a temptress."

"Do you mind?" I asked, though it was getting harder to speak now that his fingers were traveling higher.

"Not if you're mine." He pushed the skirt up and kissed the soft skin of my inner thigh. "Not if I get to unwrap you."

He kissed my pussy through the silky triangle of my thong, and I groaned, falling backward onto the mattress. In a moment, he had the slip of fabric off, and he ran his nimble tongue up my slit.

"*Gary,*" I sighed as he began to tease my center, licking my clit until I squirmed and bucked under him, teetering on the dazzling edge. "Don't stop," I exclaimed as he stood, unfastening his trousers and dropping them to the floor with his shoes and underwear.

"I'm just getting started," he said with a wicked smile. His long, hard shaft jutted before him as he lay down over me, kissing my lips, my neck, the curve of my breasts. He scooped them out of the corset top and licked and teased my nipples in turn. The hardened nubs were points of fire under his mouth. I could barely take the pleasure that radiated from them. I wanted more.

"Now, baby," I begged.

Without a word, he pushed my skirt up higher. I opened my legs for him. He guided his cock to my entrance and notched the tip in my cleft, nudging it in and out, teasing me until I moaned. At the sound, he thrust inside me.

My slick passage embraced him, pulsed as he built his cadence. I held his fiery gaze.

"Yes, Gary. I need you like this. I want this forever. I love you," I whispered. "I love you. I love you." My whispers became soft cries as he shifted, plunging harder, faster, his own face betraying his depth of emotion as he grasped my hips, crunched my skirts and took me higher. "I love you, Gary."

He came with a groan, holding himself deep inside me as he spasmed. A moment later, clenched around his pulsing cock, I wrapped my legs around him and canted upward, taking him even deeper. "Gary!" I cried out as my wave of ecstasy crested, crashing through my body, cleansing me.

He held me as I shuddered, then collapsed against me, rolled us sideways, kissed me. Still inside me. *God, yes.*

"I love you, Ez," he murmured in my ear, holding me close as our frantic breathing slowly calmed, as our volcanic heat dissipated. "Always."

He eased out of me, and we lay there for a while, caressing and kissing each other as the afternoon light seeping around the curtains mellowed into gold.

The thumping sound of the band started up outside. I giggled.

"What?"

"Think they need any help?"

"They've got it covered," Gary said, teasing my mouth with another kiss. "It's a surf band I recommended to my mom. Maybe later we can jam around the bonfire."

"If we ever leave this room." I kissed him again. "Oh, hell."

"What?"

"What am I going to do with that piano?"

Now it was his turn to chuckle. "That's what you get for interfering."

"Seriously. Those four linebackers are out there waiting for me to tell them what to do with it."

Gary traced a finger along my jawline and kissed me again. "You could send it to my place."

"Here? But aren't you moving out?"

"I already have. I got an apartment in the industrial district. It's primitive, like a loft, but it's big. It'll take your piano, no problem."

"And your drum set and pottery wheel?"

"And Pumpkin Spice." He looked at me seriously. "Even you, if you want."

I looked into his eyes, into their lagoon light, amber and bronze and flashes of green and swirling sparks of love.

"I might need to work up to that," I said.

"That's OK." A little wrinkle formed in his forehead. "I understand."

I held the steady gaze of this astonishing man who'd changed my life, who always put me first, and I knew, even more than I knew before.

"OK," I said. "I've worked through it. When can the piano and I move in?"

Gary raised his eyebrows in surprise and laughed. And he kissed me again. And in that kiss, that profound, sweet, marvelous, dangerously nice kiss, were all the answers I would ever need.

∾

AFTERWORD

Thanks for reading! Sign up for my newsletter to get fun original content, giveaways, news and cocktail recipes, and I'll send you a free story. I also have a Facebook group where readers can hang out and chat about books and life — please join us in Lucy's Lounge.

MORE ONLINE:

LucyLakestone.com
Facebook.com/LucyLakestone
Twitter.com/LucyLakestone
Bookbub.com/authors/lucy-lakestone
Pinterest.com/lucylakestone/
Amazon
Goodreads
YouTube

ACKNOWLEDGMENTS

Hugs and thanks go to the members of Spacecoast Authors of Romance for their support and inspiration, and to all my writing friends who have guided me and plied me with wine and literature. Pam Harbaugh, you rock.

Thanks so much to Open Mike's in Melbourne, Florida, for letting us film the book trailer there, and thanks to R.J. Bowen for tickling the ivories for the piano shots. Thank you to the staff at Sky Diary Productions and Velvet Petal Press and, especially, to editor and friend Holly Martin for her mad skills. More thanks go to Mr. Lakestone for his patience with piles of books and endless printouts. And lastly, thank *you* for reading!

ABOUT THE AUTHOR

Lucy Lakestone is an award-winning author who lives on Florida's east central coast, among the towns that serve as an inspiration for the hot romances of her Bohemia Beach Series, including *Bohemia Beach, Bohemia Light, Bohemia Blues* (winner of the Golden Quill), *Bohemia Heat, Bohemia Nights* and *Bohemia Bells*. She's been a journalist, photographer, editor and video producer but prefers living in her imagination, where the moon is full and the cocktails are divine. She is also the author of a novel of romantic suspense, *Desire on Deadline*.

BOHEMIA HEAT

The fourth BOHEMIA BEACH *novel*

⌒⌒

can a passion this hot be just an act?

As summer sizzles in Bohemia Beach, Penelope Locke faces a different kind of heat. She's under pressure to create spectacular costumes for an update of Shakespeare penned by hot actor Jace Edison, who's come to town to oversee the production. He's a rising star on Broadway, TV and film with a reputation for ignoring women, and just being in the same room with him fries Penelope's wiring. Jace is a tangle of contradictions behind his handsome mask, and he threatens Penelope's carefully contained emotions by treating her alternately with disdain and passion. She can't help but be tempted by his volcanic attractions, but she's been burned before. Can they get close to each other without going up in flames?

LEARN MORE AT
LucyLakestone.com

www.ingramcontent.com/pod-product-compliance
Lightning Source LLC
Chambersburg PA
CBHW021644260626
47154CB00017BA/2244